EXPIRED GAME

LAST CHANCE COUNTY - BOOK 5

LISA PHILLIPS

TWO DOGS PUBLISHING, LLC.

eBook ISBN: 979-8-88552-045-4

Paperback ISBN: 979-8-88552-046-1

Publisher: Two Dogs Publishing, LLC. Idaho, USA.

Cover design: Ryan Schwarz

Edited by: Jen Weiber

1

———

Across the parking lot, a shadow shifted. Officer Jess Ridgeman grabbed her off-duty gun from the glove box and shut the car door as gently and quietly as she could.

Whoever was there just headed around the building. She sprinted full out across the lot to a building the police department had recently combed through so many times looking for something that might have been left behind. At this point, she could practically walk through it blindfolded.

Jess headed for where she'd seen the person.

Anyone sneaking around in the dark wasn't up to something good. Whether it related to the open case, she didn't know.

At the side door, Jess leaned against the building. She breathed slowly. Listened. The night was dark and quiet, any stars up there disguised by a thick layer of cloud. It would rain before morning, according to her weather app.

Trees rustled their leaves. A street or two away a semi-truck accelerated. But she couldn't hear the trespasser.

Jess used her free hand to turn the door handle and found it unlocked—because she'd left it that way the last time she was here. No matter how many times she had to return to the crime scene, Jess would keep coming back until she got a lead. Yes, it meant anyone could enter the building. But when the plan was to catch them in the act, leaving the door open was part of the trap.

Gun first, she stepped inside and held the door so the click of it closing behind her was barely audible.

A man stepped into view at the end of the hall. As though he'd known she was here and had planned to turn the tables.

Jess clicked on the flashlight attached to her gun and moved toward him with measured steps, not wanting to be any more—or less—than ten feet away from him. She stopped—legs steady, shoulders back. "Lower your hand. Keep both where I can see them."

He obeyed that, which got her a look at his face. Two eyebrow piercings glinted in the light below a shaved head. Extremely broad shoulders—the guy was probably twice her size, but only because she was barely five-three. He had a leather jacket and jeans over black boots. On the right side of his neck, a spider web tattoo peeked out from his collar and stretched to just below his ear.

She shifted so he'd see the badge on the belt of her jeans. "What's your name, and why are you trespassing here?"

While he answered that, she'd have time to figure out where she knew him from. His face—and that tattoo. She'd seen him before.

Jess hadn't lived in town for more than two years, though she'd grown up here. They'd moved away when she was in high school. No one from her previous career with the NYPD would show up in a small northwest town, so he wasn't someone from the past. That meant she'd seen him here. In Last Chance.

She said, "Name."

"Hammer."

"Is that the name on your driver's license?"

White teeth flashed.

"Hammer, huh? Are you carrying any weapons on you?" She hadn't heard that name before, but he did look familiar.

"Yes, ma'am, I am."

Jess blinked. "Lay them on the ground and face the wall." She reached for her phone and realized she hadn't brought it with her. She'd left it on the seat in her car.

Jess gritted her teeth. He couldn't know she had no way to call for backup. She was off duty right now, and no one from the department knew she was here. She needed to keep it that way.

"Am I in some kind of trouble?"

She studied his face and figured out where she'd seen him before. *The police station ambush.* Armed men who'd worked for a local crime boss, Ed Summers, had stormed the office a few months back. They'd shot more than one person, scared everyone else, and stolen evidence. "You were there."

"What was that?"

She realized she'd muttered the words. They'd *all* been there, and while hiding in the break room keeping Ted alive and out of their hands, she'd seen this guy through the window.

"We need to talk, but I'm not arresting you." *Yet.* She reserved the right to change her mind on that later. After they'd identified him, and she had proof to back up her memories. "I have questions. You're going to accompany me to the police department and answer them."

She wanted to taunt him to let him know she'd seen him before when he'd stormed in there as part of that group of gunmen, but if she let on to this "Hammer" guy what she knew, he might feel threatened and try to escape. *What kind of name is Hammer, anyway?*

She and the other cops she worked with had caught most of the men who'd been present during that incident. This guy had remained elusive.

A fact that gave her pause now.

"Let's go."

He didn't move.

"Weapons on the ground. Hands on the wall."

Maybe he wasn't used to being arrested. But if he was someone's confidential informant in the department, then she would know. There would be a record of it in the file from that incident.

Maybe Ted knew.

No, she didn't need to think about Ted right now. They were close. Probably best friends. But she couldn't explain her drive to do her job to him any more than he could admit that he was hiding something from her.

Despite one explosive kiss that had been a serious mistake, nothing was happening between the two of them.

They were at a literal stalemate.

"There aren't a lot of options for you, so let's make this as easy as possible." She added a little more authority to her tone. Even though he was bigger, she wasn't going to let him push her around. "What happens here is up to you."

"Yeah?" He tipped his head to the side. "You're really not what everyone says, are you?"

"Excuse me?"

"By the book. Doesn't stop. Doesn't give up."

"So the criminal element of this town…talks about me?"

"Of course. You did a good job infiltrating those drug pushers targeting the high school. That was nice work."

She still had her hair dyed dark brown from that operation —her last undercover assignment. "Am I supposed to say thank you?"

He wasn't an informant.

And this guy wasn't going to be *her* informant either, though that would have been useful. She got the feeling there was seriously more to this guy than what she knew. Maybe that was the reason he'd been loose this long, even though there was plenty of evidence to get an arrest warrant. *Is someone protecting him?*

The Hammer, or whatever his name actually was, grinned again. "Just making conversation."

"We can do that better at the station."

"Yeah." He shook his head. "That isn't going to happen. I'm not going in."

Just then, Jess noticed the man had inched his way to her and was now within arm's reach. Before she could react, he disarmed her. While he dismantled her gun, Jess punched his diaphragm. He choked and coughed as her clip clattered to the floor, then he handed her back her empty gun, along with the single bullet that had been in the chamber. Acting as though she hadn't punched him at all. "This doesn't need to get messy."

"I want West." And she would accept no other outcome. Jess would never stop asking about West. She would keep looking for evidence of West's identity until she found something that led to him, their prime suspect: a local crime lord who had evaded them for months.

He took two steps back. So it might be a long shot, but he reacted.

"There's a disease in this town, and you know it."

"And you're the cure?"

She closed her mouth. Did she think that? She opened it back up. "You're not leaving."

And yet, he was headed in that direction.

Jess followed him to the door. She swiped up her clip and put her gun back together as she moved. By the time she pushed out the exit, he was nowhere to be seen.

She jogged to the end of the building and saw him down the street. Jess followed, having to go at a loose run just to keep up with his long-leg strides. Two streets down, he turned right. Hammer trotted up the steps of the community center with a phone to his ear.

Who was he calling?

She didn't like this. A biker had no business being there. This couldn't be good.

She yanked the foyer door open and strode in after him. The entryway was empty except for one person. Behind the reception desk was a familiar face sprinkled with glitter, and her signature white pixie cut. "Hey, Ruby."

"Jessica." She grinned, laying down her novel.

She looked around again. "Did a guy come in here a second ago, big dude with a spider tattoo on his neck?"

"Sure did," Ruby said. "He told me to tell you the support group for workaholics isn't until tomorrow."

Jess started at her words. "He said that?" What game was this guy playing?

Ruby shrugged, "He seemed to think it was funny."

Jess pressed her lips together, then said, "If you see him again, tell him he's being recruited for the prison baseball team."

She spun on her heel and strode out while Ruby chuckled.

Jess couldn't join her. There was nothing funny about this, not when West was still out there. Not only that, but someone in town was pimping out women and getting away with it.

The door whooshed shut behind her. Jess jogged back to her car and heard her phone ringing before she even got the door open. She grabbed it and looked at the screen. Sergeant Basuto was calling.

She swiped to answer. "Ridgeman."

"Hey, I missed the end of your shift. How was it?"

Okay, so that was weird. She'd clocked out hours ago, and he was only now checking on her? That wasn't like him at all. Jess slumped into the seat and leaned the back of her head against the headrest. "Pretty routine." She stared at the abandoned office building in front of her and tried to figure out who that man, Hammer, really was.

And whether his call had been to Basuto.

The timing fit, but that was a serious leap.

"The Calverts were at it again. But neither of them wanted to press charges, and neither wanted medical attention."

Basuto sighed. The Calverts's neighbors regularly called 9-1-

1, usually when the argument escalated to throwing things—including punches. "Anything else after that?"

Yeah. Super weird. He was definitely fishing. Like he was on to her.

"Couple speeding tickets, and a DUI." She'd been assigned to patrol the area to the east of town, between the two most popular town bars and the compound where a local club of bikers lived. Most of the bikers were out of town this weekend for a rally in South Dakota, so all in all it'd been pretty quiet.

Basuto didn't say anything. Jess fidgeted during the several seconds of painful silence.

"Two days off. Any plans?"

Jess was alone in the parking lot, her car in the corner, outside the circle of glare provided by the street lights. Watching. Waiting. "Watch TV and chill. Isn't that how it goes?"

She heard a slight chuckle in his voice. "Do you even know how to do that?"

"Usually my 'chill' involves the lake and a paddleboard, but Ellie got me hooked on Tiny House Nation, so it's not like there's nothin' to do."

"She back?"

"Sunday. Dean is picking her up from the airport." Jess had to work, anyway. So it wasn't as if she'd have been able to get Ellie herself.

Her sister was at a conference for military history college professors, hobnobbing with her crowd while she was on sabbatical from her position. Everyone knew she'd settle here permanently, but Ellie hadn't moved all her stuff from New York State yet. Just what she needed to occupy Jess's guest room.

"Okay, well I just wanted to check in," Basuto said. "You have a good one."

"Copy that, Sarge." Jess hung up the phone before he could ask any more weird questions. Had that Hammer guy called him? Maybe that was just too bizarre. She wasn't quite yet ready for such a wild theory.

Jess drove home trying to figure it out. Back to an empty house—that is, until Ellie got back from her trip.

After her grandfather—the previous police chief—had passed away following a protracted battle with cancer, Jess's sister Ellie had come home as well. Then Ellie had managed to bring down a homicidal town founder, along with discovering a decades-old body buried in the hills above town. Now she was dating Dean, the town's unofficial EMT who was starting a treatment center for trauma victims.

Jess had to listen to Ellie on the phone with Dean when she was home. Then hear all about everything sweet and wonderful Dean did by text when she was at work—usually while trying to avoid Dean's brother, Ted.

Jess looked at her phone. It was past eleven in the evening already. She still hadn't replied to Ted's three texts from earlier. If she did that, she'd have to answer his questions and admit she wasn't going to spend her weekend at home watching TV. She didn't mind spinning the sergeant a line. But tell Ted something that wasn't the truth? She couldn't do that.

Jess also wasn't going to let this go until she'd brought them down. Before the past repeated itself, and she had to relive the worst moments of her life.

2

———

"She did *what?*" Ted lifted out of his seat on Conroy's couch to pace across the room. The chief had been shot by a sniper a few weeks ago. He was back at work part time and supposedly taking it easy under the watchful eye of his fiancé.

Except when Conroy had plans with the "boys." Which Mia didn't know meant he was working the Founders Case with both Ted and Sergeant Basuto.

Ted spun to the sergeant. "Who was that who called first anyway?"

Basuto glanced at Conroy, who gave a short nod. The chief was pretty pale and tired looking. But it had been a long day.

Basuto said, "He goes by 'Hammer.' He's undercover FBI, and he's been working in town for months. First as one of Ed Summers's men. Now he's trying to identify West."

Just like they were. "So this is an FBI case as well. Does Jess know that?"

Conroy said, "Given Tate's connection to the FBI, via his brother-in-law—who is Hammer's handler—you could say this is a case we're working with federal assistance. And no, she doesn't know the FBI is taking point."

Ted clenched his teeth.

The last thing he needed right now was the FBI in town.

"Not to be confused with the FBI who've been calling. Asking to speak with you."

Ted said nothing.

"You haven't given them your statement yet?" Basuto asked.

Conroy lifted a brow. "They've had your father in custody for two weeks now. It's important to tell them what you know."

That was the part Ted didn't get—or didn't want to. "Surely the testimonies they got from Stuart and Kaylee, along with Kaylee's brother, is enough evidence. Maybe they don't need a statement from me."

"It's part of the investigation, Ted." Conroy leaned forward in his armchair with a wince he didn't bother to hide—since Mia wasn't here to see. "They need all the information that's available so they can get the full picture of everything your father's done. After all, he didn't get to be CIA director with all the black ops operations going on under the table without help. There could be others working with him."

Basuto said, "Same as how we know the bank manager wasn't alone."

"I thought he was a scumbag customer, not just a Russian sleeper agent." Ted could hardly keep it all straight. This town was nuts, but it was his home.

Ted wanted to care about the FBI's case, about justice. But he *needed* to have nothing to do with his father. The old man was in FBI custody, so why couldn't it be over? It wasn't like he would be able to hurt anyone else.

So no one needed to know.

Right?

It was bad enough that Pierce Cartwright had been arrested as Adrian Pierce West. The town was reeling over the use of that name. Though, Ted figured that was just his dad thinking he was hilarious. Using an assumed name that would get everyone in Last Chance up in arms.

Adrian Pierce West, recently appointed to CIA director, had

since been identified by the FBI who arrested him as also being Pierce Cartwright.

Now everyone knew Ted and Dean's father for exactly who he was.

Or, they thought they knew the full extent of it.

Ted strode back to his computer and pulled up the photo, desperate to change the subject. "We only have two days to figure out where the Founders next meeting will be. That's got to be the priority, not me returning a phone call."

The image showed six men dressed in military fatigues. All young, given their ages at the time of their service in Vietnam. They'd come home and founded the town of Last Chance.

Since neither said anything, Ted continued. "Of the six men in this photo, the only ones still in play are the fire chief and the owner of that restaurant on the highway."

"Pie flavor of the week is chocolate cream," Basuto said. "If we have to arrest him, I'm not going to be happy."

Conroy's lips curled up on one side. "The others are Chief Ridgeman, your father, the bank manager Silas Nigelson, and the doctor who tried to kill Ellie, right?"

Ted nodded. "Then there's whoever took the photo. We have three dead and one in FBI custody. But one of the other three *has* to be West, right? They're all involved in running this town. Legally and illegally, most likely, given their occupations. We figure out which one is in charge, and we can close the case."

"You think they're using burner phones to communicate?"

Basuto nodded. "Ones we don't know about."

"If they are," Ted answered Conroy's question, "which I do think is the case, then they don't know we're tracking their phones. Otherwise, they would leave their personal phones at home."

Conroy scratched his jaw. "There's no way to predict where they might go next?"

"No rhyme or reason." Ted pulled up the GPS history he'd

loaded onto a map. Three points were marked. "Once a month, in the middle of the night, they all show up in the same place. But it's so random, there's no way to get ahead of them."

"But we know it'll be two nights from now." Basuto folded his arms. "So we just have to follow them that night."

"Unless they get the impression we're breathing down their necks and they change it up completely." Ted thought about it. "And I'm not even sure we have two days. It's never the same day or the same length of time between meetings. It's far more general than that. Whenever their schedules converge, and they decide to meet up for whatever reason."

"One of them is *West*."

Ted heard Basuto's tone. "I'm as motivated as you are to figure this out."

He didn't even want to think about what'd been happening under their noses in this town. It turned his stomach what they had uncovered. What the bank manager had been involved in.

Jess wasn't the only one looking into it. But what she did on her own time put her at risk.

Conroy said, "We have to stick with the book on this one. We have probable cause to surveil, but until we have evidence of wrongdoing, anything more would be harassment. We're already skirting a line."

"Maybe your dad can tell us who is who." Basuto lifted his chin, a hard look in his eyes as he stared at Ted.

Because Ted had confronted him about his gung-ho determination? Maybe he just didn't like the fact Conroy's girlfriend —now his fiancé—had been hired as the Lieutenant instead of him. Ted didn't have the mental or emotional energy to figure out what the sergeant's problem was. He had enough going on.

Basuto said, "Your dad is in that picture, so he's involved. If someone in town is a crime boss and that person is also a founder of this town, then your dad probably knows who it is. Right?"

"I'm not talking to him." Just considering making contact with his father made him want to race for the door and run.

No. He was going to stay here and fight his way.

Basuto studied Ted's expression in a way that made him want to squirm. "You're not keeping anything from us, right?"

Ted held back any sign of a reaction. Any move he made would reveal the truth to these two men he respected. Good cops. They didn't need to know who Ted really was, or what he'd done.

"Can we just figure this out?" Ted pointed at the police chief. "Conroy looks exhausted, and we've all had a long day. If Jess is going to get in over her head chasing down one of these men, then we need a way to mitigate the damage done."

Conroy said, "Damage to her, or damage caused by her?"

"Yes." Ted had no illusions Jess wasn't going to get into trouble one of these days. She didn't want to let this case go. Their investigation was being kept quiet, and she didn't like how long it was taking.

"So talk to her." Basuto lifted one dark brow. "After you talk to the FBI. Jess will listen to you because you guys are…you know."

Ted stood again. "What is with you?"

"Sit down."

He obeyed Conroy, but said, "The Sarge needs to back off."

Conroy shot Basuto a look that said, "enough."

"They have a thing." Basuto lifted his hands.

"Not right now." Ted didn't look at either man. He kept his attention on the computer instead.

"Woman troubles?"

"Sergeant."

Both men fell silent.

"I'll do what I can to make sure she's safe, just like everyone else in this department. What's going on personally between Jess and I is our business."

He glanced at them, the sergeant and the chief. Ted wasn't a cop, but working for the Last Chance Police Department was the only legitimate job he'd ever had in his life. And it had kept him from spending years in jail.

"This is about Chief Ridgeman and the debt we all owe him," Ted said. "Keeping his granddaughter safe."

That was all it was. Ted's feelings for her were wrapped up in the gratitude he owed her grandfather. And the guilt that while the old man had done so much for him, Ted never quite managed to leave his old life behind.

The last thing he needed was for the people in this town—least of all his brother, or Jess and her sister—to find out the truth.

"If that's what you're going for, fine." But Basuto shot him a look. "Sure. It's all about respect and loyalty." Before they could argue with that, Basuto stood. "I have to get home."

His shift started early, so that made sense. But there was still more that Ted didn't get about the sergeant. He'd been working more since Conroy was injured, and he seemed to grow terser and terser with every day that passed. Hopefully Conroy would be back to work soon. Or the lieutenant would figure out what was going on and intervene.

Ted didn't want to be alone where Conroy could ask questions he didn't want to answer, so he shut the laptop. Basuto was already at the front door.

Ted said, "I should be going too. My brother will be wondering where I am."

Conroy lifted his chin. "Send me everything. We'll put together an operation; see if we can catch the founders together and record their conversation."

Ted nodded. "Understood."

He wound up walking with Basuto through the parking lot of Conroy's condo complex. Ted wanted to ask him what his problem was. But what would be the point? He needed to keep things simple, not get tangled up in interpersonal issues.

There was enough of that with Jess and their shared kiss.

Now, instead of getting together, they were in some weird, not-friends/not-dating zone he didn't know how to get out of. Ted had to watch everyone around him pair off with someone and find happiness. Conroy and Mia were engaged. Tate and Savannah had eloped and were currently on their honeymoon. Stuart and Kaylee had gotten married in a quiet ceremony. Now Dean was asking Ted to help him work out a proposal for Ellie, Jess's sister.

His own brother. Her sister. Together.

Thanksgiving dinner was going to be a nightmare unless they could be around each other without things getting emotionally charged. *Yeah, right.* He should book a vacation and disappear for the rest of the year.

"Later."

Ted glanced across the parking lot at Basuto. Lifted his chin. After the sergeant turned away, he sighed and leaned against his car door. Sometimes keeping up the pretense of being an upright member of the police department and the community they served was too much. Even going home where he lived with his brother and their friend Stuart *and* a whole private security team of four guys wasn't exactly comfortable.

None of them knew, any more than Conroy did.

As much as Ted tried to bury the past, it was still very much alive and part of his life. Only in the stolen moments when he was alone could he take a full breath and be honest.

He'd thought for a while that he might be able to tell Jess the truth. But he couldn't. She would turn him in for sure.

Ted's cell phone rang. He tensed for a second before forcing himself to relax. *You need a vacation.* This couldn't last forever. Holding all the dissonant fragments of his life together. His grip was slipping.

The screen illuminated.

"No." That number was…

Ted threw the phone away like it had caught fire. It bounced off the front seat and fell to the floor. Only his dad knew that number, and he was in federal custody. The guy couldn't make phone calls.

The alternative was that he'd told someone else how to contact Ted. But who had his dad revealed that secret to?

And what else had he told them?

3

____

"This is a warrant." Jess held it out for the new bank manager, a sixty-year-old man in a suit to replace the previous sixty-year-old bank manager who also always wore suits. Silas Nigelson not only happened to be a founder of Last Chance, but also a Russian sleeper agent from way back in the seventies. No one had seen that coming.

Jess continued, "The warrant grants us access to Silas Nigelson's computer along with any other electronic device he had access to through the bank."

The bank manager took the paper. His gaze drifted down from her face to the nameplate on her uniform shirt. She saw the tiny inflection in the skin around his eyes.

Yes, her last name was Ridgeman. The police chief before Conroy had been her grandfather. Maybe he was just confused because Jessica Ridgeman, normally a blonde, had gone brunette for her last undercover assignment. Who knew? _Don't care._

"So if you'll show us to the right office, we won't need to disrupt any of your employees." She motioned as she spoke to Ted, who stood beside her in his customary black skinny jeans and red Converse shoes. In deference to the fact they were out of the office today and representing the department, he had a blue button-down shirt pulled on over his rock band T-shirt. Though the shirt remained unbuttoned.

His hair fell over one eye in a way that made her want to brush it back while he looked at her with those caramel-colored eyes. He'd shaved this morning, but she preferred the stubble he got after a long shift or if he skipped a day.

The new bank manager said, "Right this way."

As they passed the counter to the back hall, Jess swiped a business card from the stack. Garfield Thieles. She pocketed the business card and had to fight the urge to shake her head. Where did they come up with these names? Made her and Ted look almost normal. Which was just a crazy thought.

Garfield trailed ahead of them, his shoes clipping the floor as he strode faster than necessary down the hall. Ready for them to get this done and get out.

She glanced at Ted. His attention was on the artwork, so she elbowed him in the arm.

"What?" Those caramel eyes.

She didn't know what to say. If he let her in, she might be able to help with whatever had him twisted up in knots. He thought he was hiding it, but she could read him. She knew he wasn't all right. No matter that he tried to convince everyone otherwise.

In the end, she settled on a neutral, unemotionally-charged conversation. "Where do you want to go for lunch?"

"I don't have time for lunch. Too much to do." He looked at the screen of his smartwatch. "Soon as we're done, I have to get back to the office."

"I could get lunch and bring it to you if you need help."

"I'm surprised you have time, what with your solo investigation into the criminal world of Last Chance."

Jess stiffened. He knew. How on earth did he know? Of course she hadn't been able to keep anything a secret.

"Yeah, I know. So does Basuto. And Conroy." His gaze darkened. "Newsflash, Jess. You aren't fooling anyone."

"I wasn't trying to."

"Then why go vigilante in your off hours?"

"I'm trying to help. What if I find something?" Even the tiniest chance she might be able to find a clue, a lead. Something they could use to identify West and uncover the horrible operation that had been going on in town—and likely still was. Their actions could save the women involved. Get them free and in a place where they could heal and rebuild their lives.

They stopped just outside the door, and he turned to her. "You could get hurt."

Jess motioned to her uniform. "I could get hurt every day. Just like you. Anything could happen, and we'd never know it was coming. But I'm not sitting on the sidelines because I'm too scared to take a chance. Not if I can *help* someone."

This time things would be different. She wasn't going to let those women down.

"You help people every day." He frowned, about to say something else, when the bank manager interrupted.

"The terminal is in here."

Ted stepped by her and into the room which opened into an expansive office space where half a dozen people worked. Most turned to see her and Ted at the door with their boss.

Garfield waved Ted to a desk. "From here, you can access the network. Nigelson had files saved locally on his computer, and those are on a flash drive which contains a copy of his hard drive." He glanced at her, a politely bland smile on his face. "Of course, his computer is now my computer. But we copied everything just in case. I'll have that brought over." Garfield snapped his fingers, and a woman hurried over.

She wasn't much older than Jess and wasn't familiar. *Sally Peters* was printed plainly on her ID badge. Garfield gave her orders, and she rushed to obey.

Jess wondered how much of Nigelson's files they'd altered in the process. A way for the bank to save face after their name was tarnished when the truth about Nigelson—and his daughter, who had also been employed here—came out. Silas and his daughter were both dead now. Whatever they might find here would be added to the FBI's case against Ted's father, who had been behind an international operation that had agents undertaking all kinds of missions. Assassinations, intelligence gathering, and so much more.

Garfield left him to it. Ted typed on the computer keyboard faster than anyone she'd ever met. It was almost mesmerizing, though she couldn't get drawn in by him. Not only did he need space to get on with it, but she was also here to protect him. Partners watching each other's backs—except she was the one carrying a gun.

Jess paced the space in front of the door. Then wandered the length of the room. Five minutes later, she made it back to Ted's side.

He didn't look at her. "Find something to do."

Jess sighed. Inactivity sucked.

"Somewhere else."

She walked away, ambling around the room like she had a place to be. Like she appreciated doing nothing.

As she passed, Garfield's lackey tensed.

Jess kept moving. No sense giving away the fact she knew she made Sally Peters tense. Jess's gaze strayed to the woman's computer screen and snagged on the image of a woman she'd met once. A long time ago.

She turned towards the desk and planted one hand beside Sally's white-knuckle grip on the mouse. Jess put her other hand on the back of Sally's chair and leaned down. "Huh."

She read Sally's post on social media. It linked an article from a small, sensationalized Brooklyn newspaper—online only —and Sally had added commentary of her own. An article Jess had not yet seen.

The mouse hovered over the Send button.

"Did some research on me?"

"Uh…I…"

"Don't bother."

Sally shoved her chair back, running over Jess's shoe. She didn't let on that it hurt. Sally backed up in the chair but didn't stand. "You have no right to be in my personal space."

Jess grabbed the mouse and clicked, "cancel." The woman's image remained, in her mind. *Rest peacefully, Nicole.* She would see that face when she closed her eyes tonight and tried to sleep.

"That's my business, not yours!"

"No? That's slander. Or is it libel?" She tapped her lip. "Ted!" She called out to him across the room. "Remind me, what's the difference between being nice and keeping your mouth shut about things you know nothing about, and mouthing off using bully tactics for everyone's online entertainment?"

She couldn't quit seeing the photo, even though it was gone. Pain sliced through her chest as though she'd been wounded. The memory she'd buried since she came here resurfaced.

Trying to wash away the past hadn't worked; it was still there in her. Ready to jump up at any moment, whether she liked it or not.

Across the room, Ted said, "I'm busy. I'm sure you can handle whatever it is."

Jess turned to Sally. "He's right. I can."

She should at least look guilty, but the woman's cheeks had pinked. Shame that she'd been caught. Not embarrassed and sorry for what she was about to say about Jess online—as though social media gave anyone permission to tear another person apart and get away with it.

Jess decided to give Ted a pass for not jumping up and wading in. The fact she would have and always did, was just her. He was right. He was busy. Her thing didn't need him, because she *could* handle it. That was true as well.

"What are we going to do now, Sally?"

"Get out of my face." Her cheeks reddened further. "You think just because you're a cop, you can throw your weight around, and I'll do nothing? That I'm supposed to just let this go, roll over and play dead?"

"I don't know you, right? We haven't met before." She didn't think they had. Jess made mistakes like anyone. Who knew what some of the people in town had decided about her from just seeing her once, or misconstruing something she said. Taking it out of context.

Sally's eyes narrowed. "I know who you are."

O-kay. "And the reason you think it's okay to bad-mouth me online is....?"

"It's the truth. Sometimes the truth hurts." She lifted her chin, her gaze hard. "Deal with it."

Jess grinned. "Deal with it?"

"Are you laughing at me?" Sally stood, pushing her chair back into the walkway. "You think you can do whatever you want. All you cops do. Well, your boss will be hearing about this. I'm going straight to the mayor. You'll probably get fired."

She brushed past Jess and clipped her arm in the process. Definitely on purpose. Sally strode to the door and hauled it open. Jess was right behind her. She cast one glance back at Ted, still busy. He would be fine for a few minutes. This was important.

Sally started, but kept walking. "This is *harassment*. I should have known."

"That I'd follow you so I can state my case to the mayor?" That would be a hit or miss. Although Conroy tried, the Mayor didn't always throw his hat in with the police department. Despite the fact they were on the same team, one that also included all the civilians living in Last Chance, there could sometimes be contentions.

At the end of the hall, she stepped out into the front-facing area of the bank. Sally started to walk faster on her tiny heels, making a beeline for the other side of the room as though trying to escape this whole situation. She was the one who'd created it. Was Jess supposed to just back off when someone wanted to post hateful words about her on the internet?

Sure, she couldn't control what people posted. Or others' opinions. Trolls trashed people online every day—even strangers—tearing them apart because of a disagreement.

It was ugly, but she'd never thought it would happen to her.

The front doors of the bank flew open and four men poured in. They wore gray overalls and black ski masks and carried automatic weapons.

Jess reached for her gun, unsnapping the clip that held it secure.

Sally grasped Jess's weapon and kicked the back of her knee in one fell swoop before Jess could pull her gun out herself. Pain ricocheted down her leg as she fell to one knee. When Jess looked up, Sally had the gun pointed right at her face.

"I wouldn't want you to get me killed too."

4

—————

The second she left the office, Ted clicked through to the internet site. Not that he was hiding anything from Jess… okay, he was hiding *this* from Jess. But he didn't want her in here, just in case he actually found something. She could read him. Most of the time he liked that, but the fact was sometimes it wasn't handy. Like right now.

He sighed, whispering to himself, "She can't know."

One of these days, he would be found out. Someone would discover one of the many things he'd kept to himself. Since the day the previous chief, Jess's grandfather, had hired him, he'd promised to sever all contact with his father.

Then he'd been ordered to find the old man.

Neither Conroy nor Ted's brother Dean needed to know Ted had been aware of his father's location this entire time. After all, he wasn't interested in being caught unawares by his dad showing up unannounced.

Ted planned to split town before that happened.

Now that his dad had been arrested, Ted could finally breathe. He didn't need to check on his father's location. The FBI were the ones who knew where he was.

He'd found the link embedded in the wider bank network. It

hadn't taken long to look through what the bank manager had given him. After all, there had been barely anything on the flash drive or in Nigelson's files. So what if the wider network wasn't listed on the warrant? That was bank business, and he wasn't getting into their transactions or records. The former manager's files had been completely sanitized of anything "sensitive" relating to the bank and its customers.

This website was nothing related to the bank. It just happened to be here. Now that he'd found this, buried in the network server, it was clear Nigelson had conducted his *other* business at work, though it was...extra-curricular. He hadn't even tried to hide it.

None of what Ted found now would be admissible in court. It may not even relate to the case, considering it might have been planted on the database—or added to it—after Silas Nigelson was killed.

So who put it here?

While the front page loaded, he waited. Upon signing in, he would then be taken to a database.

The title and image that loaded made his stomach roil. But that wasn't the whole of what sickened him about this business. Ted immediately recognized the construction of the database. His father had paid him to build this particular program. His own two hands had put this system together. Not so it could be handed off to a local crime boss and used to sell what it was peddling right now. No, Ted had been sold a line about humanitarian efforts.

Then again, everything his father had ever said had been a lie.

But using something Ted put together for *this*? Well, he shouldn't be surprised West had his hands on it now. If he was honest with himself, he should have guessed all along given the connection between Pierce Cartwright and the founders of Last Chance. But for the way his father had manipulated Ted for years, he had been so twisted up he'd never even thought to be skeptical about what was happening below the surface line he'd been fed.

For his self-preservation. Both because he hadn't wanted to know, and because he'd been threatened. The lives of his brother and his friends and the people of Last Chance, put at risk because Ted decided to rock the apple cart as it were.

"Hey, you can't look at that stuff on bank computers!" The woman strode over. She was probably in her fifties and looked like a Sunday school teacher at her decently-paid job. "That's just not right. We have firewalls." She waved an arm, gold bracelets jingling. "Get rid of it. Gross!"

She reached for the mouse. The way Jess had done with that assistant woman.

Ted didn't touch her, but he got his hand between hers and the mouse. "Whoa. Hold up one second, and I'll tell you this is a police investigation." He showed her his ID badge. "I'm Ted Cartwright. This is for a case."

"This?" She pointed at the screen, clearly not convinced. The look of disgust on her face matched how he also felt about this whole thing.

The business itself, and whoever was behind it. And his part in it, if he was going to be honest. Ted had tried desperately over the years to let go of the guilt and shame of all his father had forced and manipulated him into doing. Now all his guilt and shame were plain to see, reflected on this woman's face— her name tag read Barbara.

"I'm sorry, Barbara, but yes." He looked at the screen. "I'll minimize it and—"

"I can't believe you're looking at something like that. Cops are nasty, apparently."

"It's part of the job. Doesn't mean I like it." He hoped she'd understand. That, or realize it had nothing to do with him ogling the female form. "I won't be long, and then I'll be out of here. I just need to make sure I have everything relevant to the police investigation."

"Silas." She muttered the bank manager's name, then frowned. "Is that Sally?"

Ted blinked.

"I mean," Sunday school lady continued, "Now that I can see past the whole *underwear* thing to get a look at her face, it does kind of look like Sally." She pointed at the screen—the woman on the home page.

Ted hadn't looked much past registering that she wore lacy nightwear. Now he focused on her face. Barbara might be right. It did kind of look like Sally.

Ted asked, "How well do you know her?"

"Not *this* well." Barbara winced. "Yikes. But she's only worked here for a few days. She started last week."

"Ma'am." He didn't need her getting in the middle of this. Not any more than she already was. "Can you please find my partner and ask her to come back here?"

Where had Jess gone anyway? She'd been bearing down on Sally, doing her thing by fighting crime single handedly—or a woman bad mouthing her. He sighed. *Should have brought a radio.* If he had, he'd be able to have the dispatcher radio her immediately to get back here instead of calling Bill on this stranger's phone to ask that favor.

Sally might be involved in something other than assisting the new bank manager.

Ted inserted his own flash drive into the port on the tower by his leg and started copying the database so he could go through the programming code later. Figure out how long this had been going on. Then he would report to Conroy what he'd found—provided it was relevant to the case.

The woman huffed.

Ted didn't have time. He needed to finish this.

"Please. Just go and find my partner. She left with Sally." The second he said it, Ted wondered if that meant Jess might be in danger at this moment. He dismissed that idea as soon as he thought of it. She could take care of herself, and Jess was the first person who would tell anyone who asked that exact thing.

Still, just to be safe, he sent a text to Basuto. There was cause to request backup, and enough had happened in Last Chance the previous few months that he wasn't about to risk anyone getting hurt. Not if he could help it.

Barbara muttered a comment but walked away. Ted looked around to check and see if anyone else was staring at his computer screen. When he was satisfied no one else cared and that the few people in here were occupied with looking at their own business, he pulled his flash drive out and headed to the Command Prompt window. From here, he'd be able to find out which terminal put the database on the network.

He would also be able to remove it.

No one would ever know his involvement in this case. Or what was turning out to be a connection he'd never seen before.

Just the idea of having his name—his programming signature—on it made him want to pick up this monitor and throw it across the room. But what would getting into a rage serve to do? It wouldn't help him think clearly. Right now, answers were what he needed. Not an emotional reaction.

Jess had no idea what he was dealing with. She didn't want to know even though she had asked him. He could tell she liked the idea of them opening up to each other more—deepening their relationship. But the surface-level friendship they had going on was only serving her so far. She didn't have to give up her independence for anyone else. She didn't have to sacrifice to be with him.

Even if they started dating officially, he still didn't think she could ease up on her dogged determination to get to the bottom of each and every dangerous situation involving an innocent person. The woman simply didn't sleep if a missing person's case came across her desk. Especially if it was a woman or a child.

He was all-in to help. But he knew his limitations.

His weaknesses.

She would sweep him along for the ride, or he could disembark. They'd go their separate ways. Either way, she'd sleep well knowing she'd done everything she could for the people who needed help. And not once would she admit what there was in her past that drove her to it.

Ted had read her NYPD file, but too much of her undercover work hadn't been reported. Who knew which person she'd lost while on duty impacted her most? She didn't let go of her emotions. Not ever.

Ted, on the other hand, couldn't risk opening up about anything. Because once she found out, his whole life would be over. All he'd worked for since her grandfather hired him would be gone.

He would lose everything.

Which was why he was tempted to simply delete the whole site. Or any record of it on this system.

If he only took it off this local network, would the truth come out later?

Ted worked for the police department. *Can you really betray everything you stand for?* His finger hovered over the mouse button, and he chewed on his bottom lip.

Delete.

One button and he'd be free of this. He could solve Jess's problem and bring the operation down with the loss of their system. And he could solve his own problems at the same time.

His finger continued to hover.

Just one click.

"I don't think I'm going out there." Sunday school lady rushed back in, breathy. "There are men out in the foyer. With *guns.* And they're not here for good reason." She raced to a desk and reached to press a button under the counter.

A gunshot blasted.

The woman's body jerked and red blossomed on her sweater. A second later, she fell to the ground.

"She hit the panic button." A gunman standing by the door turned to look behind him down the hall. He swore. "She got to it."

Out of sight, someone else exclaimed loudly.

Ted shifted. Ouch. He was on the floor. His fingers swiped through a collection of dust and dirt under the same desk he'd been sitting at only a second ago. When had he hit the ground?

He couldn't tear his gaze from the woman on the floor, blood pooling around her body.

Ted pulled in a ragged breath and reached for his smartwatch to call for help.

Where was Jess?

5

"You picked a bad day to rob this bank."

The closest man hauled Jess to her feet while Sally held the gun on her. Jess glanced at the bank manager's assistant. "An inside job. It's a classic for a reason."

"Please let me shoot her." Sally didn't take her focus from Jess.

The man still holding her arm shook his head. "Not here."

So he was in charge. Sally was an underling who took orders. Also, they planned to kill her. Or, at least, they weren't opposed to it.

Of the three men who'd entered behind him, one moved across the room. He knew where he was going. The money guy? The other two fanned out, yelling at the customers and staff members. In just a matter of seconds, everyone was on the ground and ordered to turn over their cell phones.

"Won't be long before the cops show up."

His eyes flashed, the rest of his face covered by the ski mask. "Guess we'll have to be quick then." He shoved her around and then stuck the gun in her back. "Hands up. Isn't that what y'all say?" He jabbed at her spine with the barrel of his weapon.

Jess stepped forward. Sally was close enough that Jess could have reached out and grabbed her gun back. The one pointed at her spine stopped her though. Any move she made, he'd shoot her in the back.

Not here.

What was their plan?

Were they reacting to her presence, surprised she was here after casing the bank for days to find the best time to rob it? Or did they know already that she was going to be here?

Whichever it was, Jess had no intention of letting them know Ted was here. She would do whatever it took to keep it a secret.

She spread her fingers as she walked. "No one needs to get hurt." She pointed at the customers and staff, now rounded up into a group of five sitting beside the counter in a huddle on the floor. "You can let these people leave now. I'm not trying to toot my own horn, but I'm a pretty valuable hostage. Things go sideways, I carry weight. You know?"

She was waffling. Also, she didn't want things to go sideways.

Since no one said anything, she continued, "Let these people go. There will be fewer variables that way, and if someone innocent gets hurt, you'll be in more trouble than you need to be."

Plus, one of them could call the PD. If no one had already.

He chuckled.

"I'm a cop. I have to at least try to save the innocent people you're terrorizing."

"Yeah, that's what I am. A terrorist." He still sounded amused. "Isn't everyone a terrorist these days?"

Jess didn't figure he needed an answer. "Where are we going?"

Sally was the one who said, "That other hall over there."

The gun jabbed her back.

Jess gritted her teeth. "I think you should consider letting those people go." She didn't want to see anyone hurt, but being forced to leave, knowing innocent people were being hurt might be just as bad. She slowed her step and spoke over her shoulder, even though two guns were pointed at her. "Please, let them go."

Sally snorted. "Wow, bleeding heart much."

"They have nothing to do with this. Take the money and go. No one needs to get hurt."

The blow came out of nowhere.

"You were saying?"

On hands and knees, Jess breathed through the pain that cut like a blowtorch through her skull. She worked her jaw side to side and blew out a long breath. *Ouch.* He'd slammed the butt of his gun against her temple. Faster than she'd been able to react to the blow.

Sally lifted her foot. Jess twisted and caught the kick, bracing against it. But the heel of Sally's pump jabbed into her abdomen. She blew out the breath. Not nearly as much force as the blow to her head.

Sally thought it was hilarious though.

Jess ignored the pain in her head and her side, rocked back on her feet, and stood up. Teeth gritted.

"Now move."

She strode forward, hands raised again. To a hall she'd never been down before. Sally opened the door to a storage closet and shoved Jess in.

The gunman said, "I'll go round up the stragglers."

He wandered off, leaving Sally alone at the door of the closet. Jess stood beside one of those huge, yellow mop buckets, one side containing dark gray water.

Sally stared at her, still holding the gun.

Jess lifted her chin. "What?"

Didn't she have people to terrorize? Once Sally shut the door, Jess could get to work figuring a way out of this.

Until then? There wasn't much she could do that wouldn't result in her getting shot for her troubles. Jess's whole body tensed. She swayed slightly as pain rolled through her head. It was like the world's worst migraine—and she knew exactly what those felt like.

Jess reached up and touched her temple. Enough to know there was no blood, just a huge knot.

Sally chuckled. Before she could shut the door, Ted was shoved into the storage closet beside her. His jaw set. Eyes burning with suppressed anger. He held his right arm against his front with his left hand.

He stumbled into the room, and she reached for him.

At the door, the gunman stood watching. Then, with a flick of his wrist, the door slammed shut.

Jess touched his elbow and shoulder. "You okay?"

Ted flashed gritted teeth. "I don't need help."

Or sympathy, apparently. "Sorry." She stepped away. Circled the room for another door. No windows. She tried the door handle. It didn't turn. They'd been locked in. She spun back to him and planted her hands on her hips. "What happened with you?"

"They shot one of the bank employees." He shut his eyes for a second.

"Is your wrist broken?"

He shrugged one shoulder and looked around.

"I can probably kick the door open, but that doesn't solve the problem that we're unarmed."

The corner of his lips twitched. He tapped the screen of his watch. "I'm clear."

"Copy that." The voice that came through the tiny watch speaker had a tinny quality and crackled slightly.

"Is that Dean?"

The voice answered, "Hi, Jess. Sergeant Basuto is already out front and the bank is surrounded. He wants to make contact before he orders a breach."

"He thinks he can talk them down?"

"What's your read on them?"

For the duration of Jess's conversation with Dean, Ted stood watching her. She met his gaze. "Four guys, one woman. Sally. She works at the bank. I'm not sure what their endgame is."

"To rob the bank?"

Jess mulled that over. "Yeah, maybe." She didn't have enough of an idea otherwise to give any kind of definitive answer. "Either way, we need to get out of here. And we need weapons."

They were also both hurt.

"We're on our way." Dean said, "Sit tight. We'll come to you."

The screen of Ted's watch flashed. "He hung up."

Jess circled the room again. No matter where she was in the room, she was close enough to reach out and touch Ted. "You should move over there." She got between him and the door, motioning him to retreat farther across the storage closet. "Just in case."

"So I can watch you die as well?"

Her stomach churned. "That wasn't exactly what I had in mind. I will be between you and the door though. I'm the cop."

"And I'm just a useless IT guy."

"We both know you're way more than that." He wasn't going to miss her tone, or the look she shot him. "But this isn't about either of us. It's about those people out there, scared out of their minds. Wondering whether they're going to die at any moment, or if the police will storm in and rescue them. Which, sometimes, is just as scary."

She'd seen people react to the sudden influx of SWAT officers. It could be overwhelming. They looked fierce and commanding because they were *supposed* to. Some victims got scared. Some even fought the police trying to rescue them. For the officers, it was always a balancing act.

"Scary or not," Ted said. "It's for the best."

"Too bad people don't usually want what's best for them." She wasn't referring to herself, of course. Jess accepted what came. Ted was the one who looked for the very best he could be and for the very best he could have.

Which was part of the reason their relationship hadn't progressed.

Apparently, she wasn't *the best* for him.

"So Sally was in on it?"

When Jess turned to him, he continued, "She's connected to your case." He seemed reluctant to explain but told her about a database on the bank network. An internet link. Sally's picture on the home page.

"She's part of it."

He nodded.

"So there's a connection between these bank robbers suddenly deciding to steal money today of all days, and a woman who was their inside informant and a part of West's operation." Jess tapped her fingertips on her leg.

A connection.

Was West the driving force behind this group of bank robbers? No, all the crime in town couldn't be attributed to him. That would mean no one had free will or could operate without his permission. She didn't think things stretched that far in terms of his hold over Last Chance. Alternatively, they'd been employed by him to throw off the police.

As West had done when Jess's sister had been looking into their grandfather's past.

She kept tapping.

Throwing off the police. That meant the fact she and Ted were here was a threat to West. Which meant they were close to stumbling onto a lead, or evidence, that would point them to him in some way.

"We're a threat to him." She felt the pull of a smile on her lips. "That means he's scared."

"West?" Ted's tone indicated he didn't agree with that assessment. "More likely covering himself. Cleaning up his operation like he's been doing."

"If I was him, I'd have cut my losses and left town months ago. When we realized how far his operation stretched."

"But it all has to do with the founders, right? West is one of them. So why would he leave a place he helped start? He's entrenched in life here. It's his home."

Jess didn't like that. "Means he's even more motivated. Maybe desperate. He needs to keep his name out of this. Make sure no one finds out who he is."

She winced. Desperation might cause West to make a mistake, but it was also a dangerous place for all of them to be.

Staring down the barrel of a gun that shook. Tensions high. Everything on the line.

Realizing her enemy might be just as determined as she was to finish this didn't sit well. It caused that knot to twist tighter in her stomach. *That's why you have to do this.* The cost of failure would be high. Too high.

The door flung open. Sally and the gunman stood there. Sally glanced at him. "I've got it!" She even grinned. "I'll tell them he died because she couldn't protect him. That you killed him, and she just let it happen cause she couldn't do anything about it, and then you killed her too."

"Anyone ever tell you you're bloodthirsty?" The gunman grinned.

Someone behind him called out, "We've got the cash, and the kid's program is uploading the virus. The rest will be transferred within minutes."

The gunman nodded. "Let's go."

Ted sucked in a breath, stiffening.

Sally grinned. "Welcome to life as an accomplice. Of course, no one will know I was involved. I've got my story all worked out." She stepped back.

The gunman waved his weapon. "Let's go. It's got to look like you were both killed trying to stop us."

Jess flinched.

"Of course, you don't succeed."

6

____

The kid's program is uploading the virus.

Jess didn't seem to have realized what he had. They were shoved forward into the hall and led to the stairwell at the end. Where were they going?

Framed as accomplices.

Murdered here. Today.

The kid's program is uploading the virus. They had to be talking about him, and no one else. He might be in his mid-twenties, but nearly everyone thought he was younger. Or treated him as though he was. Usually it bothered him. On occasion, it came in handy.

These people had a connection to his father. Or, at least, a connection to another founder—maybe even West—who knew his dad. Who was it this time? No one with a conscience, that was for sure. Otherwise they wouldn't be so happy at the idea of ordering a team to murder Jess and Ted while their friends waited outside.

Would Dean get here in time?

His brother would set the world on fire if he thought it would protect Ted. Too bad Ted knew it was fueled by the guilt Dean felt over leaving Ted with their dad all those years ago.

But Dean had needed to escape. Ted was *glad* he'd done it. That only one of them remained in their father's grasp. Dean deserved to be free.

Jess stopped in front of him at the stairwell door.

The gunman got close. Ted saw her flinch. She was at the breaking point and wouldn't do well if she was hurt anymore. Ted didn't want her hurt more either.

"You don't have to do this."

There were two gunmen with them, and neither seemed to care that he was talking. One held a duffel bag stuffed full. Money. That wasn't what they'd come here for, considering how determined they were to set a scene that made it look like Jess and Ted had tried to stop them.

So elaborate.

For whatever reason, the plan was for them to die here today. No matter what else happened, that was their strategy and not monetary gain. They also didn't seem interested in any alternative ideas.

Ted tried again. "Who is behind all this? If you give us a name, we can make it worth your while."

Everyone had a price, especially people who regularly did all kinds of unsavory things for money. Either they were invested in the outcome, or they were just here for the payment. Time would tell. But he had to at least try and get them to change their minds. It was by far the safest option to convince these men to stand down. Turn themselves in. Roll over on whoever hired them.

The information would be worth whatever it cost.

The only other way they would get out of this without being murdered in cold blood was by fighting these two men.

Ted was going to save that option as the last resort.

Jess shifted. The gun aimed at her, lifted to point at her face, and the man holding it said, "Open the door."

She reached back, grasped the handle, and opened it. Ted was shoved through first. Jess never turned her back on the gunman. Not until doing so would mean an inevitable fall down the stairs. She held the stair rail as they descended.

Where are you, Dean?

Ted had tried to be self-sufficient for so long that being desperate for his brother to rescue him left a bad taste in his mouth. But Dean had been a Navy SEAL. If anyone could resolve this without Jess and Ted being injured in the process, it was his big brother.

The memory of that woman falling, shot right in front of him, flashed across his mind. A low moan escaped his lips.

Jess reached over and grasped his hand. A show of solidarity. The quick, tight squeeze of her fingers around his. Trying to reassure him.

He shot her a tight smile. As much as he could muster right now when there were guns pointed at their heads, and they were being walked to their deaths. She thought she had to protect him. She was determined to do it, the same way she thought she had to protect every other innocent that came into her life.

Ted didn't plan on telling her *again* that he didn't need her help. He'd grown tired of the same old conversation they'd had plenty of times before. There was no sense—and likely no time —to tell her again now. Not when it was clear she hadn't listened and probably didn't plan to.

They were about to be murdered.

If he was going to be exposed as being part of it, that might be for the best. Otherwise, he would have to face everyone he knew finding out. *No, death isn't a good answer.* It was never satisfactory as a way out—especially not when he didn't exactly have his life right with God.

Now's as good a time as any.

But when it came down to it, he didn't know what to say. *I'm sorry.* Ted didn't enjoy being a victim. He needed to take responsibility, not hide it anymore. But he also needed to control the fallout. It couldn't affect an investigation.

The district attorney would use any excuse to undermine

their investigation. She'd never liked Conroy and had no love for their small-town department. If his misdeeds came to light, it would cast a shadow on every case he'd worked. Ted couldn't risk jeopardizing a court case that could bring West down. Whoever West was, he should be in jail. Not free because of a technicality Ted could have avoided by doing the right thing and coming clean.

No. He would make sure that when it all came out there were no repercussions with the police department. They'd never forgive him otherwise. Jess most of all was about loyalty and justice. They would at least understand why he'd done what he'd done.

While she would not.

"In there."

At the bottom of the stairwell, they stepped through a doorway into what seemed to be a boiler or utility room of some kind.

Jess glanced at him. Both men were behind them now. Ted caught the look on her face, she was ready to act. Determined to do something about this situation and unwilling to wait any longer.

Ted spun the second she did. He sideswiped the gun with his forearm and kicked the gunman where it would hurt most, then brought up his knee and slammed it into the man's face.

He grabbed the gun, turned to Jess, and saw her locked in a battle with her guy.

Their gun went off. Ted ducked on a reflex, adrenaline from his own fight rushing through him to heighten everything—even while his vision tunneled. He shook off the sensation and kept his hold on the weapon in his hands.

Part of his attention stayed on the downed man and his duffel of money. Unconscious, for now.

Jess elbowed her guy in the face and got his gun. She brought the butt of it down on his temple, and he collapsed. She spun to him.

Ted backed up a step. "Whoa."

"You're okay?" She glanced at the man on the floor.

"What do we do now?"

The skin around her eyes flexed. "Secure these two and head upstairs. You contact Dean and I'll—"

"I'm already here."

His brother's frame filled the doorway. "You okay, Ted?"

He nodded. "We both are. But Jess could use an ice pack for her head."

She glanced at him.

"You guys head upstairs. We'll take care of these two."

Ted noticed Stuart behind him and lifted his chin.

"You okay, kid?"

He shrugged. They collected the gun from him and took over. Ted followed Jess up the stairs. Before stepping through the door, she turned to him. "Are you really okay?"

"We're not dead, right?"

She didn't buy him brushing it off with humor. Her eyes narrowed. "How did you take that guy down?"

"I kneed him. Twice."

She said nothing.

"Zander taught me some fighting skills. Figured one day I'd need to protect myself." Ted shrugged a shoulder. "I guess he was right."

"You know, you act all nonchalant, but I'm thinking that's not true."

"What are you talking about?" They needed to get this conversation done so he could get upstairs and mitigate the damage that would be done when his name was dragged into this.

"You play stuff off as no big deal." She studied him with an all-too-knowing gaze. "But it's not, is it?"

Ted pressed his lips into a thin line. What did she want from him? They'd gotten away from those guys, and they had a lead in the process—West didn't want them alive. The bad guy they were chasing felt threatened enough he'd retaliated. Talk about showing your cards. He'd made a move and exposed his thinking to them.

Ted and Jess, together, were capable of bringing him down.

She took a half step closer to him. "Thank you."

"For what?" He did a half-shrug.

"Helping. I wouldn't have been able to take both of those guys down by myself. I figured we'd end up dead, but I figured it was worth the risk. You helped, and it saved our lives."

"I know you'd never go down without a fight."

A tiny smile curled up the edges of her lips. She closed the space between them another inch. Ted looked down at her, since she was in her work shoes with flat heels. What were her intentions here? Was she just happy to be alive, wanting to enjoy the experience of that feeling? Remembering their kiss.

She said, "You did good, Ted. I was surprised. But that's not a bad thing."

Ted leaned down slightly, letting her show him what she wanted. Jess was like a wildfire. He'd tried to grasp it once already, and he'd been burned in the process. Neither of them wanted to give up what they held most dear, and yet the attraction was still strong between them. They were a great team.

She lifted onto the balls of her feet and touched his arm. He felt her breath on his face and closed his eyes as their lips touched in the gentlest of—

Someone cleared their throat.

Ted stepped back. Jess spun around, cheeks red. Basuto stood at the open doorway. The one he hadn't even heard move. Nor had he heard their sergeant arrive. Too wrapped up in the rush of what might happen.

"There's work to do upstairs." Basuto's eyebrow rose. "Maybe you guys can save that for later."

He disappeared behind the door. Jess followed him without a backward glance, leaving Ted in the stairwell by himself.

He hauled the door open and trotted up behind them. Jess

seemed embarrassed, but Ted just couldn't muster that emotion. That was the problem. Maybe they shouldn't be around each other. That would certainly be easier.

Was that how they were going to bring down West, by working separately instead of combining efforts?

Ted sighed.

Jess shot him a glance, but he waved her off. This wasn't about what was, or wasn't, happening between them. There would be time after West was brought in for them to have the conversation.

It's not you, it's me.

That would be the safest thing. A way to maintain what they had; a good friendship, and solid careers. Neither of which he was prepared to risk.

The last thing he needed was for her to discover everything just because he put his guard down for a moment to let her in. That would be the worst possible thing for him. Jess was entirely too astute. Of course, she would figure it out.

Until then, he had bigger problems than his life being in danger. In order to adequately protect the department from the mess that was his past, there was something he needed to do.

Ted had to scrub evidence.

7

"We know you're part of this."

Jess watched through the glass as Basuto leaned against the wall of the interrogation room. Mia sat at the table with him, the sergeant and the lieutenant interviewing Sally Peters about everything that'd happened at the bank.

Jess had told them as much as she'd remembered about Sally and what Ted had told her about the database he'd found on the computer. A link between this woman and West's operation at the warehouse.

Jess wanted to get in there and ask a few questions herself.

"Hey."

She spun to find Conroy shutting the door behind him.

"Should you be up?"

He shot her a look. "Get me a stool if you're concerned about me or if you're questioning the level of care and instruction I receive from my doctor."

She rolled her eyes. "Fine. You haven't been pushing it." The chief had been shot by a sniper just a few weeks ago. "It surprised me to see you standing."

Seemed like that was happening a lot lately. She was being thrown—first by him, then by Ted. Different situations for sure, but it spoke to the fact she'd been oblivious of things in front of her. Not paying enough attention to people who were close to her. People she cared about.

Jess sighed.

"Okay?"

She touched her forehead. The lump was still pretty big. "I'm guessing when the painkillers wear off, I'll have a great headache. I think Ted hurt his wrist, but I'm okay."

"Maybe I should get you a stool." Before she could chuckle at his words, Conroy motioned to the window. "Are they getting anywhere?"

Jess didn't want to sigh *again.* "I doubt she'll talk about West. There's nothing we can give her that will void what he'll do to her if she talks."

So many people with ties to West had been killed. She wondered about the spider tattoo guy she'd met on Friday night. If he wasn't a bad guy—which he hadn't seemed to be—he should watch his back.

She was used to picking up on small nuances and details others missed. He dressed the part, sure. Maybe it was her undercover work that made her think twice about their interaction. He hadn't been violent. He'd wanted her to let him go. If she'd been in the same situation as an undercover officer, she would have done the same thing.

Who was he?

"So we book her for the bank robbery," Conroy said. "And we get nothing else?"

"Until we find some evidence from the men." Forensics could tell them who those gunmen were, and then they'd start to dig into their lives. Their phones. Once they ID'd them, it wouldn't be long before they would have plenty of places to ask around. "Then we'll be turning over every rock we get, hoping for a hit on West."

Conroy nodded. "Did we run her prints?"

"Donaldson is going to come tell me when he gets a hit."

They'd taken her fingerprints when they booked her for being an accomplice to the attempted armed robbery of the bank. Until they knew her real name, any attempts to get more out of her would be stymied.

Conroy wandered over to lean against the wall. "Doesn't seem like she wants to say much."

"They even switched off asking questions. She has said nothing."

"But she hasn't asked for a lawyer."

Jess answered Conroy, knowing it was something between a question and a statement. "Maybe she doesn't want anyone to know she's here. Until it hits our system and word gets out that way."

Conroy nodded, a slow and measured movement.

Jess turned her attention back to what was happening in the interrogation room. At least watching them meant she wasn't thinking about Ted. Which meant, she would only end up sighing again. Quite frankly, she couldn't handle the unresolved feelings. Open case. Relationship in limbo. Her sister wasn't quite settled. The chief wasn't quite healed. And for whatever reason, Basuto's recent behavior made her wonder if he didn't approve of her as an officer.

Jess focused on the woman again. Sally Peters. "I just…"

When she said nothing else, Conroy said, "What?"

"She isn't beaten down. She's not one of West's victims."

"Maybe she recruits girls. Trains them."

"I know things like that exist in the world. And I see plenty in this job. You know, there's a reason I left New York and came here."

"Because your grandfather was sick."

"That was a real good excuse. And timely." Jess folded her arms even though her whole body was stiff. "Truth was, I couldn't hack it."

"I know that's not true."

She shrugged one shoulder, not willing to face her boss. "Maybe it is."

"I know you lost an innocent."

"None of us are innocent. The bad guys are right about that, at least." Jess shook her head. "People are just people. We make the choices we want to make, and some are born or forced into a life as a victim. But none of us are innocent."

Some people didn't want to be innocent. That was the truth she'd learned. Whether they fought back or, through choices, sabotaged their own life and the lives of others, didn't matter to so many. Bad guys just did whatever they were going to do and everyone else had to simply deal with the fallout. Jess didn't even know what to think anymore. Life wasn't close to black and white. There was evil, and there was good, but she could barely tell the difference anymore.

Especially when she was playing a part.

"Put together a proposal for an undercover operation. I'll take a look, but I'm gonna tell you now, Jess, I don't want you anywhere near what happened in that warehouse."

She glanced at him and saw some of the things he'd seen as a cop in his steady gaze. Surely he didn't know he was letting that shine through, but sometimes it was better to let some out than hold it all back and suffer for it.

Before she could tell him she didn't want to go undercover like that, any more than he did, he said, "We're going to find West the old-fashioned way. Investigating. Following leads."

She nodded.

"I'm sorry, but I don't think undercover is a good idea for this one."

Had she said that? He was the one who brought it up, not her. The last thing she wanted was to have to face that. Again. Did he think she would jump at the chance to be dragged into prostitution and sex trafficking? Jess's stomach flipped over, and she realized she hadn't eaten all day.

No. And not just because she wouldn't eat for days being

back in that world. Yes, she was good at undercover work. Her grandfather had let everyone know that part of her skillset. But it had pigeonholed her since then.

She'd been assigned to several cases that required undercover work. Now? Jess wanted to make detective. She wanted to investigate cases from start to finish; not just spend all shift responding to calls.

She wanted *out* of being the go-to for every clandestine operation the chief could come up with that required a female in her mid-twenties.

Jess opened her mouth to say just that, so Conroy would be clear on what she wanted, when the door opened.

Kaylee stuck her head in. "Hey, guys. Have either of you seen Ted?"

Jess shook her head. "Not since the bank."

"Me either." Conroy looked at his watch. "He should be back here by now." The chief followed Kaylee out.

Jess slid her phone from her pocket. No new notifications—texts or calls—from Ted, or anyone.

The door shut.

Jess went out, drawn more by worry over Ted than the nil contribution she'd made to the interrogation. They hadn't even entertained the idea of letting her in there. But how could she learn if they didn't let her try? She wanted to believe this was only about it being such an important case for them. She would continue to tell herself that. Spare herself the hurt.

Conroy had Mia's desk phone to his ear. "Sure?"

When she neared, he looked at her. Shook his head. Then into the phone, he said, "Thanks, Dean. Let me know if you find him."

He replaced the handset on the base.

"What's going on?"

He frowned. "Ted was headed back here. Dean says he left, but that was forty-five minutes ago. Even if he stopped somewhere, which—"

"Ted doesn't do. Ever." As much as it infuriated her, he didn't stop for coffee. He packed his own lunch. He ate at home. Stopping somewhere on the way here, especially without telling *anyone*, didn't seem like him at all.

And not just because she'd offered lunch and he'd turned her down.

Conroy nodded. "He should've been here by now."

Jess turned away. She strode to the back hall and the ten-by-fifteen closet he'd converted into an office. Supposedly it was so he'd be closer to the "network closet," whatever that meant. She figured it was because he didn't want to be around people to distract him all day. Same reason she preferred being out in her patrol car.

She checked that no one was in the hall and grabbed the key from the top of the door frame. It wouldn't be a secret forever, but it had worked so far. Jess let herself in. Ted wasn't inside with the door locked.

She glanced around. Every surface was covered with circuit boards. Keyboard. Mouse. Multiple monitors. More than one iPhone. There were even the guts of something that looked like it might've once been an Xbox. The whole place was an electronics graveyard.

Where are you?

She sent another text, asking him to check in, and wondered if Dean had that app set up where he could find Ted's GPS signal. Did they do that? Surely Ted would know if Dean had done it—no way could he keep that from a tech genius. And his older brother was the kind of guy who'd keep tabs on the younger brother he thought was helpless. That alone made her doubtful.

Admittedly, Jess had also thought of him like that…before today. Maybe not that he was helpless, exactly. No one with the skills Ted had to infiltrate computer systems was without defenses.

But seeing that he'd taken down a gunman? She'd practically swooned. All the way to pressing her lips to his and pretty much embarrassing herself when Basuto had caught them nearly kissing.

The whole thing was a disaster, and not just because it was obvious she'd underestimated him.

Maybe, right now, he was totally fine. Could be he was just doing his thing, and here she was underestimating him all over again. Jess probably didn't need to worry about him. He'd stroll in just fine. Or call and say he'd blown a tire on a back road and had to change it.

"Jess!"

She sprinted back to the main office. Dean was there now, as was Stuart who looked seriously pale. Both men lived with Ted. And she got the feeling Stuart considered him a younger brother nearly as much as Dean did.

"What is it?" She glanced between them, but no one said anything. "*What?*"

Kaylee walked over and set a hand on Jess's arm. Kaylee's hand shook.

Jess said, "Someone talk."

Dean started to, but Conroy interjected, "We need to find Ted as soon as possible. His life could be in danger."

"Someone already tried to kill us earlier. What else is new?" To her consternation, Jess's eyes filled with tears.

"The FBI is on their way. Pierce Cartwright escaped federal custody. They think he might be on his way here."

Ted's father was free?

"What?" She glanced around. "No."

Could he really have escaped the feds and made it to Last Chance this soon? How was it even possible he'd gotten to Ted so fast?

She saw the color bleed from Dean's face and knew Ted's experience to be far more visceral than even that. He refused to say much of anything about his father. All she knew from what Kaylee told her was that, most recently, he'd been appointed to the position of CIA director. Before he was arrested.

She blinked. "How could this have happened?"

Kaylee had been targeted by Pierce Cartwright. Jess spun to her, and the other woman nodded. Fear in her eyes. "I know."

Stuart came over to Kaylee.

"He's loose," Kaylee whispered to her husband.

Stuart took her hand and turned to the room. "We're going off the grid until Pierce Cartwright is back in FBI custody." To Dean, he said, "Find Ted."

8

———

A light shone above him. Ted blinked and saw the inside lid of a car trunk. A man stood in the opening—one of the gunmen. He wore a ski mask.

Ted gasped.

The man stared down at him.

Ted managed to groan out a couple of words. "What…" He didn't know what he was saying. Or if he'd even said anything.

He couldn't even remember the last thing he'd been doing.

Not to mention how he got here.

The masked man reached in and hauled him out of the trunk. Cool air brushed at his face, then he was inverted over the man's shoulder. Air pushed out of his lungs, and he groaned at the pressure against his abdomen. His arms swung free. He realized the smartwatch he always wore on his right wrist was gone.

The left one slammed against the back of the man's leg and pain erupted in his wrist like fire. With nothing in his stomach, he just dry heaved.

The man started to walk, jostling Ted with every step. He tried to think about what had happened. How he wound up here.

All he remembered was Jess. A moan escaped his lips. They'd nearly kissed again, and he'd wanted it. Only Basuto had interrupted, snapping them out of the dream where their lives were free of problems, and all they had was a serious case of infatuation. Back in the real world, where she was determined to find West, and Ted's job was to make sure that when the case was completed, the evidence was solid.

They couldn't afford for the founders to continue getting away with whatever they wanted. He was as just as driven as Jess to bring them down, but they had to do it right. If all they had was tainted evidence or electronic data that clouded the facts, what good would that do?

It had to be airtight.

The man carrying him stepped inside. A few paces later, Ted was tossed on a couch. He bounced, and his head hit a solid wood arm. He rolled over and dry heaved in the direction of old, stained, threadbare carpet.

"Pull it together."

The man opened a laptop on the coffee table while Ted leaned back and tried to settle his equilibrium. Did he recognize the voice? Ted would have to hear more to know for sure. Instead, the room spun around him. He made a circle with his lips and sucked in a long breath before pushing it back out.

He needed water, but this guy looked like he'd murder Ted just for asking for a concession.

The laptop screen illuminated. The man tapped the bottom of it, clicking on the touch screen. A video call rang. Seconds later, someone answered. The screen changed, but it was too dark to see the person who sat there.

"Ted Cartwright." The voice was distorted. He couldn't even tell if it was male or female.

He said nothing, just leaned his head back against the couch as it dawned on him this wasn't an unfamiliar experience. How many times had he been dragged into a clandestine conversation with his father? Too many, given the answer was more than one.

The distorted voice said, "You've seen my database. You wrote the program, so I'm sure you built in a back door for yourself."

He stared hard enough his eyes burned trying to make out the features of this person, but it was next to impossible.

"You will get me into my database and lock out Sally Peters."

Text scrolled across the bottom of the laptop screen. Admin credentials that belonged to Sally? He'd found her access to that database on the bank network.

The police had her in custody. He remembered that from when he'd followed Jess and Basuto back into the offices. Right before he'd sat down to remove the entire database from their system. He had it on the flash drive.

The drive had been in an evidence bag. He'd taken it with him. Walked to his car.

He remembered dropping it, and he remembered pain.

Play along. That's what will keep you alive while you figure out a way to talk yourself out of this.

Instead of it being his thought, it was his father's voice that rolled through his head. Along with the sludge feeling that always came with it. The slow-moving stain of guilt and shame over everything he'd done. The people he'd seen hurt. The things his father had forced him to do.

Ted remembered collapsing onto the asphalt of the parking lot right before he lost consciousness.

He'd been hit on the head. Which made sense, considering the awful headache he had right now. He shifted and held his wrist against his front, moving to the edge of the couch seat. "One-handed is going to take me a while."

The screen changed. "I've got as long as you need."

Given the distorted voice, he'd have guessed this was his father.

Except his dad was in federal custody. His father wouldn't be mixed up in Last Chance business anyway. Although as a founder residing in his home base, his dad had quickly moved on to bigger and better things. And he'd grifted his way into the top spot at the CIA. Nothing but a con man, he'd fooled so many people.

The same way Ted had fooled Chief Ridgeman. At least, that was how it felt sometimes. Like right now, when he didn't feel so much like a kidnap victim. No, this had a familiar feeling to it—like so many situations he'd been in as a teen. Dragged by his dad into penetrating some computer system or other, taking the data or transferring all the money out.

How was this any different?

Besides, he could send out a GPS signal from the computer. He could add a line of code that would collapse the whole database, preventing others from using it. Or find a way to track everyone who logged on and send that information to the police department. Or he could even gather every piece of information stored in the database and dump it onto a newsgroup website. Be done with it. Expose the whole thing.

"But if you don't get this done," the dark figure gestured off to the side, "my friend here...?" His voice trailed off. At least, Ted assumed it was a man. The build was wrong for most women. Or maybe he was just a sexist jerk who knew nothing about the varieties of femininity. His head hurt too much to figure out the answer.

The man in the room with him reached into his jacket and pulled a gun from a holster under his arm. He pointed the Glock at Ted.

Not wanting to stare down the barrel at his demise—again, since the same thing had happened multiple times today—he instead looked at the screen of the computer, which now showed the program for the database.

Ted clicked with one finger, using the laptop mousepad, and discovered the caller he was on video chat with had remotely connected to this computer. He could potentially control anything and everything Ted tried to do here, overriding any attempt to communicate with anyone. Or block his attempt to destroy or expose the database.

So he was tech savvy enough to know he should keep tabs on Ted's activity. But did he have enough knowledge to know everything Ted was about to do and what it meant?

And how much did Ted want to risk?

"Get in your backdoor. Create admin credentials for me, and delete all of Sally Peters' access through the login on the screen." That text scrolled across the bottom again.

He had no choice but to do this. Ted could add extra code to make sure he could get in later. And he always had the copy he'd put on that flash drive.

Wherever it was.

He looked at the gunman who pulled something from his back pocket with his free hand. "Looking for this?" Ted's phone was in the evidence bag along with the flash drive. "I disabled the GPS, so don't think anyone's going to be able to find you."

Were they going to kill him when he was done here?

Not for the first time today did he wonder if dying might not solve a lot of his problems. Not Dean's or Jess's or the police department's, as they would all be left with the repercussions of his actions. It would be suicide. They would find out everything. He would only be trying to escape his own guilt.

He stared at the flash drive. Things were unraveling. Instead of helping the case, it had suddenly grown even more complicated.

He was going to have to fix this as well.

"Get on with it!" The gunman lurched toward him, shoving the Glock right up against Ted's cheek.

"Okay." He held up both hands. "Give me a second to figure this out."

He ran his hands down his face, scrubbing them on his cheeks. Being careful of his wrist which felt broken. Tears gathered in his eyes, but Ted sniffed them away. Crying wasn't going to win him *any* points with these guys. They thought he was a pawn. Just like his father had.

Ever since the Chief offered him a job instead of jail time, Ted had tried to live like he was in control of his own life. That wasn't true, though, was it? He only had to look around to know he lived in a world among people who thought they could use him for whatever they wanted.

"The clock is ticking," the man in the room with him said. "And I figure you can still type with a bullet in your leg."

Ted stared at him.

"Get on with it."

He turned to the computer and figured just doing this was his best chance of surviving. If no one was able to find him, and he did this job, would they find his body later? West had lasted this long not allowing anyone to get any information on him. He'd remained maddeningly elusive so far.

Ted's background made him more like West than the good guy he tried to be every day. Sooner or later that would backfire. Everyone would find out that even the former chief had been wrong about him. He was nothing but a fraud who'd managed to hide the truth from them for years.

No matter how much he tried to be the man Chief Ridgeman thought he was, or could be, Ted was a low-life.

A lackey for the criminal underworld.

No point denying it. Or trying to hide it. Everyone would know. All the cases he'd worked on would be suspect. Criminals would go free on technicalities. He would have to live with the fallout of trying to do the right thing and come clean with the fact he'd lied.

He was better at this.

While he typed, the man in the room with him pulled Ted's phone out of the evidence bag. He tossed the bag onto the coffee table. The flash drive still inside hit the wood, sounding like the crack of plastic.

Ted winced.

"Something important?" The gunman eyed him.

Ted looked back at the computer like it was nothing, even though he'd given away the fact that flash drive was something. More leverage.

He hit a few keys, one handed, holding his injured wrist across his lap. If he was rescued before he could finish? Well, that would be too bad.

The gunman tapped and swiped his phone. He grunted. Then he grabbed Ted's injured wrist. He cried out. The gunman held his thumb against the screen, and there was nothing Ted could do about it.

Then he held his gun against Ted's chin and took a picture. "That's good. You look pretty scared. She'll probably tear out of that police station in a rush to come and save you." He chuckled and strode away. "This is gonna be fun."

Ted stared at the man.

What was he going to do?

9

Jess's phone buzzed. She stepped away from the group conversation to check it, just in case it was Ted. Or someone with information. She'd texted a couple of contacts asking around. One was a confidential informant she utilized on occasion. The other was a high-school-age kid, the son of a local criminal she'd met doing undercover work recently.

She brushed back the fall of her dark hair and unlocked her phone. Her appointment to return her hair to its natural blonde wasn't for two more weeks.

All thoughts of her looks evaporated as she stared at the incoming text.

"Everything okay?"

Jess nodded in answer to Mia's question but didn't look at her lieutenant. Otherwise Mia would realize everything was definitely not okay.

She moved to the break room and leaned against the countertop before she looked at it again.

Ted. With a gun to his chin. Underneath it, the following words:

Tell no one, or he dies.

Followed by instructions. A time and a place. She looked at the clock on the wall. Half an hour? That was hardly any time at all, and they wanted her to be there. Too soon for Conroy to mobilize everyone, scout out the area, and set up an operation to take down whoever this was. Or was there enough time? Ted's life was on the line. They had to at least try, didn't they?

She strode out of the break room. "Conroy?"

Tell no one. Were they watching even now? That might be how they got to Ted in the first place, because someone in the police department gave him up.

"What is it, Jess?" Conroy held his phone away from his mouth. "I'm getting an update from the FBI right now."

She looked around at the people here. Had one of them given Ted up? His father had escaped. The old man was out there, and he'd used the name West as an alias. That was far too much of a coincidence to not be relevant. Or the real West had told him to use it as a way to rub it in their faces.

They couldn't catch him. Or so far they hadn't, at least.

So was this West or Ted's father? It made her sick to think his dad would put a gun to his own kid's head. More relevant might be the fact he probably hadn't had time to get all the way to Last Chance from wherever he escaped the FBI—at least, not in time to kidnap his son.

"Do you have anything?"

She spun to find Dean standing there. "I…" She didn't know what to say. *Tell no one.* But Ted's older brother was a former SEAL. He wouldn't bring this to the police if she asked him to keep them out of it.

If she really was going to go it alone.

"What, Jess?"

"I'm just worried about Ted. I don't want anything to happen to him." No matter what she did, and what the outcome was, he needed to know that.

"We're all worried."

"This has to be about West."

Dean tipped his head to the side. "You think?"

"If I was allowed to talk to Sally, I think I could prove it. After all, they targeted us earlier."

"We don't know it's related. Do we?"

They also didn't know it wasn't. She was tempted to remind Dean that out of the two of them, only one was a cop. Her.

Before she could say anything, Dean patted her shoulder awkwardly. "He's going to be okay. As soon as we have a location, we can go get him." He let his hand drop. "One of Zander's men is trying to find GPS on either Ted's watch or his cell phone, but it's taking time. The FBI will be here in about ninety minutes. We'll find him."

She didn't even know what to say to that. It would be too late.

She had to get out of here without arousing suspicion, or whoever took Ted might follow through on their threat to hurt him. If she went, would she be able to save him? Or would she end up drawn into a plan to get something from her in exchange for him?

Dean wandered off. Conroy was on his call, still. She wanted them to realize she wasn't okay—so she could encourage them to follow her. To track her phone and be led to Ted's location.

But no one paid her any attention.

All she could do was hedge, unless she just came out and said it plainly. They'd follow her. *No.* There was too much risk with that plan. Whoever had Ted might be watching the police station. They'd see the activity if everyone suddenly left right after she did.

Jess had to do this herself.

She quietly grabbed her car keys from her locker and sent a text reply.

What do you want?

She wasn't going to stand around. And she wasn't going to go in blind. She needed information.

There had to be a way for her to get the help she needed

while keeping the fact she'd tried to reach out to her colleagues to herself, so that whoever was behind this didn't find out. She couldn't wait for the FBI. That would take too long. Dean could help. He certainly had the skills. Stuart was pretty much a loose cannon as well as a former clandestine agent and current food prep guy at the diner. But he'd taken Kaylee and gone, "off the grid," whatever that meant.

The reply came a few seconds later.

A TRADE. YOU HAVE TWENTY-FIVE MINUTES.

He wasn't going to tell her what he wanted. She had to show up to find out. Going in blind didn't sit right with her. It also didn't make her any less determined to do exactly what he was asking. For the sake of Ted's life, she would do *anything*. He didn't need to know that. Or maybe he was counting on it.

Earlier today, someone had tried to kill them. That had been part of the bank robbery plan, but it had gone wrong. They'd foiled that plot. Sally was in custody.

Did they still need to die?

This could be about West needing both her and Ted murdered, so they'd no longer be a problem. The coincidence factor once again. This time, the idea made her want to smile. *Good.* She wanted to be a problem for the biggest bad guy in town. A big enough problem he thought she should be murdered because she was determined to bring him down.

Or she knew more than she thought, and that knowledge made her a threat.

But what could that be?

Jess pulled on a bulletproof vest, armed herself, slid her jacket over it, and zipped it up. It would be pretty obvious what she had on. Unless she snuck out the back way.

Sending everything to Dean's phone was a risk. A serious risk. She'd have to pray they weren't in her phone and couldn't see who she told. If she disobeyed their orders and Ted died because of it, would she ever forgive herself?

She bit her lip. Maybe there was a better way to get the

word out. She just needed to figure out what that was. Ted was always the one who worked out those technological problems. Jess could talk her way into any group, gang, or organization. She could don any persona and get information for the police department.

None of that was going to come in handy right now, not when it counted more than it ever had. As it stood, she'd have to take this guy down herself. Kill him, probably. She'd taken a life before. It wasn't something she wanted to do again, but if it was going to be her or someone else, then she would defend herself with lethal force. *After* she knew Ted was still alive.

Jess headed out of the locker room.

Bill stood in the hall, stretching out his legs. The dispatcher was sixty-four and as spry as any of them. He was just a little... grizzled. And four inches shorter than her. "Jess."

"Hey."

She saw the moment he realized she was leaving—and that her jacket was too big. Bill always knew when any of them were up to something. She couldn't say the same about him, though. He acted cordial enough, but what did they really know about him?

If someone in the police department was working for West, it could just as easily be Bill as anyone. Maybe it was even *more* plausible.

He lifted a bushy white brow. "Can't wait for the FBI?"

"Please don't tell Conroy." She looked at the time on her phone. "Not for twenty minutes or so." She touched her hands together in prayer position in front of her, the cell phone smashed between them. "Please."

He pressed his lips together and worked his jaw around. It looked painful, and she thought she heard some clicking.

Jess winced. "I have to go."

"Do you have a way to find Ted?"

"I hope so."

He studied her. "Do you need backup? I can call Donaldson."

Actually, that wasn't a bad idea. Donaldson might be younger than her, and the rookie of the department, but he was a good cop. And a solid guy.

"I'll enable the GPS on my phone. If I don't text you in half an hour, can you track me and send him?"

Bill nodded. "He's on shift, so I'll try not to assign him anything that might come in. Unless I think it's you."

"Thanks."

He shrugged like it was no big deal when they both knew that, in some situations, protection in the form of backup could save a life. This department had been through enough in the last few months to make them all aware of that.

She headed out the back door, her stride fast enough it discouraged the officer just arriving from doing more than wave.

She nodded, then picked up her pace to jog to her car. The place he wanted her to go was a state park. The bottom of a trail, gravel for a parking lot. One roofed sign with a map indicating where the trails led. She and Ted had mountain biked up there a few times. She preferred that to biking or walking in town. Anywhere she could get away from the every day and do something different.

Would they get the chance to do it again?

Her phone rang as she drove. It was Mia. What did she want? Calling to check up on her or because Conroy asked her to find Jess? She didn't answer it.

The parking lot was empty. Night had fallen hours ago. This was pretty much the longest day of her life so far. And considering it might be her last day of life on this earth, maybe that was fitting and God was giving her the gift of each of these last minutes.

She got out of her car, shut the door, and leaned against it. Waiting. Nothing happened.

Almost five minutes later, another car pulled in. She memorized the plate number but didn't risk texting it to Bill. The driver would see.

As he put his car in park, she wondered if this was the spider web tattoo guy. He might have seemed nice enough for a bad guy, but for all she knew, he could be working for West. Trying to fake her out. Whatever thoughts she'd previously had about his allegiances didn't play into this situation.

He opened his door, but the dome light in the car didn't come on. A hood shrouded his face.

Fear walked with cold fingers up her spine. This wasn't good.

Jess tensed, her fingers itching to reach for her gun. Inside her car, her phone began to ring.

He strode toward her but stopped at least ten feet away.

"Where is Ted? I need to know he's still alive."

"He's alive." The voice was gruff, and not one she recognized. "Ted works for us now."

Then he lifted a gun and fired it at her.

10

—————

The gunshot sounded muffled. Ted blinked, realizing he'd been knocked out again. This time by some kind of stun gun. He groaned and sat up.

You did it too fast.

Like it was his problem the job that West had him do had taken less than ten minutes? He'd tried to drag it out as long as possible, but typing one fingered just to go as slowly as possible wasn't something he was capable of doing.

Now it was over. He'd done exactly what West wanted him to do—with a little of his own magic added to the program. If he could find a way to access it from a remote location, he'd be able to get inside.

If.

Just the idea of all the finagling he'd have to do to make it work gave him a headache. Or he just had a headache.

Considering the version of the database he had on that flash drive didn't include the latest update he'd just been forced to make, it was virtually useless except as evidence after the fact. A history of what they'd done, and who was involved. It could be used to make their case. Conroy would likely consider it a win.

Ted wasn't so sure he could be positive about it. It wouldn't tell them who West was or where to find him.

Ted blinked again and realized he was staring at the torn material on the roof of a car. He sat up. Hands bound. Fire. His wrist, it felt like fire. The sensation made him double over, hissing because the last thing he wanted was to go through those dry heaves all over again. It had been bad enough the first time.

He groaned, laying back down on the backseat of whoever's car this was. He heard a muffled thud, and a man cried out. He realized he could hear fighting.

Figured. The kidnapper gunman guy—whoever he was—currently stood with his back to the car, struggling with someone. Hopefully they'd hurt him. Or kill him.

Ted usually wasn't so bloodthirsty, but he was having a bad day.

He sighed. Sitting around wouldn't help things. Maybe the gunman's assailant needed Ted's help. He wouldn't be useful staying in the back seat, waiting for someone else to kidnap him all over again. He'd been handed off between bad guys plenty of times as a teen. Mostly when his father farmed out his services in exchange for a favor. Ted would have to hack some computer system or take down some kind of network. A power grid. A fiber optic system. Didn't matter.

Same job, different city. Sometimes different countries.

He got his legs in front, leaned his elbow on the passenger seat back, and climbed into the front. A backpack lay in the foot well, passenger side. Ted kept his head low and rifled through it. As soon as he was seen, he would need a way to defend himself.

Another gunshot went off.

He ducked, sucking in a breath, and glanced over. Whoever the gunman was fighting with was smaller than he was. Dark hair swung around. Not anyone he knew, considering the object of his thoughts was generally a little powerhouse blonde.

Ted rifled through the backpack. He found rope and a

camping shovel in the bigger compartment, along with a folded-up tarp.

He didn't want to know what that was for, but he was pretty sure he could guess. This guy planned to bury Ted. After he murdered him.

The driver's window splintered. Ted only realized after the fact that a bullet had shattered the glass. It embedded itself in the passenger window, not far from the back of Ted's head. Had he been leaning an inch or two back instead of hunched over, he'd be dead right now.

Ted checked the smaller front compartment, keeping lower than before even though his previous position had saved his life.

"Bingo." His bound hands lit on the grand prize, and Ted pulled out his watch with the fingers of his good hand. Ignoring the vomit-inducing pain in his other wrist, he tapped the screen.

It wasn't broken.

He'd have to… And then… The screen flashed as it rebooted. He kept his head down and waited that forever-yawning expanse of time while his smartwatch came back online and connected. Not to his phone. This one worked independently of his cell. It connected to a satellite, much like a sat phone. Limited capability. But he could get a call out even without a cell signal.

And that was what he did.

"Ted?" Dean's voice came through the small and tinny-sounding speaker on the watch.

"Dean." He nearly whimpered. "You need to come here."

He didn't even know what he was saying. All he knew was he needed his big brother. Everything he'd ever said about goal setting. About inner strength. About drive and growth. All of that stuff went out the window. He was injured, in danger, and he needed his big brother.

Again.

Déjà vu much.

"Ted." His brother's tone was so relieved a tear rolled down

Ted's face. Dean said, "You need to tell me where you are." It sounded like he was already on the move though.

"You don't know?"

"I think Jess does. She left a while ago."

Ted frowned. He glanced at the window. *Dark hair.* "She's here."

"What?"

"She needs backup."

"Send me your location."

Ted touched the buttons on either side of his watch. It vibrated for a second in his hand.

"Got it. Ten minutes."

Another gunshot went off. Ted yelped and flinched so hard he nearly smacked his forehead on the dash. How come he'd never known gunshots were that loud? He gritted his teeth. "Make it five."

Ted left the line open, the watch on his seat, cracked the door, and got out. He wobbled a bit and put his knee down. Better than his hands. He probably had a broken wrist, or so he figured.

Jess cried out.

Ted scrambled for the backpack and got out the camping shovel, which he managed to open up to its full length. By the time he had it, the world was spinning around him. He took a minute and breathed through it.

The urge to pray was strong, considering how bad things had gotten today. But how could he do that when he had no right to ask God for anything? He wasn't a good person. No matter that everyone else thought he was—that only meant Ted had succeeded in fooling them all these years. Especially his brother. Dean was always talking about God and going to church. As though that would solve all of Ted's problems.

Ignoring his errant thoughts, Ted scrambled to the back bumper. Jess lay on her back on the ground. Above her, his kidnapper had both hands on her throat, squeezing the breath out of her.

"No!" He scrambled up, hoisting the shovel above his head and sprinting to her while everything in him cried out.

The gunman twisted.

Ted saw the weapon at the last minute. He brought the shovel down. *Oh, well.* If this was going to be the end, then at least everyone who knew him would keep thinking he was a good guy. Maybe even a hero.

Jess jerked her whole body. The gunman tipped to the side, dislodged by her movement. The weapon slammed into Ted's ribs a split second before Ted slammed the shovel down on the man's shoulder. Too bad he'd been aiming for the head.

As the gunman's body folded at the spot where he'd been hit and fell to the side, Ted realized the gun had no bullets left. Empty.

Ted collapsed onto the ground.

Jess grunted. The gunman was up on one knee, trying belligerently to come at Ted again with his gun. She scrambled up and took the shovel from Ted—even though his fingers didn't want to let go—and slammed the gunman in the face again.

His body crumpled to the ground.

Jess landed on her behind with a whimper of relief. "Ted?"

He looked up at her not too far away but didn't get up off the ground. "Hi." His voice sounded thick, gruff. He cleared his throat. Or tried to. Emotion collected in a lump. He tried to swallow it but felt moisture run from his eyes down the sides of his head to his hair. Ted lifted his hands and covered his head. *Ouch.* He bit his lip.

"Hey." He heard her shift, then felt her hand on his arm. "It's okay. We're okay."

"Are we?" He lowered his hands and shot her a look that indicated just how much he agreed. Or didn't, as the case was.

She touched his shoulders. Ted stretched the fingers on his good hand to touch her face and said, "Are you okay?"

"What do you say we call an ambulance and let someone with years of medical training make that determination?"

Ted made a face. "Fine. Only because I'm pretty sure I'm going to need a cast on my wrist."

She gasped. "You hurt it more?"

He managed to shrug one shoulder, though it was clear she didn't seem to buy his attempt at nonchalance. "It's been a really long day. I haven't yet had the chance to have it looked at after I injured it earlier. What with a bank robbery *and* being kidnapped."

She bit her lip.

"There's more?"

Jess nodded. "Your dad escaped federal custody."

Everything in Ted stilled. His hand dropped from her soft cheek.

"Don't pull away, *please.* Don't pretend everything's fine when I know it isn't."

"So you've seen through me this whole time," he said. "Is that it?"

"You thought you were fooling me?" One eyebrow rose.

"I guess you're the only one good at acting." And she was. Jess was the best at undercover work. But no one else had ever realized he held so much back.

Before she could object to his comment, he continued, "It doesn't matter. Not right now. Unless you're planning on going after West."

"I am, but you're right. I need your statement, and we're going to interrogate this guy." She motioned to the unconscious man, his back to them. "Plus, Sally Peters. There's a lot of work to do, but it all gets us one step closer to identifying West."

He nodded, and yet his thoughts strayed to his father. Would the old man come here? He'd caused more than enough damage already. And if he was trying to avoid the cops, why come to a place where people knew him—a place they'd assume he might go?

No. Ted didn't think his dad would show up. But at least now he knew it had been his dad calling before. Not someone else. He hadn't told anyone anything.

Jess started to speak.

Ted heard a rustle, but only in time to watch the shovel come down and slam into Jess's head.

She crumpled on top of him, unconscious. Blood coated him from a head wound in her hair. He scrambled out from under her, grabbed the first thing he could find—the empty gun —and slammed it into the man's arm as he came down with the shovel again. This time to hit him.

He launched up, tackled the guy, and they hit the asphalt. He heard the moment his attacker's skull hit the ground.

He got up on his knees over the man. A red haze fell over his world. Jess was down. She could be dead from a skull fracture, and he'd been laying there thinking about his dad?

He'd let it happen.

He lifted the shovel, determined to give payback. If she was dead, then this guy would be too. That was only fair.

"Ted!"

He twisted to see a handful of people, guns out. Including his brother. "Put the shovel down."

It clattered on the asphalt, and he lifted his hands.

11

"For the record—" Her sister threw the car into park. "—you should be at home. Isn't that what the doctor said?"

Jess unclipped her seatbelt and reached for the door handle, trying not to turn her head too much. Or too fast. The hospital had given her some good meds. It still hurt, though. And it was making her grumpy.

"I slept at the hospital. I was there all night," she pointed out. "I can sit down as well here as I can at home, and I'll feel useful."

She pushed the door open and got out. Why argue? That would take energy she needed to conserve for the fight ahead.

"Are you even listening?"

Jess didn't turn. Her sister did that thing where she talked over the roof of the car, usually with one foot still inside. She'd seen it so many times Jess could picture her in her head.

She had to be here. Why argue trying to convince her sister of that?

"No one is saying you need to feel useful right now, let alone actually *be* useful."

Jess hoped it was just her head. "Is that supposed to make any sense?"

Ellie approached her around the car, smiling as she moved. Dean was with Ted. She knew that much. And maybe more, even. What she'd heard from Donaldson in the middle of the night gave her pause.

Her sister said, "You should be at home, doing nothing. Not even thinking about work."

"Resting?"

"You make that sound like a moral failing."

"In the middle of a case like this?" Jess shrugged one shoulder. "Maybe it is."

"Sure, if you didn't look like you're about to pass out."

"I don't look that bad. Do I?"

Ellie shot her look.

"Wow." Jess shoved at her shoulder while her sister laughed. "So we'll do this quickly. I just want to check in."

Too much had happened yesterday. Despite her injuries, she'd told the truth. In the middle of a case like this, there was no way Jess would take a day off. They had to bring down West. Then they'd be able to take a day off. She might even go on vacation.

Ellie made a noncommittal but very opinionated noise.

Jess ignored her and went to the front door. Inevitably, thoughts of Ted slipped in. *It looked like he was gonna kill that guy.* Donaldson had been practically speechless, retelling the details of how they'd found her and Ted. And the unconscious man Ted had been about to kill. Or, so it looked.

No way. No way would he kill someone.

He'd been standing over the guy, shovel in hand. Donaldson had told her every second of how they'd raced over just in time to see him about to "deliver a death blow." As though that made any sense whatsoever.

Jess believed anyone could be driven to kill another person —it just depended on the circumstances.

She'd been unconscious. He'd been alone and freaked out. She didn't know where his head had been at. But apparently it had been serious enough he felt the need to strike out at the kidnapper. Who knew, maybe Ted had been hurt somehow in a way they didn't know. Or terrorized. Could be he was only taking the control back. Regaining the power he'd lost.

All she knew? Dean had told Ellie that Ted didn't want to see her.

Jess sighed and pulled open the door. Her sister caught it, and she stepped inside first.

Jess had been unconscious on the ground, and he'd tried to kill the man that hurt her. It turned out his hit to her head hadn't been that bad. They'd put one staple in her head. Sure, it hurt. But it would heal.

"Jess!" A fresh face hopped off her stool and rushed through the security door to swamp her in a hug. Ruby.

"Hey." She circled the woman's middle with her arms. "Wow, that's way better." When Ruby pulled back, Jess said, "I knew there was a reason I came here."

"Oh, you." Ruby nudged her shoulder. "I know you don't mean that since you had no idea I'd be here covering for Kaylee. Not to mention, Officer Workaholic doesn't know how to take a day off."

"You know what they say," Jess fired back. "Crime never sleeps."

Ruby made a face at Ellie over Jess's shoulder, then said, "Literally no one says that." She set her hands on her hips. "Don't let Sergeant Basuto catch you here."

"Too late."

Jess didn't look at him. She moved through the open door and strode to him, both her hands up. Palms out. "I know I'm not cleared to work."

He folded his arms across his chest. "Then why are you here? If you wanted an update, you could have called."

"I know." She lowered her hands.

"Jess!" Conroy stood at his door, a wide smile on his face.

Mia, his lieutenant and fiancé, was right behind him, trying to peer over his shoulder.

"Hey, Chief." Might as well keep it professional.

"I'm sure Officer Ridgeman was just grabbing something," Sergeant Basuto said. "And then she's going to be on her way. Home. To rest."

Conroy smirked. Mia wiggled around him and moved to Ellie, where the two had a low conversation with their heads together.

Jess needed to figure out how to hang out here. She didn't want an update. Wasn't here to grab something. And she wasn't going to leave. She would be way out of the loop if she went home.

She glanced at Conroy. "Has Sally Peters said anything?"

He shook his head. "We've ID'd the man who took Ted, though. He's at the hospital under guard."

"Who is he?"

"Local guy with a long list of priors. He used to work for Ed Summers. Did a couple of years before that for breaking and entering after a stint for assault with a deadly weapon."

"So he's been around?"

Conroy nodded. "After we arrested Ed, we lost track of him."

There were a few like that. She'd halfway thought that guy with the spider web was the one behind it, but their attacker hadn't been nearly as big as him.

"Are you really okay?" His gaze softened. She knew he genuinely cared. He'd been a cop and a good guy she respected when he'd been her lieutenant. Now he was her chief, a title previously held by her grandfather, and there wasn't a decision he made that she didn't agree with—or at least know he had everyone's best interests at heart.

And when had she ever been able to say that about a boss?

"I'm okay."

"You just want to feel useful."

Jess decided to just go for it. "I'd like to talk to Sally. See if she'll give something up to me that she might not with anyone else."

"I already tried." Mia stepped up to the side, keeping professional distance between herself and the boss. He wasn't her fiancé at work, when they were chief and lieutenant. "But I think it's a good idea. Wear her down. Keep coming at her, using every resource at our disposal." She studied Jess's face. "But I also think you should give yourself a day or two. Try it then."

So long as the lieutenant was going to allow it, Jess didn't mind what qualifiers there were going to be. She nodded. "Okay. Sounds good."

"Good." Ellie nudged her shoulder. "See? Everything is in hand, and you can go home to rest."

Jess pressed her lips together. No way was she going to argue with her sister in front of two superiors.

Ellie grinned. She totally knew it.

Jess turned back to Conroy and Mia. "Maybe tomorrow afternoon? I'll see if I can get Sally to flip on West."

Conroy said, "Intel from Ted is that West had him shut her out of the operation. She's been cut loose."

"So she has no reason to defend him." That only made Jess want to go in there right now. Not wait until tomorrow.

"She's not going anywhere." Conroy gave her a pointed look. "No reason you can't rest and do this tomorrow. Take some time, figure out how you're going to broach it with her."

Okay, that made sense. Given how much her head hurt, she probably wasn't firing on all cylinders. "Yes, Chief. That sounds good."

"Good." He grinned. "Because you have no choice. We don't interrogate on our days off."

Jess smiled back at him, and Ellie laughed. Even Mia looked to be fighting a smile.

"Let's go." Her sister tugged on her elbow, and Jess let her sister steer her while the lieutenant and chief headed back into his office.

Jess wasn't ignorant that their relationship occasionally crossed into personal territory at work. No one could keep their boundaries that straight all the time and small towns had their own rules about basically everything.

But she knew Conroy and Mia never played favorites with any officer over another. They all got a fair shake. And the two of them had plenty of people who kept them accountable— including members of the city council and the pastor of the church in town. The whole police department did that, too.

Animosity against anyone in a police uniform was one thing, but most folks in this town loved Conroy. They were coming to love Mia, now that she was back in town. It was clear they made each other happy, and this town was their home.

Who could begrudge them the life they wanted after all they'd been through?

Now that she'd been standing for a while, she was feeling the effects of the long day yesterday. How many times had she been hit on the head? Enough she'd lost count.

Sergeant Basuto stood in the walkway.

Jess stopped in front of him. "Sergeant?" She lifted her chin. Things had been weird since Conroy was shot by a sniper. Basuto had stepped up to fill the gap since Mia had been spending most of her time helping Conroy recuperate.

Still, something was going on with him she hadn't figured out.

"Get some rest, Ridgeman."

She nodded. "Understood."

As she walked with her sister to the door and gave Ruby another hug, Ellie frowned at the sergeant. Jess didn't want to get into it. Not while she had nothing but a hunch and speculation.

Besides, she had enough problems of her own without wading into others'.

If she was going to target someone that needed "help," it would for sure be Ted. That guy was hiding a serious amount of *something*. She hadn't worked that out either.

Jess sighed. Her sister opened her car door for her, and she shot Ellie a look. "Thanks."

Ellie giggled.

She leaned her head back on the headrest and closed her eyes, not wanting to lose this train of thought. Right after being kidnapped, Ted had been…well, he'd been Ted—not in a state of shock and disbelief that he'd been targeted. No, it was more that he took it in stride. That was half the problem, him being his normal self. Whatever that was, it had been brooding behind his eyes for longer than the two years she'd known him since she moved back.

His dad.

That was her guess. Though, how that made him roll with so much when most people would freak out, she had no idea. She'd expected to have to talk him through the shock. No. He'd been upset, but that was more about being in pain. Her sister told her he'd badly sprained his wrist.

What had his dad done to him? Whatever happened, it seemed like West didn't even ruffle him.

First Basuto. Now Ted. She didn't want to suspect either of working for West, or at least being influenced by him, but the truth was she didn't know. They were longtime residents. She'd grown up here but had been gone too long. Jess was treated like a newcomer.

Now, more than ever, she knew she had to root out West. Before the disease spread any further.

And it was going to be up to her.

12

Dean shoved the door open over Ted's shoulder. "Go ahead."

Ted glanced at his brother, but Dean had already turned back to the car. He stepped into the house. They both lived there with Stuart who now worked for Hollis at the diner. Ted's father had ruined Stuart's life as much as he'd ruined both Ted's and Dean's lives, and Stuart had now seen fit to take his wife and go "off the grid." All because of Pierce Cartwright.

Then there was Zander and his three teammates. The four of them were operators on a private security team; a business that Zander ran. All off on a mission right now.

That left him and Dean in a house that had two floors but multiple bedrooms. Ted's army of reprogrammed robot vacuums took care of the square footage, and the rest of them split the bathroom and kitchen chores on a rotation.

Ted knew it was more like living in a military barracks—since basically all of them had had that kind of lifestyle at one time or another, except for him. But to him it still felt like a family. The kind who stood together when a threat came. Like Zander had helped Stuart before. Like Ted had helped Dean and Ellie. The way they all would bind together if Ted's father showed up on their doorstep.

Unless the place was quiet and empty. His family busy with their lives.

Dean stepped in the front door. Ted turned in the foyer. Dean's expression softened from concentration to compassion. "The boys got a call early. They hit the airport pretty quickly."

Ted nodded.

"I prefer it when they're here, too." Dean squeezed the tendon between Ted's neck and shoulder. "I don't have to take out the trash as often."

"Pretty soon you'll be married to Ellie, living…" Ted frowned. "Where will you be living?"

"I don't know yet. And there's no rush." It seemed like he was trying to reassure Ted.

After everything that had happened to him yesterday—and the reason his left arm was currently in an athletic wrap—he figured that made sense. Dean had probably freaked out after finding Ted with his hands tied together and about to kill a guy with a shovel.

Of course, Ted explained he'd just been about to make sure the gunman was completely knocked out. Not trying to end his life.

Of course, none of them believed him.

Ted slumped onto the couch.

"Hungry?"

"Not really." He laid his head back and closed his eyes. Dean might be a former Navy SEAL, but he was also the town's unofficial EMT. Lately, he'd been getting fewer calls for that as folks knew he'd been focusing his efforts on setting up a therapy center in the mountains for people needing to work through their trauma.

If he told Dean he should be first in line, his brother would freak out. So he'd never said anything. So far, he'd been dealing with it fine. Right?

A little voice in his head tried to tell him otherwise, but Ted pushed that thought aside. Which only left the way open for thinking about Jess. The crack of that shovel against her skull. He knew she was fine; Ellie and Dean had both reassured him of that. But hearing it over and over in his mind. Seeing her fall. Feeling her weight slump against him. Ted couldn't shake it.

"Tea?"

He shrugged one shoulder.

"I'm sorry no one is here."

"It's not Christmas morning. Or my birthday. And Stuart did the right thing taking Kaylee as far away as possible from…"

He didn't even want to say the name.

Ted tried, in general, not to act like a disappointed kid when he wanted to hang out and the boys weren't here. He was a grown man, nearly twenty-five. They weren't his brothers. But he still missed them when they were gone. Especially in such a big house. It echoed when it was empty, reminding him way too much of the days after Dean left for the Navy. When Ted had been alone with his father.

Or just alone.

His dad hadn't always needed help with a con he was running. As far as Pierce Cartwright was concerned, when Ted didn't serve a specific purpose, he was a nobody.

Ted shuddered. "Is he really loose?"

Dean perched on the arm of the couch. "I can't believe the feds lost him. Though, considering how Dad is, maybe that's not so astounding."

"If anyone can escape federal custody, it's him."

"They're saying he charmed a female agent."

"Gross." Their dad was like…old. Super old.

Dean chuckled. "You'll be wrinkly one day, and you'll be whistling a different tune."

"If I live that long."

He heard Dean shift onto the couch and opened his eyes.

His brother said, "I'm not sure I want to dig in with that right now. Could be you're just suffering from acute lack of filter, considering the meds they gave you."

"Yeah. That's probably it."

"When it was clear you'd been taken?" Dean shook his head. "I couldn't breathe."

"Now you know how I felt when you were off on SEAL missions, and I had no idea if you'd call or if someone would show up with a piece of paper and condolences."

Dean stared for nearly a minute. "I'm calling it ALF. Acute Lack of Filter." He dug his phone out of his pants pocket. "Maybe no one has copyrighted that, and I can have Ellie ghost-write a book for me. Dealing with ALF."

Ted's shoulders shook as he tried—and failed—to suppress the chuckle. "Every family member of a military serviceman or woman, cop, or any other first responder goes through the same thing. You felt it. It's not pleasant knowing someone you love could be in danger." He shrugged one shoulder. "We deal. Because it's the right thing to do."

"I did not want to deal," Dean said. "I wanted to start shooting West's men."

Ted smiled.

"Tell me what happened."

All the humor he had been feeling dissipated. Ted stared at the photos on the mantel because the last thing he wanted to do was go over—again—what happened. The pictures were ones Zander had put there when they moved in, making it more personal and less like the barracks they were used to from military life. Above them hung an ocean scene, a photo one of the boys had taken in Bali on a stakeout. Or a vacation. Ted couldn't remember.

"Bro."

He glanced at Dean, still not wanting to discuss it. "I already told the cops everything. You heard it all. West had a job he needed me to do, and I did it. I lost the flash drive from the bank somewhere in the process of it, so we have nothing on the database."

"The one you wrote."

Ted nodded. Yes, he'd told them that much. Considering it was a lost lead, he hadn't figured it would have the same impact it would've had otherwise. Not an in-your-face reality, but more of an abstract concept. Something Ted had done an indeterminate number of years ago.

Long enough he'd practically forgotten it existed.

His bother continued, "That had to have been hard, realizing it was your handiwork that allowed these people to do what they've been doing. Using innocent women to make money."

He wanted to fire back that no one was innocent, but that didn't always go down well. Dean would only wonder why he was so cynical. He'd have to tell his brother that was something he and Jess had actually agreed over.

Instead, Ted picked at a thread on the hem of his shirt. "There's nothing I can do about how my work is being utilized. Dad sold all kinds of things I programmed to all kinds of people. There's probably code I wrote in some Chinese government network."

Dean made a face. "But you put a virus or a worm, or something, in West's system, right?"

Ted shook his head. "I gave myself access to the database at the same time I made him admin credentials. If I come across the program again, I can use that to access it. Otherwise, no. I wasn't able to destroy it."

Dean let out a long breath.

"I thought they were going to kill me. Instead the plan was the same as it was at the bank. Kill both me and Jess. Like that will stop the cops from going after West?" Ted didn't get how that worked. Cops didn't scare easily. At least, not the ones he worked with. "I didn't have enough time to get creative. I did what I could as slowly as possible without arousing suspicion."

"Okay."

Ted glanced over.

"You don't have to convince me. You kept yourself alive, and you probably saved Jess's life. I heard she was pretty banged up fighting that guy."

He bit his lips together.

"You still don't want to talk to her?" After nearly a minute of quiet, Dean said, "I know it was scary. These are the times we need to pull together, not push the people we care about away."

"You don't even like her."

"That's not…" Dean's denial fell flat. "I didn't understand her. Now I know how driven she is, and when you were in trouble, she waded in without hesitation." He sounded proud of her. "Either way, she's going to be my sister-in-law when I marry Ellie. I'm glad I've come to appreciate her, even if she does kind of drive me crazy still."

Ted huffed out a breath. "You should see her undercover. No fear. She'd walk into molten lava if someone needed help."

"Why is that a bad thing?"

Ted scrunched up his nose in a shrug. Protecting people unable to protect themselves wasn't a bad thing. Jess was noble, but the reason why she was so driven to do it was what stumped him every time.

He just didn't understand. She seemed to have her reasons. And it didn't seem she had any intention of ever telling him what they were.

"You like her, right?"

"Sure, but it's complicated."

"Except when it's the simplest thing in the world."

Dean was only saying that because he was in love, working on a proposal for his girlfriend. How quickly people in relationships forgot how it felt to be single. On the other side of things. Sure, there was a dance where two people opened up to each other. But it didn't always work like that.

Sometimes one had no intention of opening up. Ever.

And the other was equally as stubborn.

For entirely different reasons, they were both determined to leave the past behind. Except his was currently rearing its ugly head.

He squeezed his eyes shut. Too much would go wrong if his dad showed up. If everyone found out he'd been his dad's pawn far longer than Chief Ridgeman ever knew. That he'd let the former chief down so thoroughly…

Ted didn't want to think about how it would go down.

"Everything is going to be okay," his brother said. "The FBI will find Dad. The police department will identify which of the founders is West. You'll be part of it, testifying in that way you do where you have to explain yourself because nobody understands half the technical stuff you're talking about."

Ted grinned. "I think that might've been a compliment."

"You know it was."

"I don't need my ego stroked just because I feel crummy. This isn't a pity party."

"Good." Dean sat forward on the couch, forearms on his knees. "Because I want you to call the FBI back and tell them what you know about Dad."

"Just like that?" He wanted to be sick again. "Maybe I will take that tea."

"Coward."

"After everything? You're going to say that about me."

Dean squeezed the bridge of his nose. "Okay, fine. You're the farthest thing from a coward, and I know that. It was a cheap shot." He lowered his hand to his lap. "You don't think I want to be the one with the information? I'd make sure he's nowhere near you *ever* again."

That sounded pretty final. As though Dean might've entertained the idea of killing their dad.

But he hadn't tried to do it.

Ted swallowed. "I would rather believe he'll never come here because it's too obvious."

"That's the goal. So give them what you know, and they can make sure he's caught before he even thinks to bother you."

"That makes sense."

Dean gently shoved the side of Ted's head. "Time to face your fears, bro. And I'll be right there with you."

Ted could only wish that were true.

13

———

Jess rang the doorbell. The camera in the corner of the eave lit up with a red light, though she'd heard Ellie say that it was always recording and not just when someone showed up. Not only Dean, but also Zander and his team, were worried about security.

A good thing, considering someone had tried to kill her and Ted twice yesterday.

The door swung open and Ted stood there. "Uh…hey."

Jess shifted, feeling the weight of her off-duty gun holstered on her hip. "Hey. Ellie told me to come and pick her up."

Ted frowned. His arm was in a sling, and his hair was mussed as though he'd only recently woken up. "Dean and Ellie went for a walk. They said they were going to get lunch and go see a movie."

That made no sense. Jess was sure she was supposed to get her and bring her home. But that wasn't what her brain lit on. "They left you here unprotected?"

Ted started to speak, then just shook his head.

Jess sucked in a breath through her nose while she tried to figure out what on earth was going on. Sure, they were both in danger, but she had a gun she'd been trained thoroughly to use and could take care of herself.

Given what she'd seen of Ted, he could take care of himself as well. But he had a badly sprained wrist. She only had a headache. And a tiny staple in her head.

"Also—" Jess leaned in for another sniff. "—what is that smell?"

Ted barely stepped back. She just about managed to not bump his arm as she wiggled between the door frame and his body. "Sorry." She glanced up at him, their faces close.

His eyes flashed. Then he turned away to shut the front door.

Jess kept going toward the kitchen where a pot simmered on the stove. Behind her, she heard Ted press buttons on the alarm panel. She laid her hands on the counter at the breakfast bar. "Why does that smell so good?"

She glanced over her shoulder.

Ted cracked a smile. "Stuart left soup in the fridge."

She turned to him. He just stared at her, so she said, "Is it okay if I stay for lunch? Ellie told me she was going to go grocery shopping, but she didn't do it yet."

He sighed. "Fine."

Jess watched him trail around the counter into the kitchen. "Everything okay? How's your arm?"

He shrugged one shoulder, then pulled two bowls from the cupboard one-handed.

"Need some help?"

"No."

She hopped up on a stool, and he set a bowl in front of her. Jess used the spoon to stir it. "Chicken noodle."

He flopped a loaf of bread in front of her. It rolled onto its side. A second later he put a knife and tub of butter next to it.

"Want two slices?"

He came around to the stool by her, carrying his bowl.

"Sure." He slid onto the seat beside her. "It's definitely a soup kind of day."

"Right? Overcast, dim, and kind of dreary." She frowned. "Why would Dean and Ellie go for a walk on a day like this?" And why lie to her, saying she needed to pick up her sister, only to ditch? Unless Ellie was conniving to get Jess and Ted alone to talk to each other.

So that was it.

Jess wasn't the one who'd resisted a conversation. Dean and Ellie were the ones who said Ted didn't want to talk to her in the hospital.

She swallowed her bite and forgot everything. "So good."

He chuckled.

"How'd you sleep?"

"Not great." He lifted his hand. "This thing is kind of uncomfortable."

"Is that just a fabric bandage? I thought they might put a cast on."

"They're supposed to check again in a few days after the swelling goes down."

"Oh." She handed him a buttered slice of bread.

"How's your head?"

Jess touched the spot where they'd stapled her and winced. "Hurts, but no permanent damage."

He didn't look super convinced.

"I'm headed to work this afternoon. Conroy's letting me interview Sally Peters, since everyone else is busy with the bank robbers and the kidnapper that we arrested."

His expression was guarded. He took a bite, then said, "Yeah?"

She nodded. It hurt. "Anything you think I can use to get her to flip on West?"

"He wanted her out. Surely you can appeal to her ego, as it were, considering he dropped her like a hot potato."

"I guess when you work with people like that, you have to expect betrayal."

"You really do."

She tried not to react. "Sounds like you might know something about that."

He shrugged one shoulder. "I lived it. Watched my dad do it to others, and to Dean. When my brother left for the Navy, it was like he was dead to my dad."

"That had to have been hard. Feeling alone."

"It was." He dipped buttered bread in his soup and stuffed it in his mouth.

Jess bit back the urge to jump on the line of conversation and make him talk when he was chewing. She concentrated on her soup, chasing chunks of chicken around the bowl with her spoon.

If he was going to open up, finally give her some clue as to what went on inside that head of his, not to mention act as though he trusted her, well, then, Jess was going to have to open up to him.

It was the last thing she wanted. Vulnerability was uncomfortable, to say the least. But if it got her information on West's operation in the process? Maybe even a lead on where his dad might be—that would be a win for her, considering it would mean she'd helped a federal investigation.

A win-win as far as she could see.

Not to mention they'd be in a place where they trusted each other more. Right now, she had to focus on this case since they were in the middle of something serious. But if they came out of it closer and stronger, then how could that be a bad thing?

Jess shifted the handle of her spoon in her fingertips, twirling it in the bowl. "You know, I was NYPD before I came here."

It hadn't been a question, but Ted nodded anyway.

"About a year into my time there, I worked undercover with a major crimes unit. They were trying to bring down three guys who ran what was essentially a high-end prostitution ring. Like making it shiny and classy changed what they were doing." She made a face. "Destroying lives."

"You were undercover?"

"We knew of a couple of girls that went missing, ones who fit the profile we had on them. They got me inside in a way I caught the attention of one of the men. Pretended I was down on my luck, just got fired. Couldn't pay my rent. Not hard to believe. Just enough I was able to tell the lieutenant where the meet would take place. The hotel they worked out of." The more she spoke, the more choked up she got.

Ted twisted to put his good hand on hers. "What happened?"

"Somehow they knew. I showed up, and there was a dead woman in the hotel room."

"Did they catch the murderer?"

"It was hired out to a local mob guy, and he never said who hired him. Cash. Untraceable. No record anywhere. The guy I connected with—the one who was part of the operation—turned out to be a front. Just someone they used to make the initial contact. He knew nothing." She paused. "Major crimes...I figured they laid low for a while and kept operating."

"So it was a bust."

"A dead girl, all for nothing."

"You know they were probably going to kill her anyway," Ted said. "Otherwise it would have been someone else. Someone expendable."

"I'm surprised they didn't try to kill me." She didn't even want to think about the fact that girl had been dead either way. Especially not considering the level of cynicism in Ted's tone. She hadn't known he was that much of a realist. Usually he was all about what they could learn, how they could grow. Do better next time.

"No matter what," she said, "I failed. A girl was dead. The detective in charge of the case asked me out. He thought that since the case was over, I'd want to get together." She shook her head, still not able to believe he'd dismissed her grief and shock at having discovered that girl. So severely beaten and murdered.

Jess hadn't had a romantic relationship since. And she hadn't entertained those feelings again—not until she got to know Ted.

"Her death wasn't about you," he offered. "It was simply convenient, and it had the desired effect if it meant they could send a message and carry on unheeded."

"I got an email a month ago from the lieutenant. He's a captain now." She felt a small smile curl up the corners of her lips. "They took down the whole operation."

Not only had she not been there to see it, but she also hadn't assisted in any part of it the last three years the case had been ongoing.

"That's good." Ted stacked their bowls but didn't get up.

"I know it's a good thing." She ran her thumbnail along the edge of the counter. "I just wanted to be there when they were arrested."

"Like with interviewing Sally Peters? Seeing it through to the end. Being there when we ID West and bring him in."

She shrugged one shoulder. "At least making sure no one innocent is hurt just to send us a message."

"So far he's just been messing with us," Ted said. "Or at least, that's what it feels like."

She nodded. This was supposed to have been about getting him to open up. Would he reciprocate now that she'd told him the worst there was in her past?

When he said nothing, she asked, "Are you doing okay with the workload you have on this?"

"I'm supposed to be behind the scenes, and yet I seem to be targeted every time I turn around."

She nodded. "I know how that feels."

"We'll get there." With one hand he brushed back hair that had fallen over his forehead. "I could do without having to worry my dad could show up anytime I turn around though."

"I'm sorry. It's crazy he escaped custody."

Ted nodded. "Right? I have a video call with the agent in charge at six, and I'm supposed to give them all the intel I have on him." He blew out a breath. "One day I should just write it all down, then people can stop asking me."

"A memoir." She nudged his good hand. "Hey, maybe Ellie will ghostwrite it for you."

He chuckled. "Dean said the same thing about an idea he had." She smiled, enjoying the moment. It wasn't long before Ted frowned. He turned to the front window. "Do you smell smoke?"

"I—" Before she could say she didn't, Jess realized she did. "Yeah." She hopped off the stool and drew her weapon.

"Are you going to shoot the fire out?"

"Maybe." She grinned. "But I'm not taking any chances, considering."

"Fair enough."

The doorbell rang.

She followed Ted to the screen where he tapped a button. No bigger than an iPad Mini, the tablet illuminated with the image from the front-door camera.

Two firefighters in full gear stood on the doorstep.

"Open up!" One pounded on the front door with a gloved fist. "You need to evacuate immediately!"

Ted stepped toward the door.

Jess's instincts fired. "Wait!"

But it was too late. He'd already turned the handle. The door swung in at him.

14

––––––––

Ted narrowly dodged the door before it hit him. Two firefighters in full gear barreled through the door.

"Whoa. What are you guys doing?" The smell of smoke filled his nostrils. Especially now that the door was open. What was burning?

Ted figured half the police department was already on their way here. The huge house was on the outskirts of town, tucked back in the trees in the foothills. The only other structure was the barn next to it.

He frowned. "Is the barn on fire?"

Jess still hadn't raised her gun. But neither had she put it away.

"Guys."

The one closest to him turned. "Wheys da flush dry?"

Given the breathing mask that covered his face, his voice sounded muffled. Ted couldn't recognize the voice or face, so he didn't know which of the town's fire department first responders his voice belonged to. Or even what he was saying.

The man closed in on him.

Jess said, "Easy."

The man pushed his masked face into Ted's, enunciating his words this time. "Where is the flash drive?"

"Wha——" Ted realized what he was talking about. This man wasn't here to put out any fires. He worked for West. "The one from the bank? I don't have it. You guys do."

He'd left it on the coffee table in the house he'd been taken to after being kidnapped. Had the police retrieved everything after they arrested the kidnapper? His kidnapper was in the hospital. Was the guy awake?

This was getting to be just too much.

"Back up." He lifted his good hand, palm out. "And get out of my house."

Since Jess had her weapon still loose in her hands, he turned to the alarm panel. He'd never actually used the "in distress" function but knew how to do it. The signal would alert everyone who lived here via their cell phone. At the same time, it would contact emergency services, and help would come in less than five minutes.

Assuming they had that long.

The firefighter after the flash drive shoved Ted in the back, causing his finger to glance off the alarm panel before he could press the emergency button. Then he slammed Ted backward, pinning his sprained arm between his body and the wall.

Ted cried out.

Jess's gun went off. He twisted to see her fire again before he could say or do anything. The man behind him jerked back and fell against the wall.

"Go!" she yelled. "Let's go!"

Ted's brain caught up to what was going on. He ran through the house, down the hall, and around the corner toward the back door. Zander had a mirror hung up in the corner to nullify the blind bend.

Ted stopped around the corner and leaned against the wall.

Jess raced around, nearly colliding with him. "Come on!" She tried to reach for him as she moved, but he shook off her hold on his good arm and studied the angled mirror. The fish-eye view of the front door was clear.

"They're down."

"No blood." She tugged on his arm. "They're not down. Come *on*."

"I need my phone." They had to call for help.

"I have mine."

He saw them at that moment. The first firefighter jogged down the hall. Ted turned to Jess, ushering her along. "Come on."

She huffed.

He figured that was a pretty good reaction since they were both injured. Anytime either one of them was over tired, or in pain, they tended to snip at each other. Who didn't? And who, on realizing they did it, didn't try to work on that tendency within themselves?

He sure did. It was part of being the man Chief Ridgeman had thought he was.

All his attempts at growth were to live up to his expectations.

Jess shoved the door handle and held it open, her gun trained past him as he raced through it. Outside now, he tried to figure out where they should go.

The guys had drilled him on emergency procedures. Evacuation plans. He knew they were still working on the idea of a panic room in the house, but all they'd done so far was ask him to figure out how to get satellite TV in there. They hadn't built anything yet.

He headed for the warehouse, glancing back over his shoulder to make sure she was with him.

Jess hauled a two-by-four leaning against the house over to the door and wedged it under the handle.

He slowed. "Good thinking. Now *come on*."

The smoke was worse out here. Ted rounded the corner of the house and saw the warehouse. His cry was audible.

"What?" She nearly bumped into him but managed to stall her momentum before colliding with him. "What is…oh, no."

"They'd just renovated the inside." He wanted to collapse and cry over all Zander and his team's hard work. Lost now.

"That's what you're worried about?" A bang on the interior of the back door distracted him from her ire for a second. Then she continued, "They probably set that fire to draw us out, knowing we were alone in the house. Only we never smelled it, so they got impatient and knocked on the door."

The back door she'd wedged shut splintered as the fire-fighter inside the house kicked it open. His boot stuck in the door.

Ted nudged her. "Save the debrief for after this is done. Go!"

The firefighter shoved the rest of the door open and stepped out, a gun in his hands. Ted raced toward the warehouse. It would be dangerous and there was a lot of smoke, but he figured it could give them cover as they circled around.

Why hadn't he worn his watch today?

Okay, he knew why, considering he'd been inside at home with the alarm on. He didn't wear it twenty-four seven.

"Give me your phone."

Before she could dig it out of her back pocket where she kept it, a firefighter rounded the warehouse. The other one. Coming from the direction of the house.

"Go!" He jerked on her arm with his good hand. They raced for the carport, under which Zander had parked his rusty broken-down truck. The one that didn't run. And no one except him was allowed to touch.

What sounded like a mortar detonated inside the warehouse, immediately followed by a steady pop-pop.

"His ammo stash."

Zander kept his ammunition locked away. Had it not all been in a fireproof safe, or was it something else entirely that was exploding now? The heat of the fire drew beads of sweat down Ted's back as he ran.

Right behind him, Jess coughed.

She slowed, and he saw her glance back. "They're coming. They saw us." She dug her phone out as she ran, fumbling between the gun and the cell. Trying to slide her thumb across the home button.

"Make an emergency call."

She nearly ran into a tree.

"Watch out."

"Take it." She shoved the phone at him. "And go."

What was… Ted had no time to even finish thinking the question in his head before she half-shoved-half-threw the phone toward his hands and reached back with her gun. She squeezed off a shot at the firefighter closest to them.

Dirt kicked up beside his foot.

The man never slowed, only lifted a gun of his own. A revolver. The muzzle flashed.

A tree beside him exploded. Ted fumbled and dropped the phone. He slowed to go back.

"Don't!" She practically shoved him over. "Go. Go."

He's shooting at me.

For some reason, it irritated him that she'd fired and the guy's return shot was aimed at him. Now he'd lost the phone. Where were they going to go? There was nowhere to hide out here. And fewer places than that where they could call for help. "They probably followed you right to my doorstep."

It wasn't like they gave out their address. The guys were super picky about security. He doubted West—or his dad, for that matter—knew where he was. And that was the way he liked it.

"You think this is my fault?" Another shot rang out, and she ducked her head. "They're after your flash drive."

"The one I don't have?" He shot her a look but dropped the conversation.

The last thing they needed to do was find a spot to hide out here and give away their position by arguing.

"Why do you guys live so far from town, anyway? We'll probably be dead or captured before help gets here." She huffed out a breathy sigh. "I can't *believe* this is happening *again.*"

He'd rather figure out the why of it after they were away from two firefighters with guns currently chasing them. "Does it matter? Just go."

"No one is coming. No one even knows we're in trouble."

He said, "So give me the gun. I'll distract them, and you go for help."

"So they can kill you?" She shot him a look.

Ted kept tromping through the brush, even though he wanted to quit. His arm hurt. "Who cares? You get help, and you'll have more leads to find West."

"My grandfather didn't give you a job so you could martyr yourself for the police department in some misguided attempt at a thank you."

He shot her a look that time. "That's not what—"

Crack. Splintered bark from a tree stung his cheek.

Jess fired two more shots. "I'm nearly out of bullets. But with any luck, so is he."

"Do you even believe in luck?"

"You know what I mean."

Did he? Ted wasn't even sure. He slowed. Mostly because he had to.

"Come on."

"I can't." He shook his head, unable to believe she was still moving.

"My grandfather believed in you. And you're just going to quit now?"

If this was her idea of a pep talk, it was awful, and she should not quit her day job. Ted slowed, headed for a downed tree at a jogging pace, and didn't bother answering her. That would take energy he didn't have. Mental headspace he needed to pour into figuring out how to get them out of here.

Where were they anyway? If they'd headed northeast, they would be going up, but this terrain was mostly flat. That meant they'd reach the edge of the sledding hill soon enough.

"You think you're not worth saving."

"Does it matter? We're probably dead either way. They're right behind us." And she was standing out in the open. Sure, she scanned the area beyond where he hid, but instead of crouching like him, she made herself a target.

If she wasn't going to hide…

"We should keep going."

Jess frowned. "He's looking at his phone."

"Can you steal it from him?"

"Maybe if he was dead. They have to be wearing protective clothing, otherwise they'd be dead already."

And yet he and Jess were not. They were injured and on the run. Which meant the odds were seriously not in their favor.

Ted got up, biting back the groan. "Come on." They had to keep moving.

Thankfully she didn't argue. The gunshots had died down. Maybe the firefighter was saving his ammo also. Or he knew something they didn't about what lay ahead.

Ted shook his head. No, that would only be a problem if…

He looked around.

"What? What is it?" Neither of them slowed. Jess glanced as he'd done, but didn't say more.

Ted shook his head. "I'm just thinking about what we're walking up to. There's a spot where the drop off on the sledding hill is pretty steep. Zander skis down it."

"We'll have to be on the lookout for—"

Another gunshot rang out. Ted twisted to look back, ducking as he moved, but kept walking. Jess grasped his arm, her gaze in front of them. She gasped.

His foot missed the next step, and Ted started to tumble.

15

Ted toppled over, pulling Jess with him over the edge and down the abrupt ledge of the hill. The sensation of falling rushed against her with the wind, and she waited for the end to come by way of a bullet to the back.

One second alive. The next, gasping her last breath.

But it never came.

Ted hit the ground first. She landed on his stomach, her body splayed across his. She saw his arm hit the ground, and she flipped end over end. The grade of the hill was too steep to slow them down. Ted cried out, the sound cutting off quickly. Too quickly.

Jess landed beside him the next time. Her head slammed on the ground and a spiked branch dug into her temple.

She cried out, all while trying to bite the sound back. Before she could figure out why Ted had gone silent, they were already on their next circumvolution of somersaults. Over and over, end over end. She couldn't get a good angle on where they were headed, they were going so fast.

Breathlessly fast.

Her head felt like someone was trying to pry it open. She

reached out in a desperate attempt to grab onto something—anything—to slow her down even a little bit. Her fingers slipped through all the brush and twigs she grasped for. She was going too fast to stop herself.

Ted clipped a tree stump, his legs jerking awkwardly. He looked like a ragdoll. *He's unconscious.* Jess grasped his arm. Her elbow twisted awkwardly underneath her. She couldn't help reacting to that aloud. They needed some serious help.

Jess didn't usually ask God for help, but this was crazy. The firefighter guy at the top of the hill would probably shoot them if they didn't die first on the way to the bottom.

She gasped. *Help. Please.*

What else could she say? God was God. She didn't usually need Him, but these were extenuating circumstances. She would have to work out her theology later. Like whether she had the right to ask Him for anything.

The tops of the trees entered and then exited her vision, replaced over and over again with the jagged ground cover of the forest. Like she was in a giant washing machine. With pinecones. Jess cried out and tasted blood. They continued tumbling down the hill, picking up speed as they went. Dirt and grass kicked up. Birds scattered into the sky. Her forehead slammed into Ted's collar bone. This wasn't exactly her idea of a good day.

Would they ever stop? She wondered if there was a bottom to this hill. Even as they continued to roll, she tried to train her eyes on a stationary point downhill in front of her. Three rotations later, she saw where they were headed.

Then she wished she hadn't.

A cliff-like ledge. The prelude to an icy mountain river. There was no way to put the brakes on before they plunged over the side. Except there was a tree coming up. She hissed out a breath. *This is going to hurt.* Ted was unconscious, his body limp. Not even able to brace himself each time he tumbled over. It was up to her to stop them before they hit the bottom of the hill.

And dropped off into oblivion. Going over the edge and sailing through the air before landing in the river—ice cold from snow runoff.

Every January first, a group of high school kids—and other daredevils—jumped off this ledge into the water. More than a few times, they'd had to get Life Flight to the area to airlift someone to the hospital because they'd hit their head and developed hypothermia. It never got warm. If she even thought she would go into the water while paddle boarding, Jess always wore a wetsuit.

Jess grasped onto Ted's arm, winding hers through it. Yeah, this was *really* going to hurt.

She leaned back and hauled him toward her so they were one, descending the hill feet first instead of on their sides. It slowed their momentum slightly. She only tumbled onto her head once as they flipped over headfirst. But she got her other arm out, ready for it.

Ready.

Set.

Jess grabbed the tree. It slammed into her forearm, and she grasped the rough bark with her hand in a death grip. She had to stop herself and Ted. He outweighed her and would be no help.

Ted kept going.

Her teeth snapped together, and she bit down to avoid crying out as they rolled around her grasp on the tree. She felt her skin give way, a horrific sound and feel of her arm as it shredded, but she held on.

She gritted her teeth and quit thinking about all the ways this could fail. She had to hang on.

When she had killed enough of their momentum—and the skin on her arm—she finally let go. They rolled a few feet and Ted slid out of her grip, but eventually they stopped.

Jess blinked up at the sky. Her head pounded. She moaned and tried to roll over, ignoring the mess that was now the inside of her arm. "Ted." She gasped out a breath and looked up at the top of the hill.

Thankfully, there was enough tree cover no one could see them. Would that firefighter hike down to look for them? *Please, God. No.* She couldn't defend them in the state she was in, and they still had no way to call for help. Until someone got to Ted's house and realized the barn was on fire, and they were missing, who would come looking for them? And where would they start the search?

She'd told Conroy so many times that the department needed a K9. Usually they were drug dogs, or they found people hiding from the police. But a search and rescue dog was so much cooler.

Is that helpful right now?

Maybe not, but she was getting desperate.

Cold air ruffled her clothing. She checked her ankle to be sure, but she already knew she hadn't brought a backup gun with her. She'd have to change that for next time. But it didn't help right now.

Ted moaned.

She crawled to him, laying her hand on his shirt. The wounds on her forearm made her grit her teeth. She was making a giant mess on his tee, but who cared?

"Ted. Wake up, Ted." She used her cop voice and repeated it a second time.

I don't want to be alone.

She still couldn't believe he had been so determined to get himself killed just to save her. Of course, she'd have done the same. She was a cop. She'd sacrifice her life for his without a second of hesitation. Was he allowed to do the same? No way. Not when he'd been in such a defeated place. That wasn't nobility. It was giving up.

Not something she'd have thought he would ever do.

Yielding was one thing. Though, she'd never done that

either. It was probably why she and God had nothing but a cold détente between them. Jess didn't give up control. Not even for a God everyone said was good. She'd have to experience it for herself.

But this was about Ted, not her spiritual vacancies.

"Wake up." She whimpered. "Please." She shook him with her good hand. "We need to get out of here."

His arms and legs shifted, and his eyelids began to flutter.

"Please. I know it hurts, but you have to wake up."

His lips puffed out and a moan escaped.

"Please."

"Jess?" His eyes focused, and she found herself in a locked gaze with him.

Seconds stretched out, every breath she took rushing through her ears like the wind in a tunnel. "Hey. You okay?"

He blinked, and the moment broke. "Jess, your arm!"

Thankfully, he didn't shout. She wasn't about to do anything to let the men who'd shot at them know where they landed. "We need to get out of here."

"But—"

She cut him off, sitting up. "We have to go."

Ted sat up. When he started to sway, she helped steady him. This wasn't good. What if he couldn't walk? What if those men found them again, and they fell over the edge for real this time? Her arm—and her pounding head—would be numb from the cold water, but she would also develop hypothermia.

They'd have to carry each other out. Better to simply walk from here. However they were supposed to do that, when she had no idea where they even were, was a mystery to her.

Ted pulled off his sweater one-handed. Once she figured out what he was doing, she held his sling while he tore off the bottom of his T-shirt. She glanced away, not wanting to be distracted by the sight of his abs right now. She helped him put the sweater back on, but he ignored the sling.

He offered her a tight smile and reached for her bleeding arm. One bandaged palm holding her hand, and the warm fingers of his other hand wrapping the shirt like a bandage around her scratched and bloodied arm. "Here."

Jess swallowed down the acidic taste in her mouth as he tied it off. "I think I'm in shock. I can't really feel it."

"Don't worry." He offered her an apologetic smile. "You'll feel it later."

"Thanks."

"We can arm wrestle our injured limbs for use of the sling."

Despite everything, she felt herself smile. "Put it on, Ted."

Jess looked around for her gun. All she saw was pine needles and grass. A few rabbit holes. She'd seen them on some of the early mornings they'd hiked the foothills together.

Ted groaned but clambered to his feet.

"Do you see anyone?"

He held out his good hand, and she clasped his wrist with her good hand to leverage herself up on her feet. Her head swam. Ted's arm slid around her waist, and she leaned into him. This time he steadied her. Each holding up the other when they were too weak to stand alone. She smiled against his sweater. They were a team.

When she looked up, his gaze was on the top of the hill. "I don't see anyone."

"I can't hear them coming either." She scanned around them too. "But they will. Soon enough, they'll climb down to make sure we're dead."

"You don't think they'll assume we're too injured to get up?"

"Maybe. People underestimate us all the time." She shrugged one shoulder. "What do you think?"

He looked down at her. Nodded. "I think we might be good."

A quip she shouldn't say rolled through her head, birthing a smile on her lips.

"We survived. Again." He matched her smile with one of his own.

"Sure did." She wanted to comment that they couldn't be kept down. That West wasn't going to beat them. Instead she sobered her mind, "But it's still a long way out of here. We have no weapons, no protection, and no help."

"Someone will realize we're missing. They'll look."

She wasn't so confident. "Until they find us, we should keep moving."

"Okay, but you just forgot one thing."

She frowned. "What's—"

Ted's head swooped down, and he pressed his lips against hers.

Oh. Jess wound up clinging to him, and it occurred to her that she didn't especially like it when the woman in a couple did that. And yet, here she was doing that exact thing.

Then she realized she was overthinking this. It would be much better to just relax, and be in the moment. If they weren't going to possibly be found at any time.

Ted's chest shook, and she realized he was laughing. He pulled back a slight amount. "I can hear your brain working."

Jess said nothing. She reached up with her good hand to touch the back of his neck, tugging his mouth down to meet hers once again and decided to just get lost in it.

What was the point in worrying? Or overthinking this. It only served to remind her of all the reasons this wasn't a good idea.

Plus, being in the moment kept her mind off the pain in her arm—the one loosely wrapped around his waist now. And it almost made her forget the pain in her head.

A twig snapped.

Jess's body tensed. Under her arm, she felt Ted shift. They both looked toward the sound. A uniformed firefighter, his clothing mussed, held a gun on them.

She shifted, moving a hand to point at him. Palm out. "Hold—"

He pulled the trigger.

The gun clicked. Nothing but the echo of the click. Jammed, or out of bullets.

The man muttered a curse, and Jess ran at him. She launched herself toward his middle in a full-out tackle.

16

Ted barely had time to react before she'd tackled the guy to the ground. The man let out an "oof," apparently as surprised as Ted over what Jess had done.

He moved toward them. When she pinned the man's hand out to one side, Ted stood on his wrist. "Got it."

She moved her hand, her arm soaking blood through his shirt now. How she wasn't crying because of the pain, he didn't even know. But she held her arm to her front and settled her weight astride the man's chest, with one knee on his other arm.

Jess tore off the man's helmet.

He blinked at them, like someone going outside to the sun after being in a dark room.

"Anyone you recognize?"

It took him a second to figure out she was asking him. Ted shook his head, then realized she wasn't looking at him. "No."

"Me either."

The man struggled but didn't have much fight in him. He seemed out of breath. Probably from running after them. Coupled with the amount of sweat dampening his hair, his bloodshot eyes, and the look of his front teeth, Ted figured this guy had been promised a fresh score of meth if he terrorized them.

Kidnapped them.

Killed them.

Jess held her shoulders straight and tight. "Who is West?"

The man grinned that macabre smile and lifted his head off the grass to snap his teeth at her. If she leaned down, he would probably bite her.

Ted leaned more on the man's hand.

Jess yelled, "Who! Tell me now."

The man only laughed.

"Who sent you to try and kill us?"

His body shook under them. Was he high right now?

Jess let out a cry of frustration. Then she punched the man's nose. "Tell me."

He howled in pain, unable to cover his face because they had his arms pinned.

Ted didn't like that they'd been caught unaware. If that gun hadn't been empty or jammed, or whatever happened to it, then one or both of them would be dead right now.

The reality that they'd been kissing, and it had nearly cost their lives, wasn't lost on him. It also wasn't something that would be lost on Jess. With that solid core of "cop" she had in her, born and raised to wear that blue uniform, she would absolutely regret being caught off guard.

After all, that dogged determination of hers to solve every crime in Last Chance so no one ever got hurt was the reason their relationship hadn't progressed.

He was hiding entirely too much from her to successfully date her. She would figure it out sooner or later. She would realize he was a giant fraud and that would mean losing her faith in her grandfather—and tarnishing her memory of him. She didn't need to realize that Chief Ridgeman had made a mistake hiring him, believing he could do the right thing and go straight.

Jess grabbed the arm beside his foot. "Ted."

He lifted his foot, and she hoisted the guy over by his arm, turning him onto his front. She patted down the bulky uniform.

"Protective gear?" She'd shot this man and the other one who had been with him earlier, but neither seemed to have suffered for it.

"Looks like it." She pulled out a cell phone and tossed it onto the grass.

"We should keep an eye out for the other guy."

She nodded. "Got it. Can you call for help?" She motioned to the phone.

"Sure." He wanted to feel useful while she was doing her cop thing. Ted scooped the phone off the grass and studied the top of the hill. It was hard to see through the trees, what with all the branches disguising the ridge.

Behind him he could hear the rush of the water below. Fifteen feet down was the edge that attracted so many people wanting to jump off of it and into the icy river. Just for fun. Not him. Ted had been involved in enough life-endangering experiences, he sure didn't need to go seek them out.

After all, that was why he had an injured arm and was stranded in the middle of nowhere. They were about two miles from his house. Two hard miles of uphill hiking he wasn't looking forward to.

Ted thought about who to call and settled on just the emergency number.

"9-1-1 this is—"

"Bill, it's Ted."

"Ted! Where are you?"

Relief washed over him. His knees nearly buckled, so he locked them straight and kept watching Jess while he explained everything. She didn't need to be caught unaware again. Not with her arm bleeding like it was and with a possibly-high man who could hurt her.

"Donaldson is closest."

"Good." Ted said, "Send Dean as well. Jess is bleeding."

Bill's exclamation made Ted move the phone away from his ear. He winced. Bill said, "What do you mean, *bleeding?*"

"I mean bleeding." Ted saw the corner of Jess's lips curl up into a smile, but she didn't look any less frustrated at this situation. She was apparently as happy about this as he was. "She scraped up her arm on a tree. Pretty badly."

"This is unbelievable…" Bill's voice trailed off into muttering Ted couldn't hear. "…the two of you have been through."

"I know." Ted shoved hair back, but it only fell forward again. Of course he knew. It had been happening to him this whole time. His arm *hurt.* He was well aware of the danger they'd been in—repeatedly—over the last few days.

"Who's the guy?"

Ted didn't answer Bill's question yet. Instead, he said, "Jess, can you roll him back?"

The man was limp as she turned him.

Ted took a picture with the phone and then said, "I'm texting you a photo, Bill. Can you run it through our system and see if you can get an ID?"

"I'll send it to Mia. One sec." The line muted.

Given Bill was the emergency dispatcher, it made sense Ted wasn't the only one he was helping. What else was Bill doing? Fielding other calls, walking someone else through the worst day of their life? Right now, Ted was having nearly the worst week of his. Except for those couple of moments he'd been with Jess. When the reasons why they shouldn't be together anymore dissipated, and all he could think about was the attraction between them.

Which was precisely why Jess wasn't looking at him, and why she had been so intentionally rough with the man on the ground.

Now that the guy looked to have passed out, she was sitting back on her heels. Pain catching up with her.

Ted didn't wonder that he could read her so well. Jess thought she kept her feelings to herself. And he'd seen her undercover. She'd been a completely different person and it had birthed in him serious respect for her. However, when she was hurt? Different story.

"Ted?" His name was muffled.

He put the phone to his ear. "Yeah?"

"Fire crew is headed to your house."

"I heard some nasty stuff explode. They need to be careful with the barn." He shivered at the idea of firefighters showing up. "What about Dean?"

"ATV's. I have his GPS, and he's about two miles from you."

Ted said to Jess, "The cavalry is almost here." They should be able to hear engines pretty soon. "Then we can get back to town."

She nodded but didn't look at him. "No wallet on this guy. Does Bill know who he is yet?"

"No." Bill would have told him. Probably they'd find out later from the lieutenant or Sergeant Basuto. Ted rolled his shoulders. He wanted to sit down and not get up for several hours. But doing that out here wasn't going to be helpful.

He blew out a long breath.

"We'll probably get nothing from this guy. West has kept his identity secret this whole time. It's unlikely he'll mess up now. A guy like this can't be relied on to keep his mouth shut."

Ted switched the phone to his bandaged hand. He set his other on her shoulder, which he squeezed. "You can't assume we won't get a lead from this. That's just exhaustion and pain talking."

"It's also realistic."

Nothing he could say here would satisfy her. Besides, she had the right to feel defeated if she wanted to. Ted tried to see the positive side of everything. But even he had to fight the urge to consider all his attempts at proving he was a good guy were for nothing. Or that her grandfather's faith in him had been misguided.

In this, he could use his work for the police department to get them a result. It didn't matter what he'd been into in the past. What his dad had dragged him to participate in. What mattered was finding West and bringing him down.

Who cared that Ted was nothing but a fraud? Okay, so *Ted* might care about others' opinions, but it didn't need to be relevant right now. Or he was just too tired to worry they'd all find out. That was a problem for tomorrow.

He needed to focus on what he could do *right now*. ID this guy. Go through all the evidence they had. He might have only one working arm, but he could use dictation with his computer and type one-handed.

Ted straightened, satisfied that at least he had the right outlook. Jess would come around. He was sure of it. Probably in time for him to lose faith again, and she'd end up helping him next time. Wasn't that how relationships worked? One person picked the other up, and they helped each other along.

Unless there were too many issues to work through, and the relationship failed.

Or never got started in the first place.

Ted tilted his head. The sound of ATV engines that belonged to multiple vehicles rumbled their way. He strained to see who it was. How many people. If they had medical equipment to treat Jess's arm or handcuffs to arrest their attacker. Or both.

Both would be great.

"Can they get down here?"

He said, "I guess we'll find out." Though, he'd seen Zander and his team navigate all kinds of terrain. Still, it wasn't the safest exercise.

The last thing he wanted was for one of their rescuers to be hurt when they were only trying to help.

He lifted the phone in his hand to shade his eyes from the

afternoon sun now peeking through the trees. Bill had gone silent again, probably dealing with someone else.

"Dean." Ellie was behind him, arms around his brother's waist. Ted spotted a second ATV. "Officer Allen." Then a third. "Donaldson."

They made up the search and rescue team in Last Chance. At least, considering Zander and the guys and Stuart were all gone right now, they were who Ted wanted to come and rescue him from whatever awful situation he was currently in. Especially since he didn't see Sergeant Basuto and his disapproving stare headed their way.

The ATVs angled down, tipping toward them as they descended the hill. They sounded like a swarm of mechanical insects headed their way. The sight was slightly mesmerizing.

Jess let out a cry. He twisted to her and saw her fall back, his gaze snagging on the blood-soaked T-shirt on her arm.

The definitely fake firefighter launched himself up off the ground. He shoved Ted back before Ted had even realized he'd moved to stop the guy. He landed on his butt and heard someone up the hill yell over the sound of the ATVs.

Ted glanced at them and saw Dean's angry face. Then he turned around again.

The firefighter guy raced to the edge and jumped over, his heavy clothing rustling as he moved. No hesitation. He just launched himself off the edge. His arms and legs pumped in the air, and then he was falling.

Ted gasped as he disappeared over the edge.

Bill's muffled voice came through the phone speaker. Ted swiped it off the ground and held it to his ear. "Bill?"

"What are you doing here?" Bill's question sounded taut. And Ted knew instantly the dispatcher wasn't talking to him.

A muffled thud followed the question. Ted frowned. "Hello? Bill?"

There was no answer, only silence.

"Bill!"

17

"Jess!"

She didn't glance over to watch her sister run to her. Jess didn't have the strength, so she just lay there on the grass on that hillside, staring at the sun. The word, "Ugh," may have escaped her lips, though she'd deny that later.

Ellie landed on her knees beside her and touched Jess's forehead.

"I don't have a fever."

"No, just a chronic bad attitude."

"I do not have a battitude."

Ellie snorted. "Sure. Whatever you say."

"I'm dying. There's no other reason you'd be nice to me at a time like this." She turned to her sister and saw the worry etched into every line of Ellie's face. "This is the end, isn't it?"

"Sarcasm does not become you."

Ted's voice cut across their conversation. "...find out what's happening!"

Jess rolled slightly on the grass to see Dean and Ted in intense conversation. "What's going on?"

They looked at her, laying on the grass, staring up at them.

Dean said, "Ted thinks something might've happened at the police station."

"Bill's voice cut off." Ted's face was pale, his eyes dark. He needed two good nights of sleep and the requisite amount of full meals.

The fact he also looked like he needed a hug wasn't something she would allow herself to dwell on right now. Jess had to push those thoughts from her mind while Ellie took her hand and held it. She figured that meant she looked like she could use a hug also.

Jess squeezed her sister's hand but didn't let go. "Did you call in?"

Ted said, "My call to Bill is still open. I'm going to hang up and call Mia." He turned away.

Dean watched for a second, then came to her. "Can you sit up?" He deposited a backpack by her hip and sat down while her sister helped her up. He unwound the T-shirt around her forearm that covered her open wounds and didn't manage to hide the wince.

"Yeah."

He glanced at Ellie and started to speak.

"Don't send me on some pointless and benign errand just because you don't want me to see this."

Jess glanced at her in time to see her sister lift her chin.

Ellie said, "Besides, it's too late."

Jess wanted to laugh. If she did, she would probably start crying instead, because she really did feel awful. Her arm hurt in a blinding way that made her want to throw up. All the rage she'd entertained earlier was gone now. It had dissipated after she lost her cool and punched that guy in the face.

She was going to have to include that in her report. She wasn't prepared for it to come out later, probably when the guy complained that the cop he'd been trying to kidnap and kill had fought back.

Jess sighed.

"You okay?" Dean waited for a second, then squirted her arm with a white bottle.

She hissed. "That's cold."

"It'll numb your arm, but I still want you to be seen by a doctor. You could get an infection all too easily."

"That would be some nice frosting on the awful-tasting cake that has been the last few days."

Ellie squeezed her other arm. "At least you and Ted are safe now."

"For the moment. Seems like every time we're by ourselves, someone tries to kill us. Or kidnap us?" Jess shook her head. "I'm not even sure what they're trying to do. Maybe frustrate us to death or something."

Dean's lips twitched.

Ellie huffed. "There is nothing funny about this. The founders are at it again, and West is threatening Jess's life."

To his credit, he frowned. "Who do you think it is? Ted identified everyone in that photo of those guys from Vietnam. So which one is it, the mayor or the fire chief are the only ones left. Right?"

Jess's brain stuttered. "Did I miss something?"

No. There was no way. She had to have misheard him. Ted had *identified* them all? And he hadn't told her?

Jess shoved away Dean's handful of bandages and got up. She strode to Ted, ignoring Donaldson's, "Hey."

She got right in his face. "You know who the founders are?"

Donaldson gaped.

Ted hung up the phone. "I don't have time for this."

He started to walk by her. Jess reached out on a reflex, and her forearm touched his shirt. She didn't know if she hit him, or if he walked into her raised arm. Either way didn't matter. Same result.

Jess cried out.

Ted spun to her, but she backed up two steps. Stumbled. Turned away from them all and bent double while tears streamed down her face. She sucked in a breath, forcing down the bile that rose.

"We need to go." It was like Ted didn't even care that he'd withheld serious information from her. He said, "Bill might be in trouble. I can't get ahold of Mia, and no one is answering the phone at the office."

She straightened and turned.

Ted twisted to face her. "We can talk about whatever your problem is later on."

Then he walked away. Donaldson frowned after him, then said, "Come on. You can ride with me."

"Thanks."

Dean jogged after them, Ellie beside him. "Your arm still needs bandaging."

"I know." She winced. Dean had her sit on the ATV seat and wait while he wrapped the scratches and gouges on her arm. The inside of her forearm was basically shredded, but after a one second glance, she didn't look at it again. Not until it was covered with the white bandage.

"It still hurts."

Dean's lips twitched again. "I'll call ahead so the new doctor is expecting you."

Ellie stiffened. Given her encounter with the previous doctor, that was understandable. The man had tried to kill her. The new doctor was a woman, but Jess had never met her. She'd been off shift when Jess was admitted after Ted's kidnapping.

"You okay?"

She blinked and realized she'd zoned out. "We should go."

Jess was as ready as any of them to get out of there. Ted had already jumped on an ATV and powered it up the hill with Officer Allen sitting on the back. She heard the cop say something but couldn't make out what it was.

"Let's go."

Jess climbed on behind Donaldson. They rode across the mountains to town, Ted speeding up ahead. A long twenty minutes later, the first ATV crossed the main street. Someone honked their horn, and Jess spotted Mia barreling down the road toward them in a car Jess had never seen before.

She flashed her lights, coming fast.

Jess patted Donaldson's arm. He twisted to see and called out, "Lieutenant, whoa!" and hit the brakes.

Mia did the same, screeching to a stop just as Ted, ahead of them, passed in front of her bumper and jumped the curb into the parking lot. The lieutenant stared over the steering wheel as they all convoyed into the parking lot.

As Donaldson pulled up beside Ted, he glanced over and seemed surprised to see her there. She could see the moment the realization hit him that she was behind the rookie officer.

A big part of her wanted to rub it in his face that she was sitting with a handsome good guy who most definitely wasn't him. But Jess didn't have it in her to follow through. Not only did she not want to hurt his feelings that way, especially when things were so complicated between them, but she also didn't have the energy to be petty. Or spiteful. Right now, at least.

Ugh. She was a horrible person sometimes.

She patted Donaldson's arm. "Go." He swung his leg off the ATV and glanced at her. She said, "Please help Ted." He was younger than her, though only by a couple of years. Donaldson was a good cop, and a good guy, but still pretty green.

Dean went inside with them as well, while Ellie came over to Jess. Her sister said, "We should stay outside until they clear the building."

Mia came over from the car carrying four bulky white paper bags with handles. She'd been to the diner and brought back a bunch of food for everyone. Something she did regularly, considering her past injuries confined her to a desk—for the most part. "Care to explain what's going on, Officer Ridgeman?"

Jess said, "Is it Friday already?" That was when she usually grabbed lunch.

Mia sent her a compassionate smile. "It's Wednesday, Jess. I just thought I'd mix it up a little."

Jess made an, "eek" face. Mia out of her routine? What on earth was happening in the world? "I think I need to sit down. I'm having the vapors."

"You already are sitting down." Ellie frowned. She grabbed two of the bags from Mia. "I think it's clear."

Dean stood at the front door of the police station, his dark brows pulling together.

"Did we really just let our men go in there and play hero for us?" Jess glanced at her sister and saw this was not the right audience. A history professor? The lieutenant, she could understand.

Jess shook her head. She shouldn't have let the rest of them, let alone Ted, go in there alone. Without her.

"Jess—"

Before her sister could argue with whatever Jess had been trying to get across, she led the way to the door. "What's going on?" If she'd had her gun and full use of her faculties, she'd have helped. Dean knew that.

"Find a seat. We'll explain over lunch."

She stepped in and saw Ted leading Bill out into the main office area. Across the counter she yelled, "Bill!"

He waved her off, but she wasn't going to accept that. Jess headed through the door beside the counter and moved right to him as he sat in Savannah's chair. She crouched in front of him. "What happened?"

"Clocked me over the head." Bill winced, and his craggy face shifted like two landmasses colliding.

Donaldson strode in from the hall that led down to the basement level where the holding cells were located. "Call Conroy."

"On it." Mia pulled her chair up to her desk. "What's going on?"

"Sally Peters is dead in her cell." Donaldson reached up to grasp the back of his neck. "By the look of it, she's been shot."

Jess turned to the dispatcher. "You were the only one here?"

Bill nodded. She could see the pain in his eyes, but before she figured out what to do, Dean handed him an ice pack. Bill held it to the back of his head. "Lieutenant Tathers was headed back, and Basuto was supposed to be here, but he had a call across town."

Jess frowned. "And the officer over the holding cells?"

Donaldson approached. "No sign of him. I'm going to search outside."

Jess was about to wobble over on her heels and fall out of her crouch, so she stood up. But her legs shook anyway, and she started to over-balance.

Ted reached out and clasped her hips. She looked up. "Thanks."

He let go like he'd touched something hot.

Jess sighed.

"I can't believe I missed all of this." Mia jerked back around to concentrate on her call. "Hey," her tone softened along with her expression. "It's me."

Jess tuned out Mia's conversation with Conroy.

"I'm going to go check the surveillance video." Ted walked off in the direction of his office.

Dean gave her a pitying look she didn't like at all, and pulled a penlight from his backpack. "Bill?"

Jess wandered off. She was way too antsy to sit down, and there was no way anyone would let her do actual police work. Even she would admit her arm hurt. A lot.

Ellie joined her at the door of the empty Chief's office.

It didn't look much different than it had before Conroy took over when her Grandfather died. Prior to that, there had been a hospital bed here. Her grandfather had wanted to spend his final days where he was most comfortable. The twenty-four-seven staff hadn't hurt.

How many nights had she sat by his bed, holding his hand, while he fought for his life? She was fighting a battle of her own right now. And she was losing.

He would be ashamed of her.

18

Ted shut the door to his office and leaned back against it. Felt like forever since he'd been in here, even though it hadn't been more than a couple of days. The place was a big storage closet that he'd asked the chief to convert into an office.

In here, he could breathe.

He could be himself, while outside this room he had to put on a face. Talk about a growth mindset. And whatever productivity tactic he'd learned most recently. They weren't lies. He charted on the walls how he progressed at the tasks he was assigned. And he tried to have a positive outlook as much as possible.

It helped combat the darkness and scarcity inside him.

Ted wandered around his desk to sink into his chair. He hit the power button on the computer tower on the floor. Then the one beside it. On the desk were four monitors. The inside two rotated so they displayed vertically and the two outside screens horizontal. He shut his eyes and listened to the fans whir.

First, he would check the surveillance to see if it was possible to ID the person who had attacked Bill and killed Sally Peters. Then, he had several confiscated cell phones to go through. Every cell that belonged to everyone associated with West that they'd arrested so far. The judge had granted them full access in order to bring down their enemy.

The more phones he had, the more data he got.

So far, he had a pretty robust algorithm running that sifted through phone numbers they gathered. The source phone number was added, along with whoever they called or messaged over the life of the phone. Based on frequency, location, and several other things—like specific keywords from messages—he was building a program that would give Ted the number of the person most likely to be the boss.

West.

After that, it was only a matter of time before they found him.

A low hum sounded from the corner of the room. Ted's eyes flashed open. Seconds later, the door handle twisted down. Dean stuck his head between the open door and the frame. "Come in?"

Ted nodded. He had no other chairs in his office apart from the one he was sitting in. Prior to the previous chief's cancer diagnosis, the cushy chair now in Conroy's office had been in here. Ridgeman had liked to come in and sit when the old chief wanted a quiet place to rest—somewhere to think when he was trying to figure something out. More than once he'd fallen asleep in the chair, and Ted had listened to his light snoring.

Now he had to play music so it wasn't deathly quiet in here.

"Everything okay?"

Ted blew out a breath.

"Yeah." Dean smiled. "Pretty much." He looked around, then said, "One sec." He disappeared and came back with a rolling office chair. Who knew where he got that from.

Ted eyed him.

"You have company. Deal with it."

"Take the chair with you when you leave."

Dean eyed him right back.

Ted logged into both computers with one swipe of his

fingerprint on the scanner between the two computers. He loaded the phone data into his program first, so it could run while he looked at the surveillance footage.

"What are you thinking?"

Ted glanced at his brother.

"Why so determined to get to work? It's your day off."

"You think I won't log this as time and a half?" Ted tried to brush it off with humor.

"We both know this is bigger than your paycheck." Dean leaned forward to pin him with a stare that was one hundred percent special forces. "You've been hedging on the hunt for Dad since Ellie first showed me that photo. Dad was in Vietnam with the founders. There's a reason this was always his home base."

"He wouldn't come back here now. That makes no sense."

Dean said, "Do you actually believe that?"

"You think he *would* come back here?"

"I think if I was the FBI, the spot where his sons—and his support system—are would be the first place I'd look."

Ted's finger stilled over the mouse button. "I'm not a special agent, and I've never been a SEAL." He motioned at the computer monitors in front of him. "This is what I do."

"So why haven't you found him yet?"

Ted said nothing.

"Did you know he was running the organization that hired Stuart?"

"Because it would be my fault he and Kaylee were nearly killed over it?" Ted understood that he'd be considered an accessory if what he'd done ever got out. But what would that matter? It didn't have a knock-on effect on the Last Chance Police Department. Sure, he'd testified in a lot of cases, but it was the cops here who did the real work.

Which was, of course, completely the opposite of what he'd decided before.

So, basically, he was in complete denial. Trying to hedge all his bets.

Dean sighed. "What has you all tied up in knots? I mean, I get that he dragged you into his stuff, but that stopped when you took the job here. Right?"

Was life ever that simple? One chapter ended and another began. Life moved on. Chains fell away, and someone walked in freedom from that point. Only if that was the case, Ted would have been different the day he'd given his life to Christ, however many months ago that was now.

Instead, nothing had changed, and he couldn't help but wonder if he'd seriously missed something about the whole Christianity thing. It seemed like God wasn't too bothered by the fact Ted couldn't seem to shed his past and move on. He hadn't changed anything about Ted, or his life.

"Please talk to me."

He was about to answer his brother when the footage loaded, and he got a look at the person who had been in the room with Bill during his phone call with the dispatcher.

"What is it?" Dean stood. Before Ted could click off, his brother tugged the corner of the screen and looked at it. "That's—"

"Dad." Ted choked the word out.

"He's here."

Dean was worried about that? Ted had bigger problems than just the fact they'd confirmed their father was in Last Chance. "He killed Sally Peters."

"Why would he come here? That makes no sense." Dean straightened. "If I was him, I'd have disappeared to Canada by now."

Ted shrugged, slightly taken back by Dean's shift in option. "If he didn't escape the draft that way, why would he do it now?"

"Maybe. He's not one to run." Dean settled on the edge of the desk. "Do you have footage from the cell?"

Ted pulled up the holding cell used for women who had been arrested. Sally had been the only occupant. "Here." He clicked play. Sally was sitting on the bench seat at the rear of the cell under the tiny window. Slumped down, she looked defeated. Or tired. Or both.

Cut off from her support. Betrayed, and let go by West.

Her body flinched, and she lifted her head. She mouthed something, and then a flash off screen erupted. She was shoved back by the force of a bullet. Her body hit the wall, and she slumped on the bench again. This time, dead.

"He shot her through the bars." Dean shifted. "Is there another angle that shows his face?"

"What are you, a cop now?"

Dean cuffed the side of Ted's head, though not in a way that hurt.

It was on the tip of his tongue to tell his brother not to treat him like a kid, but the screen went black. He stared at his reflection, saying nothing. What was the point in trying to convince his brother? Dean would always see him as someone who needed protection.

Maybe he did.

Since Ted had taken the job here, Dean thought their father had left him alone all those years. If he knew the truth, his overprotectiveness would get so much worse.

"The last few days have been crazy for you and Jess." Dean studied his face. "How are you doing?"

"I have a lot of work. If the heavens are smiling on me, I'll get a lead that will send these guys right to West's doorstep." He waved in the direction of the main office, through the wall.

"You know that isn't what I was asking."

"I don't want to talk about Jess."

Dean glanced away, his huge shoulders lifting and falling in a sigh. Ted had always wondered why his brother's frame was so much bigger than his. They both had their father's coloring, but

Ted was pretty sure they had different mothers. Though, he didn't know for sure.

No matter. It didn't change their relationship. Or it wouldn't if they indeed were only half-brothers. They were still family nonetheless.

"All this time, you knew what he was doing."

Ted opened his mouth to argue.

"You didn't want me to know." Dean got up, circled the desk, and stared at the artwork on the wall—a magic eye image of a dinosaur Ted had pinned up there years ago. He turned around. "You were supposed to have been using your superpowers to find Dad. Instead, you probably knew where he was this entire time."

"I didn't know where he was. And I didn't know he was the CIA director." Ted shook his head. "How was I supposed to know what he was doing? Or that he would work his way into that position."

Their dad was the ultimate conman. He'd used his military credentials to fool so many. People in powerful positions, so high up in government, there should have been checks. Someone should have realized who he really was.

But no one had.

"The FBI arrested him." Ted gritted his teeth. "I figured that was the end of it until he called."

"You mean 'they' right? The FBI started calling because they wanted a statement from you."

Ted stared at him.

"Dad has a way to contact you."

He nodded, swallowing. This was about to get so much worse. But there was no way Ted could control it all by himself. Not when his dad was in town now. "Why did he kill Sally Peters?"

A muscle flexed in Dean's jaw. He didn't like the subject change. He wasn't going to change the direction of their conversation now, but he'd bet they'd be finishing that conversation later.

Ted didn't like his brother knowing exactly how long he'd been under their dad's thumb.

Dean said, "He doesn't do anything without a reason."

Ted said, "It doesn't make sense why he'd risk coming here and killing her. Unless he needed something or got something out of it."

"For him, or someone else?"

"Good question." Ted leaned back in his chair, trying to think it through the way Jess would.

"One you have an answer to?"

Ted realized he'd been completely distracted by thoughts of Jess. Go figure. That had been a pretty all-consuming kiss. He shook his head, not wanting to go down another rabbit trail. "Could be he did it as a favor. He needs something, maybe from West. So he contacts him and gets the job to kill Sally Peters in exchange for…what?"

"Maybe a new ID. Or money?"

Ted nodded. "I'd believe that. He just escaped federal custody. Either he has a nest egg, or he needs one."

"Stands to reason he'd go back where his support system is."

Ted's body shuddered. He couldn't hold back his reaction. Was his dad going to call again? If he did, was that a way for them to get West? Surely if Ted got his dad to identify the person referred to as West, that would absolve him of a lot of his culpability in whatever his dad had forced him into over the years.

Now there was an idea. Have his dad roll over on West and bring the man down that way.

Use his dad. The way his dad had used him so many times.

Dean was studying him, a knowing look in his eyes. "You have a way to contact him?"

19

———

"It was Pierce Cartwright?"

Bill's jaw hardened under Jess's stare. She figured her expression was pretty intense. How else was she supposed to get the information from him?

There was more. He was holding back, and her whole plan was to attempt to intimidate him into telling her not just who attacked him.

"Tell me, Bill."

He only nodded.

That was good enough for now. Later Mia could get a statement from him, and that—along with his testimony—would be part of the DA's pile of evidence against…

She could hardly even think it.

Pierce Cartwright. Ted's dad was here. He'd killed Sally Peters. Jess shut her eyes for a second and felt Mia squeeze her shoulder.

The lieutenant said, "You expect us to believe that's all of it?"

She opened her eyes to find Bill glaring at both of them.

Of course, Mia had already figured out what it took Jess

much longer to realize. Hopefully the lieutenant wouldn't hold that against her.

Ellie looked up from her phone. "Dean says they knew that. Ted looked at surveillance. He wants to know if we found the duty officer yet."

Mia said, "Tell him Conroy and Donaldson are looking still."

Jess tried to figure out why the duty officer wasn't inside. He was either dead by now, or he'd been kidnapped. Would they get a ransom demand soon? Or would the two men find him somewhere, beyond help?

"Should I go help them?"

Mia shook her head. "Stay here, Officer Ridgeman."

She didn't argue with her lieutenant. Instead, Jess turned to Bill. "You've worked for this department for how many years?"

Bill swallowed. Not nervous. That wasn't the expression on his face. He looked more like he was choked up because he'd been caught. Guilty and maybe slightly relieved they'd discovered the truth. He didn't have to hide anymore.

Finally, he said, "Twenty-six years."

So, longer than she'd been alive. "Do you know who the founders are?" She remembered then that Ted had identified them all. He'd also kept that fact to himself for several weeks while the rest of them waited for that intelligence. "Are you one of them?"

"Of course not. I'm not old enough."

Jess rolled her eyes and stepped away while Mia kept asking him questions. Everyone in the room was listening. Ellie lifted her attention from her phone. "Dean said he and Ted are going to run an errand. He asked if I could go home with you instead, and he'd call me later."

Jess would've slung her arm around her sister's shoulder except it was bandaged. She leaned against the desk beside her and nudged Ellie with her shoulder.

Her sister shrugged. "It's fine. They're upset over their dad, and he'll probably talk to me about it later."

"He talks to you…about their dad?"

Ellie frowned. "Only a little, I think."

"Huh." She didn't want to sound upset by that. They were engaged. She and Ted were… Jess didn't know what they were.

Friends who felt like more, mixed in with some casual and ill-timed kissing, that nearly cost their lives?

Something like that.

Ellie gently nudged her back. In a low voice, she said, "You okay?"

Jess didn't even know the answer to that. She had no energy and everything hurt. Her thoughts didn't seem to want to coalesce, let alone provide any kind of clarity.

Ellie gave her a gentle smile; the kind her big sister was best at. "You will be."

"Sure?"

"I'm sure."

"You guys are *so* cute." Mia looked about ready to burst out of her chair.

Jess said, "Get over here."

Mia rushed over and hugged them both, her arms circling them and her head between the two of theirs.

"Ow."

Ellie chuckled.

Mia looked like she'd done a grave wrong to Jess.

She shook her head. "I'm fine."

"Sure. You really *don't* look like you need to go lie down and sleep for hours." Mia walked away, shaking her head.

"You aren't fooling anyone."

Jess stood. "I'm good to go."

Bill snorted. Jess spun to face him. "Something to say?"

His lips twitched. "You've been the same since you were five. Always looking for approval, seeking out whoever will pat you on your head and tell you, 'job well done.'"

"And that's a bad thing?"

He scrunched his nose up in a shrug that ruffled his craggy face.

"You're in enough trouble." Plus, he was baiting her into losing her cool.

All this time, she'd thought she could trust him. That she knew him, and he was a good guy. *Guess not.* That had been happening a lot this week. Who hadn't lied to her? Probably there were several people in that category. Jess simply couldn't think of them right now.

What she needed to do was get Bill to tell her everything so Mia would know she was still perfectly capable of doing her job, even when things were all over the place, and she could make sense of nothing.

"Is this an interrogation?" Bill lifted his chin. "Because you suck at it. Don't expect to make detective anytime soon."

Jess's whole body flinched, even as she tried to hold it back. Didn't matter. Everything inside cried out at that. Ellie let out a tiny moan.

Jess wanted to do the same.

Until she realized he'd known precisely what buttons to press to get a reaction out of her. Hurting her feelings was his intention.

Mia stood back while Jess took a step toward him. "You know Pierce Cartwright. Not just know him," Jess said. "You let him in while the place was quiet, and he not only attacked you, but he killed that woman in holding."

His stare hardened.

"What reason do you have to keep quiet about this? Because if you do," Jess said, "it only looks like you're an accomplice of West. Maybe you've even been under his thumb this whole time."

"I don't work for West." He bit out the words. "And Pierce Cartwright knocked me out."

"You weren't expecting him. But you can release the mechanism on the front door from your office, and there was no one on the desk." She folded her arms across her front, cradling her injured arm in a way that was only slightly painful, but not so painful she would pass out. Right now, there was a fine line between the two. "You let him in the front door of this house. Why?"

He just stared at her.

"Where's the duty officer? Is he dead too?"

Mia spoke then. "Did you get one of us killed? Because that gets you life in prison."

"I didn't hurt him."

"Where is he?"

"How should I know?" Bill lifted his hands.

He needed to be in cuffs. That, or they were risking him attacking one of them.

"He knocked me out."

Jess said, "Convenient. I'll give you that. Was it all part of the plan?"

"What plan, Ridgeman?" Bill shook his head, as though inconvenienced by this whole experience.

"Being belligerent isn't going to help right now." Mia looked worried, probably about the duty officer. Or about this whole thing.

A death.

A betrayal.

An officer missing.

Jess was done waiting. "How did West contact you? What was the arrangement?"

"It wasn't West. I don't know him. I don't work for him." Bill looked to the side. "I got a text from Pierce."

"Ted's *father*? The man the FBI is looking for?"

"They're on their way." Bill shot her a look. "The minute Pierce contacted me, I told them. They have access to my phone and traced the number. Who knows if they got anything, but it could help."

Mia pulled her phone and walked away, making a call.

Jess said, "You informed the FBI."

"And then he attacked me when he got here."

"But you didn't tell any of us that Pierce was on his way here."

"He needed to succeed. Otherwise he would know I was only setting a trap for him, and I would be dead as well as Sally Peters."

Jess didn't even know where to start with that.

"How can you be so callous with someone else's life?" Ellie wandered over.

Oh, right. That was where Jess should have started. "Maybe two people's lives. But not yours, is that right? So long as you're okay, who cares what happens to everyone else?"

"I'm not going to say 'sorry' like a little kid caught with his hand in the cookie jar. I'm your elder, and as such I deserve your respect."

Jess shook her head. "You've been in contact with Ted's father this whole time, and now someone is dead because of you. And you think you can demand our respect?"

"I've earned it."

"Not with this."

Her grandfather had instilled in her the need to always prove herself. People got caught up in their own problems. They'd forget how useful she could be if she didn't constantly remind them. Conroy. Mia. Even Basuto and the other officers she worked with. They shouldn't forget that this was her career, and she was good at it.

It was why she hadn't wanted to be pigeonholed into undercover work and had started to chafe against what seemed to be a consensus about her with nearly everyone in the department.

She'd decided it was time to change their opinion. Create a new culture. And yes, Bill was right that she wanted to be a detective. How he knew that she didn't want to try to guess. Probably just reaching.

Mia wandered back over. "The FBI is fifteen minutes out."

To Bill, she said, "How long have you been friends with Pierce Cartwright?"

Bill closed his eyes. "For as long as I can remember."

"You know what he did to Ted." It slipped out before Jess could snatch the comment back.

He sighed. "I've helped Ted as much as I could. Tried to be a buffer between the two of them when Pierce got angry. And those times he needed more from Ted, but the kid would've been found out." He opened his eyes.

"So you're the guardian angel. That's the angle you're gonna take?"

Mia glanced at her. "Bill, I get you've been trying to do the right thing. And you've done good things for this town for as long as I can remember—"

Jess was about to object, but she also wanted to know where her lieutenant was going with this line of conversation.

"—This is your chance to do the best thing you've ever done. For Ted. For the duty officer...if he's even still alive. And for yourself."

Jess wanted the book thrown at him. Bill was their dispatcher. How would Last Chance emergency services even run without him? It would be a disaster.

"I can't believe this." Jess ran one hand down her face. "Everyone in this town trusted you, and all along you've been working for a man who destroys lives." That list was so long she'd lost count. "And you don't even care."

"The good always outweighed the bad."

She started to argue, but Mia raised her hand. "Bill, do you know how to contact Pierce Cartwright?"

Jess saw it on his face. *You do.* All along they'd been looking for him. Especially after he'd been arrested. Now he was in the wind, and he'd committed a murder.

Jess wasn't waiting to find out. Bill needed to start talking, and whatever idea Mia had would be put into action. "Give me his number. Before he hurts someone else."

20

———

Firefighters still hung out at the house when they pulled up the driveway. Ted gathered his things from between his feet as Dean parked his SUV. They'd both been pretty quiet the drive over. Now that they were faced with the damage those two men had done, Ted figured the last thing they needed was to talk about what they might be about to do.

His sense of denial was overblown. Ted already knew that he could pretty much convince himself red was blue, and blue was red if he wanted to. Reality didn't need to factor into it. And it wasn't the same as burying his head in the sand.

Now he was double avoiding it, letting his brain mull over how it worked rather than thinking about what was going on around him.

"Need help?"

Ted shook his head. He looped the backpack strap over his good arm and pulled the door handle. Straightening out of the car hurt, but he ignored the aches and bruises all over his body. So far they hadn't lost one of the good guys. He would like it to stay that way, which meant Ted needed to be on his A game. Not down for the count because of a few injuries.

A man in dark gray slacks and a white shirt strode around

from the barn. The insignia and bars on his shoulders said who he was as much as his lightly tanned features and perfectly styled hair. Authority was like a mantle he wore along with his tax bracket.

Dean held his hand out. "Chief Hilden."

Ted realized then he hadn't been exactly right. Dean's sense of his own capabilities should be the same. He should wear authority as the fire chief did, commanding respect wherever he went.

But he didn't.

Because Dean was naturally far more understated than Steven Hilden? Or because Hilden needed the people around him to recognize his position in the community? This man was one of the founders in that photo from Vietnam. Here when the town of Last Chance first started.

A contender for the position of West.

"Ted."

He tried to smile and hoped Hilden figured he was just having a bad day. "Hilden." He wasn't going to call the man "Chief" since he already had a chief—Conroy. Ted motioned his chin in the direction of the barn. "How's it look back there?"

Hilden's tidy eyebrows rose. "Some interesting stuff your friends have in that barn."

It was on the tip of Ted's tongue to ask if they'd touched anything. As it was, Zander wouldn't be super pleased when he got home from this latest mission and discovered his team's training center was nothing but ash.

Dean said, "We appreciate you getting it under control."

They made small talk about paperwork and insurance, things to look out for so they didn't have further problems. Ted mostly tuned it out.

Both he and Dean had agreed at the office that calling their father and asking for a meet, one where their dad revealed the identity of the person who was West, was the best and quickest way to end the threat.

No more having to worry about this ongoing investigation that had enveloped the police department for months now.

Done.

Added bonus: Dean planned to capture their father at the same time.

"I'll let you guys go inside." Hilden glanced at Ted and then walked away. The fire chief probably thought Ted was about to pass out or something.

"I need lunch."

Dean chuckled and opened the front door for them.

Inside smelled like smoke. "Did the house get burned?"

"Apparently the siding outside, closest to the barn. There was some damage in here, but not from the smoke."

"They shot at us."

Dean took his backpack and set it on the breakfast bar. Ted hopped on a stool and started to tug open the zipper, his elbow holding the bag while he tugged on it. "Breakfast sandwich?"

His brother knew how he felt about those. Any time of day was a good time for one of those, especially the way Dean made them. He would never tell Stuart, but Ted preferred that to anything their roommate and friend made for dinner.

He opened his laptop and swiped his thumb print to log on.

Dean straightened from having his head in the fridge, a carton of eggs in his arm. "What do you have running?"

"Everything collected from the cell phones of everyone arrested in connection with West."

"That's probably a lot of data." Dean tugged the coffee pot to the edge of the counter and flipped the lid. He peered into the top and made a face.

Ted studied the program. It was still working. "It's populating a program designed by this guy I message with at Cal Tech. I'm testing it for him so I can give feedback about improvements he should make. When it's done with this latest round, absorbing everything into the algorithm, it should refresh the list I have and give me a fresh round of names—or confirm what we already suspected."

"Which, so far, has been what?"

"That one of the founders is West."

Dean nodded.

Ted continued, "It'll show highest probability based on frequency and duration of calls and even vocal tones depicted from voice messages and phone numbers who it thinks is the top dog. The one in charge."

West. The person behind so much of the crime in town.

"We're still calling Dad, right?"

Ted made a face. He tried to brush off the lingering tension in the air about inviting their dad back into either of their lives. "And here I thought you might've forgotten about that."

Dean laughed. "So long as you don't do it by yourself."

"Because you want to partake in the fun as well?"

Dean glanced over, egg shell in one hand and the other resting on the edge of a glass measuring jug. "I just don't want you doing this alone. That's all."

Oh, that was all? "I'd be irritated, but I actually appreciate that."

Dean looked back at what he was doing. Ted caught the edge of a smile. "If we get a location for him, we'll have to inform the FBI. Or they could argue we're aiding and abetting him."

Ted made a face. "I'd rather just turn everything over to Conroy. Let him deal with it."

"So the Last Chance PD can make their case to convict West."

"I thought that was what we were doing."

"No, we're getting Dad out of your life. West is a bonus."

Ted started to argue that he didn't need his dad out of his life.

Of course, Dean saw that and shot him a look.

Ted closed his mouth. Then he said, "I never thought I'd be free of him."

"Now is the time to do it. To get him turned over to the FBI once and for all and hope they don't lose him. Again."

Ted felt his lips twitch. "There's actually an agent who lives in town here. He's undercover. First as an investigator tailing Ed Summers, and then he moved his way up the ladder trying to get to the top."

"He hasn't figured out who West is either?"

"Conroy said that's supposed to make us feel better, but I'm not exactly on board with that. You know?"

Dean nodded. "Either way it means no one has a result."

Could they really get one by calling their dad? They would have to persuade him that rolling over on West was to his advantage. Not only that, but they'd have to trap him and bring him in after he told them the identity of the man they were after. Or get the FBI to capture him.

It would be a double cross on top of a double cross. But worth it, if they pulled it off.

"Let's just get this over with."

Dean said, "Eat first," and set a plated breakfast sandwich in front of him. It was so tall it almost toppled over.

He took his brother's suggestion and then decided he'd waited long enough.

Ted pulled his phone from the front pocket of the backpack and returned the call from just a few days ago. Had it been so recent? In some ways it felt like weeks since he'd left that meeting with Basuto and Conroy. Now his dad was on the loose, and Ted might be able to get West.

He put the call on speaker and Dean leaned against the counter while they both listened to it ring.

"Took you long enough." His dad's voice was graveled, as it had been for years. He still smoked even now.

"I've been busy running from goons sent by your buddy West."

His dad was silent for a moment, probably because Ted had never in his life talked to his father like that. Then he erupted with laugher and commented under his breath.

"What is he giving you for killing Sally Peters?"

"You tracing this call?"

Ted said, "This isn't a police operation. Dean is here, and he's listening."

"Yeah?" Pierce Cartwright asked. "You listening, boy?"

Ted's jaw hardened. His brother didn't look much happier. "Doesn't matter. You're running from the FBI. What do you need?"

"You're gonna give it to me?" Pierce paused. "Like I'm supposed to believe this isn't a trap. Trying to convince them all you've gone straight. Wait till I tell all about who you really are."

"You don't know the first thing about who I am."

"I don't know all the things you've done?"

"For you," Ted pointed out. Just talking to his dad gave him a sick feeling in his stomach. Maybe that would always be the case, and Ted simply had to roll with it.

Pierce chuckled.

Ted said, "We want West. Tell us who he is, and we'll give you whatever he promised."

"Maybe he already gave it to me."

"Did he?"

Pierce grunted, audible through the phone speaker. "How do you know you can even pull it off?"

"What is it?" Dean moved closer to the phone. "A new ID. Passport. Money. Transportation. What?"

How West had the means to provide another identity, Ted didn't know. Perhaps the money was Pierce's in the first place—and killing Sally Peters was payment.

"He's been busy."

"Tell us," Ted said. They knew West was busy. Pierce showing up demanding whatever he wanted probably didn't help West stay under the police radar. It likely pointed more search lights in his direction.

"He's gonna fake my death."

"Done." Dean didn't look so amenable. At first glance, Ted thought he looked like he was volunteering to kill their father himself. To save anyone else the trouble.

Ted mouthed, *FBI*.

Dean shrugged.

"You think I'll put my life in your hands, boy? After you told me the next time you saw me you'd kill me yourself?"

Dean had told their dad that? Ted never knew. "We can convince everyone. We're legit, and we have no reason to help you. We tell the FBI, the police, and whoever else will listen that we saw you die. You think they won't believe us?"

Pierce grunted.

"You know we're right." Ted glanced at his brother, who nodded his approval. This was a good plan. They could pull it off, double cross their dad back into FBI custody, and find West. Ted would have his father out of his life for good.

And maybe, just maybe, everything they'd achieved would mean the FBI would go easy on him when they assessed the issue of filing charges. Convicting Ted of being an accessory to everything Pierce Cartwright had done.

"Make a plan. If I like it, I'll do it. If not, you'll never hear from me again."

"Fine." Dean's jaw flexed.

Pierce hung up.

"You think he'll go for it?"

Dean tipped his head to the side. "Maybe. Depends on what we come up with."

"So, how should our father die?"

21

───────

J ess shivered. Last time she'd stood on Ted's doorstep, things hadn't exactly gone well. At least this time Ellie was with her.

"We're not staying long." Ellie was using her "teacher" frown as she knocked on the front door. That was never good.

"I know. You've told me that several times since we left the police station."

Jess was supposed to be on medical leave, though it wasn't that formal. Mia had given her the lecture about not coming back until she was fighting fit. Her lieutenant planned to get to work, employing everyone in the department to work the new leads they had.

The whole thing was a mess. Then again, it had been this way since they first heard the name West. Since they learned the founders of Last Chance hadn't exactly been the most upright. Even their grandfather hadn't come through that completely unscathed, though folks seemed gracious to let a dead man rest.

The door opened. Dean's gaze softened when he saw Ellie. Jess, on the other hand, didn't get a particularly warm reaction. Just, "He's in the kitchen."

Jess left them to talk by the door and went to find Ted.

He saw her coming and closed the cupboard under the sink where they—and basically everyone else in the world—kept their trash can. "Hey." Ted strode to the hall in front of her, holding his laptop, and headed for his room.

Jess stood at the door and watched him ease into his desk chair. She shifted the pile of clean laundry from his armchair and set it on the bed, then claimed the comfy spot. "How are you feeling?"

He pulled over a couple of odd pieces of metal from a building set and used a rivet to secure them together in an arm. "Is that really what you came here to ask?"

Jess sighed and looked at the high shelf above his full-size bed. It was littered with tiny robots, cranes, and all kinds of machines. Too many of them. She had no idea what they were or if they even had a purpose. Ted put them together while he was thinking. A way to occupy his hands with repeated movement, to free his mind to solve a problem.

She preferred hiking. Usually with someone there to talk to.

They were so different. Wasn't that a good thing for a relationship? Or were they doomed because they had no common ground except work? Jess didn't have enough past romances to glean from. She didn't want to ask Ellie, and Savannah was off on her honeymoon for two weeks.

A vacation sounded good.

Ted opened the lid of his laptop and logged in. On the screen, his program was running.

"Data from the phones?"

He nodded without turning.

"Anything yet?"

"I'll tell Conroy when it's done. I'm sure you'll be briefed."

"Why are you shutting me out?" Jess twisted so she could see him without turning her head, which was starting to hurt. "Like how you're feeling over the fact it was your dad who killed Sally Peters."

His shoulders stiffened.

"What are you guys doing?" She knew he was up to something. And he'd never pull it off without Dean finding out, which meant his brother knew. It was usually better to just include him up front rather than have to explain it all when he butted in anyway. "Please tell me."

"We're working with the FBI to get him back in their custody. Other than that, it's nothing to do with the Last Chance Police Department."

"So I'm nothing but a cop to you now, is that it?" After everything they'd been through together. All the affection they shared. Running for their lives. Movie nights, sitting close on the couch and sharing a bowl of caramel popcorn.

She stood. "I guess there's no reason for me to be here then."

If he didn't care at all, why stick around? She was nothing to him but a colleague. At least right now. Because he had no intention of letting her into his personal life, he'd relegated her back to being "just a cop."

Jess got to the door before he said, "Hold up," sounding wearier than she'd thought he was.

She turned, trying not to make it look obvious that she'd wanted him to call her back. That all she wanted was for him to ask her to stay.

Ugh. When had she turned into someone this needy? The truth was, she watched how Dean and Ellie complemented each other. How they both needed each other. But with her and Ted, he would never admit to needing her.

She studied his face. He didn't want to let her in. Had he been hurt before, letting someone in? Jess desperately wanted him to open up to her. But was that only because it would make her feel validated? She certainly would feel respected and appreciated if he talked to her about this. But that wasn't a good enough reason for him to share. He should do it because he wanted to because she made it safe for him.

Jess said, "I should go. You're right, I don't have to know

about every single thing that's happening. I just care about you, and I wanted to see if you're all right."

"Sit down, Jess." He brushed his free hand down his pant leg to his knee. Rubbing off the sweat of nerves? He did look like he was gearing up for something.

Jess wanted to walk away and mope. Lick her wounds and whine to her journal about how people were so fickle. Everyone she worked with said they appreciated her. But then they didn't act like it. She was sidelined and pigeonholed.

She wanted to be a big part of Ted's life, someone who made it better. Who complimented him and helped him out.

She eased back onto the chair.

"Are *you* okay?"

She rolled her eyes. "Probably about as 'okay' as you. I'm not supposed to go back to work until I'm a hundred percent."

"So you're working this case anyway, coming here to find out what I'm doing?"

"That's not it." Not completely, at least. "I was just worried since you and Dean left so fast. Ellie was too."

Ted's gaze was as unreadable as ever. "Thanks."

She shrugged one shoulder.

"I'd rather ignore the fact my father even exists." He brushed that fall of hair off his face.

Was it her fault that every time he did that, her heart seemed to catch?

He kept talking. "Instead, he's right back in my life, at my place of work. Murdering." His throat bobbed as he swallowed. "If I can bring him in and get him to tell us who West is—?"

She nodded. The idea they could be done with both would surely be tempting. She could see why he'd done it. Though, she wished he'd have included her in the process.

"But either way he tells the FBI about me."

Jess shook her head. "That you worked for him, years ago?"

"He has enough he can discredit me. More uh…recently. Cases I've testified on could be subject to review. Who knows what the fallout will be?" His brow furrowed, but not out of confusion. It was something else. "So how do I hand him back over to the FBI, knowing he could cost us West? Criminals will go free—and I mean more than just West—and then I'll probably lose my job."

His dad had leverage over him. That was what Ted had kept to himself all these years.

"What about your growth mindset? What does that tell you to do?"

He rolled his eyes and gave a slight shake of his head. "I have no idea what to do, but I know that if he's dead at the end of this, I won't shed a tear. And he won't be able to tell anyone anything. The fallout will be minimal."

"So you want him to be killed."

"Because I'm a horrible son, I guess." Ted glanced aside. "Too scared to own up to what I've done. I'd rather bury it all with him and move on."

"Ted—"

He shook his head. "Don't bother trying to make me feel better. It won't work. Because I've been trying to think through scenarios where the FBI is forced to kill him. So I can be prepared, just in case."

"You're not bloodthirsty."

"No? You think I haven't considered getting a gun and using it on him myself?" He lifted his good hand, palm up, then let it fall back to his lap. "We're supposed to fake his death for him. Convince everyone he's gone. It could go wrong, and he'll end up dead for real."

"That's a risk he's taking." His father had to know that. He was trusting two men he'd destroyed, men he was supposed to have raised into good guys. Who'd managed somehow to be that themselves with no help from him.

"And the risk I'm taking with him being alive is to lose everything."

"Against all odds."

Ted started. "What does that mean?"

"I was thinking about the men you and Dean are."

"I'm nothing like Dean."

"You're very different." She'd concede that point. "That's true enough. But it doesn't mean you're not both good men. Strong. Caring. Loyal. Hardworking."

Ted started to shake his head.

"I know what you believe, and that's what he's put in your head. The good you've done for years now, the man I know you are, is what my grandfather saw in you. A good guy who works to help people. To bring justice."

"That's a cover. It's not the truth."

"Maybe it's you who has that backward. Maybe it's the truth, and what's underneath—the bad you think is the real you—is what your father put there. It's not the real you, the man you'd have been if he hadn't dragged you all over the place doing his work."

"That's not… I don't."

"I get it, you know?" She could admit this to him, at least. "There's a part of me people don't see because they see what they want to."

"So it's all on them? Like your grandfather, deciding I was worth trusting when there wasn't anything farther from the truth."

She shook her head. "It's what I show people, but it's also what they decide. It's a little bit of both."

"You can't control what people think of you."

"Not always. But sometimes you can write the narrative." Part of how people treated her was how she'd taught them to treat her—which was based on how she saw herself. The whole thing was complicated. "What I'm running into is trying to get people to change their perception about me. Because I don't like what I've written."

"I want to keep mine."

"Because you're scared of what they'll do or say if they see the truth?"

He pressed his lips together.

"Do you want me to tell you it wasn't your fault? That he dragged you into situations you should never have been in. That he forced you to do things you never should've done or would have chosen to do if you'd been given the choice."

"I did choose. Some of it. And I wasn't always unhappy."

"Life is life. We all have different experiences. What matters is what you do with the future, not what happened in the past that you can no longer change."

Jess wanted to make detective, not be assigned undercover cases her entire career. No matter how Bill's words had made her feel, that was what she saw in her future. The thing, currently out of reach, that she wanted.

So what was she going to do about that?

"You should start a podcast. Like a life coach type of thing."

Jess grinned. "Everyone has one these days." She shrugged. "Who has time? We're trying to bring down West."

"You can *try* all you want. I'm going to do it."

Her grin turned into a laugh. She was about to say, "Yes," when a knock sounded at the door.

Dean opened it and stuck his head in. "The FBI is here."

22

––––––

In the front seat of the big black SUV that Special Agent Eric Cullings had arrived in and was now driving, Dean spoke on Ted's phone.

Sitting beside Ted in the middle row, another agent leaned into him, watching every keystroke Ted made on the laptop perched on his knees. He'd made a hotspot with his phone to connect his computer to the internet and was running a trace. Trying to find the source of Dean's caller.

"I know that, Dad." The way his brother said *Dad* made Ted want to wince.

The agent beside Ted used a low voice to say, "Keep him talking."

As though they all didn't know that. It was the whole point of what they were doing out here. Even though Ted had already explained to them that their father was far too smart to allow himself to be strung along so that his GPS might be tracked to the place he was standing right now.

Dean spoke into the phone. "It's a good plan. It'll work."

It had taken them *years* to find him. And that had been thanks to Stuart, Kaylee's brother Brad, and an operation that involved law enforcement from both Last Chance and Zander's team. Even then, he'd escaped federal custody.

And they thought he'd hang on long enough to be caught?

Ted shook his head, even as he zeroed in on the location. He gave Eric the closest cross streets, figuring he knew the town well enough. The guy had married local PI Tate Hudson's sister and was here often, what with having an undercover guy in town.

Dean chuckled, but it sounded like no laughter Ted had ever heard from him. "You just don't like the idea of me fake-shooting you." He paused, then chuckled louder. "You would. Just tell me when, and I'll be there."

The GPS narrowed to an apartment complex on the west side of town. Ted whispered the name to Eric, who nodded and hit his turn signal.

The idea they might actually come across his father didn't fill him with excitement. Despite being along for the ride, he'd rather be back at the house with Jess who was protecting Ellie. Ted wasn't super happy, but they needed his skills.

Problem was, he might end up having to look his father in the eye.

He would see everything he'd ever done and hated about himself reflected in the old man's eyes. And then more of what his father had done. Like trying to drag poor Kaylee into a reconditioning program so she could be "trained" to become his wife. Or talking his way into the CIA Director job.

The crimes his father had committed were unbelievable. Ted figured the FBI didn't know the half of it.

And yet, he'd come back here.

On the run from the law and faced with no men and no resources, his father had returned to where he had people on his side. Or, at least someone willing to give him what he wanted in return for killing Sally Peters.

Ted wanted to amputate him from his life, like a diseased limb. Slowly spreading the bacteria that would kill the rest of the body. His dad needed to be cut off.

The Special Agent next to him tapped Ted's arm. He looked over and the man mouthed, *You okay?* Ted shrugged. What did it matter? They were doing this anyway.

The FBI agent was cut from the same cloth as Eric. Tall, fit. Clean cut. Like a businessman, but with an air of lethality. The badge and gun said he meant business. Ted had been around cops for years, but these guys wore it differently.

If they could hold on to his father this time, they'd have a shot to bring Pierce Cartwright to justice—while Ted lost his job, his support system, and probably his freedom in the process.

Would he lose Jess too?

Somehow, from their conversation in his bedroom, he wondered if she would walk away. Write him off. It seemed almost like she wouldn't hold his actions against him—even as she refused to let him skate out from responsibility for his choices. He didn't understand it. Kind of like how he didn't understand why God would choose not to hold his mistakes against him. Paying for what he'd done made much more sense.

Ted didn't want to go to jail. But getting away scot-free? That would be worse.

The computer zeroed in on the building. It turned out to be a townhouse. Much better than multiple floors of apartments where they'd have to wait for him to come out. Or guess which floor he was on. Ted pulled up the listing and found the name on the lease.

He showed everything to the agent beside him. The townhouse was being leased to Leonard Orlando, who Ted knew was a firefighter with the Last Chance Fire Department. After several men had pretended to be firefighters lately, this could mean the whole department was being dragged into this. Implicated.

He sent it all to Conroy's email address while Eric pulled up outside the house, a couple of doors down.

Dean said, "See you then," and hung up the phone.

"We should move quickly." Eric got out, then leaned down to ask, "You want in, Dean?"

"Yep." Ted's brother shoved his door open. "Stay here."

The two FBI agents donned protective vests, gave one to Dean, and the three of them raced to the front door carrying weapons.

Ted closed the lid of his laptop and grabbed the keys from the ignition. He locked up the car and followed to the front door.

Before he got to it, the Special Agent appeared. His brows rose seeing Ted there.

"Jenkins, right?"

The Special Agent responded by saying, "Let's go. You'll want to see what we found."

Ted followed him up the steps and through the door where he abruptly stopped in his tracks. *What they'd found?* He should've said, "Who."

Ted gaped at the man on his front on the carpet, hands cuffed behind his back. "Basuto?"

What on earth was going on? They'd tracked his father and landed Basuto. Did that mean he was working with Pierce Cartwright? Or…West?

Ted just stared.

Basuto wiggled on the floor, struggling against the cuffs like any belligerent criminal. Not like a police sergeant. "What are you guys doing in my house? And let me up."

Dean hauled the sergeant to his feet and stepped back. Eric still had his weapon out. Ted stood with Jenkins at the entryway while Eric said, "Care to explain your connection to Pierce Cartwright, Sergeant Basuto?"

He blinked. "My…*what?*" He spun to Dean. "I don't know your father." Then back to Eric. "Uncuff me. I'm a police sergeant in this town. Call Conroy."

"Because you believe that, as a cop, you're above suspicion?"

He stared down Special Agent Cullings, apparently not

impressed by Eric's line of questioning. "If I'd done something illegal, I'd expect nothing less than exactly what I'd do to any other suspect. But I haven't. Why are you asking me about Pierce Cartwright?" He looked at each of them in turn. "Ted?"

He didn't want to be dragged into this. "Look…" Ted had no idea how to explain. He glanced at Eric, who nodded. "Dean was on the phone with our father, and we traced his GPS. It led us here."

"So you kick the door in?" Basuto stared them all down. "Throw me on my face and cuff me when all I'm doing is watching TV?"

Ted probably wouldn't have thought that was too suspicious.

Dean glanced at Special Agent Cullings. The knowing expression on the Special Agent's face told Ted exactly which one of them had subdued Basuto. He figured Dean may even have argued or hesitated, allowing Eric to take the lead—if he hadn't already been in that position.

Whichever way it went down, the FBI agent seemed to not see a problem with what had happened. Eric said, "My orders are to bring in Pierce Cartwright by any means necessary. Or anyone associated with him. This is a serious situation with national security stakes. Pierce Cartwright *will* be brought in. By *any* means necessary."

"Well, clearly I'm not him. And he's not here. Check."

Eric said, "We have."

Jenkins shifted. "I'll take one more look."

"No snooping," Basuto called after him as he watched Jenkins disappear out of sight. Then he glanced at Eric again. "Seriously? Raiding my house and cuffing me?"

Ted understood his frustration and anger. But facts were facts. "This townhouse is leased to Leonard Orlando." Basuto would recognize the name. The firefighter. One of the men who had chased Ted and Jess down that hill? They'd watched one man who wasn't a firefighter go over the edge, probably to his death. Search and rescue crews hadn't found anything, last he'd heard. The other man? Nowhere to be found.

Was Leonard the one that should be implicated, or was it a real possibility Basuto was involved?

The sergeant sighed. "I sublease from him. He and his wife decided to end their separation, and they're trying to make it work again."

"And my dad?" Ted wanted an answer. If Basuto knew his father, he had to know. They all did.

"Clearly this is a setup." Basuto sighed, his arms still secured behind his back. "To keep us chasing our tails and the FBI occupied with busywork that will lead nowhere."

"That means Cartwright knew we'd double cross him."

Dean said, "Or he stays apprised of what the FBI is doing somehow."

Ted figured their raid of this townhouse had also likely been seen. By his father, at least, if not by West as well. "The GPS led us here. I doubt he has the tech to spoof that."

"I'm not working with him. Or for him. Or however that works." Basuto's expression pleaded for them to believe him. "I'm being set up."

"Let's go talk it over with Conroy." Eric stepped toward him. "But if you try anything, I'll treat you as though you're Pierce Cartwright's right-hand man."

"Fine." Basuto twisted so Eric could remove the cuffs.

Jenkins returned to the room. Eric lifted his chin, and the Special Agent shook his head. Ted figured that exchange meant Jenkins hadn't found anything. They led Basuto out, and he turned to Dean. "A setup? You think that's what this is?"

"I don't think he was here." Dean glanced around. "Or, maybe he was outside. Close enough the satellite couldn't tell exactly—like when the Maps app thinks you're in the river but you're walking right next to it."

"It's more accurate than that, but you're right that there could be some margin for error."

"We still did the right thing."

Ted knew that. Their father was a dangerous fugitive. He was clever and inventive. The idea of seeing the old man again made everything inside him start to frost in pure terror. He wanted to run. Get as far away as fast as possible, so he'd never have to face any of this.

What matters is what you do with the future. Not what happened in the past that you can no longer change.

Jess had it right. He should've listened to her before instead of shutting her out.

Ted pulled out his phone and dialed her number just to check in. He didn't have to tell her he knew now that she was right. There were things he could change. There were things he had some control over, and others he had zero control over.

Ted needed to work on what he could, and let Whoever was in control of the other stuff guide that. *How do I do that, God?* His Heavenly Father hadn't been a huge factor—ever since Ted had converted and then essentially walked away from the whole thing. But if he wanted to figure out how to do this, God was probably the way to go. After all, the whole point was that He was the smarter one. The all-knowing Creator. Ted figured that meant He could be trusted.

At least, he hoped that was true.

Jess's phone connected to the call.

"Hello?" He frowned at his brother. "Jess, can you hear me?"

After a brief rustle, the line went dead.

23

———

"I'll refill the popcorn bowl." Jess swiped the empty bowl off the coffee table and stood, trying to remember where her phone was. A couple of texts weren't worth checking right now. But if she got a call from someone in the PD, she'd answer it. Only so they could tell her they'd found Pierce Cartwright. Otherwise she would just continue to spend time with her sister, pretending everything was fine, and that this wasn't about protective detail.

The second she rounded the couch and Ellie couldn't see her face any longer, Jess let her expression drop. Displeasure and probably exhaustion replaced the fake smile she reserved for mindless sitcoms. Jess much preferred drama or true crime. She didn't need to pretend everything was fine while she was alone in the…

A man stood in their kitchen.

Jess froze at the doorway. She recognized him immediately from a recent national news article. Former CIA Director exposed for private war mongering. Kidnapping. Enhanced interrogation. Illegal operations. Money laundering.

On the run.

Probably armed and highly dangerous.

"Pierce Cartwright." Jess tried to decide whether to hug the bowl to her front or hurl it at the man standing by the back door. "Or is it Adrian *West.*"

Pierce Cartwright was his birth name, and his name as Dean and Ted's father. A name he'd signed when drafted into the Army, and the name sewn onto his fatigues while he served in Vietnam. A name belonging to the man who'd posed for a photo along with the other founders of Last Chance.

More recently he'd used the name Adrian *West* to get the top job at the CIA.

His expression tightened and then flashed, widening into his winning, conman smile. Amusement. Jess felt disdain in the pit of her stomach.

She almost respected him for all he'd managed to achieve. After all, her undercover work often took her into circles like that. She knew what it took to talk her way into the inner sanctum. He'd managed to fool key players in government, fake a military service much more impressive than what he'd actually done, and be appointed by the President to the job of CIA director.

She *almost* respected him.

Instead, she cocked her hip and asked, "What are you doing here?"

Jess heard her sister move behind her as she asked him the question. Hopefully Ellie was using her cell phone to call the police department. Or the FBI.

Jess could throw the bowl, then race to the refrigerator and grab her gun from on top. It would be risky, though worth it if she could shoot him. He was closer to her weapon than she was. She might not have time to get across the room before he recovered from the bowl thrown at his head.

He blinked, ending his study of her. Ellie was out of view. Jess knew that, because he was now only looking at her.

Good. Her sister should stay out of sight until Ted and Dean's father was gone.

"You can call me Pierce."

Jess bit back a retort. Should she ask him how he managed to get in through a locked door? Why couldn't he just answer the question of why he was here? Simply, so he'd understand her, she said, "Whatever. Just tell me what you want."

"So rude."

"You broke into my house. You want me to be accommodating?" Jess eyed the knife block. Or were the kitchen scissors closer?

"Violent little thing, aren't you?"

"When it's necessary." All she needed to do was keep him here until the FBI showed up and took him into custody. She could try and subdue him, but all that was necessary was making sure he didn't leave.

Probably they were on their way right now.

Should she try and arrest him? Sure, he was wily. He might get away, or she might get hurt. Or *more* hurt.

But if she managed it, Jess would get the credit for catching a man who was currently the nation's most wanted fugitive.

"Just tell me what you want."

"And make it fast, because the FBI is on their way?" His expression still held that air of amusement.

Behind her, she heard Ellie make a strangled sound. Her sister was listening. And was she really supposed to believe his flippant question meant he wasn't worried if the feds were on their way? Jess wasn't sure whether he believed she was able to contact them, or not. Or perhaps he simply wasn't concerned over the FBI at all.

Jess shrugged one shoulder, trying to pass this off as no big deal. Truth was, it could end up being one of the most important conversations of her life.

If she managed to catch Pierce Cartwright personally, that would put her in a top-notch standing with the FBI. They might even ask her to join a task force. She could get a promotion or a sweet undercover assignment. Or both.

Just the thought of that happening had her taking an involuntary half step forward. Then she caught herself. She was better than that. Better than giving away her intentions or letting her emotions rule her. Especially if she wanted to have any hope of getting usable intel from him.

He continued that amused stare. "Maybe I just wanted to come by and see the women who have captured my sons' attention."

"While they conveniently happen to be on an operation with the FBI, tracking your location to bring you in?"

"Stuff happens."

Of course, that wasn't what he'd said. But it was how she preferred to have heard it. "Listen, *Pierce.* Just say what you have to say, because you don't have much time before the FBI bursts in and ends it all right here."

His lips curled, and his shoulders jerked in a silent chuckle. "I doubt that." He lifted his phone and shook it. "Signal jammer. Nothing in *or* out. My son has built many devices for me and has written many programs over the years. They come in handy at times like this."

So no one was coming. Jess had to solve this herself? Fine. That was actually good to know, considering she didn't need to waste time waiting for help to show when it never would. She just needed a plan. Then she was going to go for it.

All she had to do was subdue him, and she would have the career she wanted.

Not the life in Last Chance she'd settled for over the previous few years. The nationally recognized career she'd always wanted. Deep down. Respect. Recognition. Those things were so close it almost felt like she could reach out and grab them.

Jess pitched the bowl at his head. It flew across the room, and she moved. Slid a knife from the butcher block. Rounded the island and rushed at him.

He brought his arm up to block the bowl, swiping so it

thunked off his forearm and hit the floor. He dropped the phone and the screen shattered.

Jess slammed him against the door and held the knife to his neck. "Ellie?"

"Yes?" Her sister sounded breathy. Nervous.

"Get the phone. Shut it off, and then call Conroy." She bit the words out, trying not to cry over how much her forearm hurt right now.

She heard her sister move but didn't shift her gaze from Pierce Cartwright. Ted's father didn't even twitch. If he did, he'd only get cut across his neck.

His eyes flared. "You won't kill me."

"Wanna bet?" She lifted her brows. "I'm sure the FBI won't mind if you're captured dead or alive. After all, an autopsy is cheaper than a federal court case that's going to drag on for months."

"What do you want?"

"In exchange for letting you go?" She nearly laughed. "You're in no position to bargain."

"There's always room for a deal."

That might have worked in the past, keeping him from getting arrested until his silver-haired years. It might've made it so he managed to escape federal custody after that. But he wouldn't get away now.

"So," he said. "What do you want?"

"Who is West?"

His chest shook under the pressure of her forearm. "Just the world then, nothing small."

"I'll put in a good word for you."

"I'm sure that's untrue." He studied her features. "He'll never let you find out. In fact, he asked me to warn you about what happens to nosy little girls who don't walk away."

"And I'm gonna pass a message back like this is middle school recess?"

Never mind that she figured this had been his whole point in coming. He said it was to get a look at the women in his sons' lives, but she'd figured that wasn't it. Like he even cared? Like she and Ted were in an actual relationship?

No, this made far more sense.

West had sent him here on another errand. Pierce Cartwright was here to deliver a message from the man she was trying to find.

"He's got you, doesn't he?" Jess needed to tread carefully, or he would shut down. "You had to come here. Risk capture, or me killing you, just to tell me what he said." Or he would explode, and she'd be able to use the opportunity.

He said nothing.

"Why not just run instead of doing favors for West?"

"I have my reasons."

"I'd love to hear them, but it occurs to me that I don't care."

Again, he was silent.

"Oh, how the mighty have fallen. From running the CIA, king of your domain, to this?" A trickle of blood accompanied her words, but she didn't let up the pressure on his neck. If she did that, he would jump on it. "Ellie!"

"Conroy is on his way." Her sister's voice shook.

Probably with a team of officers in full SWAT gear and the same of FBI agents.

Jess said, "Get my gun off the top of the fridge."

The skin around Pierce's eyes flexed. Nervous? He should be. It didn't much matter to Jess if she wound up killing him or not. They'd probably still give her a promotion.

She heard her sister moving around and said, "Time's running out. So tell me who he is. It's your only leverage here."

He had to know there were a limited number of possible outcomes. Not many ways this could go down, and most of those ended with him either dead or back in FBI custody.

Ellie said, "What am I supposed to do with this?"

Jess wanted her to point it, loaded with the safety off, at the man she currently had pinned against the wall. But Ellie didn't like guns at the best of times.

His phone vibrated in his hand. They both heard it, but neither moved. Some kind of signal? Or it could be a way to get to West.

"Give me the phone."

He said, "I've enjoyed this. Especially the parts where you considered yourself to be in control of the situation here."

Jess didn't like the sound of that. "Hand the phone over and put your hands on your head. After that, I will allow you to turn around." To her sister, she said, "Ellie, I'm gonna need cuffs." Her sister knew where she kept them.

Jess heard her move away. That was for the best. If she was forced to hurt Pierce Cartwright, Ellie didn't need to see it. She wasn't a cop. Ellie might have been through plenty in the last few months, but she hadn't seen nearly the horrors that Jess had.

"Nicole. That was her name, wasn't it?"

Jess's whole body flinched like she'd been struck. "How do you..?" The knife faltered.

Pierce shoved her, both hands to her middle as he pushed her back. The corner of the phone dug into her ribs. Jess's body nearly folded in two, and she hit the dining table but somehow managed to not go down.

"As if you'll ever be good enough for one of my sons." As he spoke, he pulled out a cylinder from his jacket pocket.

She knew what that was.

Pierce Cartwright pulled the pin and tossed it, then raced out the kitchen door just as light and sound exploded in the room.

Blinding her.

24

The front door swung open just as Ted jumped out of the car. Jess came tearing out of the house at full speed, tripped off the front step, and fell. She landed in a sprawl, face first in the grass.

"Jess!" He raced to her and landed on the grass beside her. Ted helped her turn over to a sitting position and took a look at her face. "What happened?"

Jess's eyes were glazed over, her face flushed and not quite able to focus on him. Her attention darted all over the place. "Where is he…where did he go?"

"Who are you talking about? Was West here?"

After she hadn't answered the phone, they'd all piled into their vehicles and made their way here as quickly as possible. Even Special Agent Cullings. Though two of his colleagues had taken Sergeant Basuto back to the police station so they could talk more to him about what had happened.

When she still hadn't said anything, he prompted her. "Jess."

She shook her head. "Your dad was here." Then she lifted two fingers and pressed them between her brows, at the top of her nose. "I think he threw a flashbang at me."

Conroy crouched to touch her shoulder. "Which direction did he go?"

She shook her head again. "I don't know." Then paused to wince. "I need to stop shaking my head because it hurts."

Conroy straightened to his full height. "I'm going to get on the search."

Ted didn't want to think about the fact his father could get away with this, or that he might be on the loose still. But he also had other priorities right now. He turned to his brother. "Can you take a look at her?"

He crouched as Conroy had done and looked into her eyes. "Our dad was really here?"

"Yes." Jess's voice was shaky. "Ellie is still inside. She was waking up when I came out."

"I know," Dean said. "I see her in the doorway." He turned to Ted. "She needs to see a doctor, but the effects of the flash-bang should pass." Dean got up and moved to the doorway, where Ellie stood leaning against the door jamb.

"Help me up." Jess shifted to stand.

"Is that even a good idea?" As he spoke, Ted braced her weight with his hands on her elbows. But when she stood, it was clear her balance was unsteady. "We should get you a chair."

"Not while your father is still out there." She twisted to face him and lifted her chin. "I think I nicked his neck with my knife." Her brows crinkled together.

"You got him? What did he say?"

"He wanted to get a look at me and Ellie while you guys were busy."

Ted nodded. "We tracked his call to the source and wound up busting into Basuto's apartment. I thought for a second that he was involved, but now I'm not so sure. The FBI can figure it out."

"Is he even a suspect? I mean, could he be West?"

"That's crazy, right?" He shook his head. "This is Basuto

were talking about, right? No way is he under West's thumb, let alone the criminal we've been chasing for months."

"He has been acting weird lately, but I never would have thought this." She shut her eyes and gave herself a minute.

"We should get you to a doctor so you can be checked out." There was no way she was in a state fit to debate what had happened. She needed to give a statement so they could have it on record exactly what his father had said to her.

The idea that his father had targeted her hit way too close to home. There was supposed to be a line of demarcation between his dad's life and his life, the understanding being that they didn't bother each other. And now this is happening. Ted was supposed to be dealing with this in his way and in his own time. Now his dad had dragged in Jess. Not to mention the fact that he'd probably seriously scared Ellie.

Ted glanced at his future sister-in-law, standing with his brother inside the open doorway. Their forms were silhouetted by the light coming from inside so he could see them in an embrace. Kind of like the hug he wouldn't mind sharing with Jess right now.

"I'm fine," Jess said. "I don't want to slow down anything. If I need to get checked out, I will, but I'm just bruised from when I hit the table."

"And your arm?"

She winced. "Yeah. How's *your* arm?"

Ted pulled her to him in a quick side hug, ignoring her question. He figured they were neck and neck on bruises after everything that had happened so far. Too bad for them it wasn't a competition, because having faced down a flashbang, she might be in the lead right now.

"As long as you do," he said.

She stared up at him. "Are you trying to tell me what to do?"

"If it sounds like that, I'm sure it's only because I care about your state of being."

"That's gonna go both ways." She eyed him. "Because now

that I've met your father, I think I might be entitled to understand exactly what happened between the two of you."

"I thought you were busy trying to catch West?"

One of her brows lifted, and she managed to almost hide the wince. "I asked your father who he was. It sounded like your dad might've been…not exactly scared to tell me, but more like West is holding something over his head. He said he was sent here to warn me to stop looking into West."

"Meanwhile," Ted said. "We're out on a wild goose chase running up against what's probably going to turn out to be a red herring."

"Unless Basuto really is working for West."

He shook his head. Just the idea that someone they had all trusted could be dirty seriously rubbed Ted the wrong way. Even though he hadn't always done the right thing, he'd always figured he could trust the others in the police department. They were good people. Good cops. The kind who tried to help as much as they could, knowing that some people genuinely needed the assistance.

And now West might have wheedled his way into the department? That meant Ted was no longer the weak link. He hadn't been targeted or blackmailed. It may have been someone else, namely the sergeant who had been running the department after Conroy was shot by the sniper. Mia was the lieutenant, but she was also Conroy's fiancé. She'd divided her time between the hospital and helping him convalesce and the department and her duties there.

Basuto was the one who had been taking the lead. If he had been targeted, that would make sense.

None of them could have anticipated this.

Ted needed to get back to his computer so he could pull his thoughts together and figure out where they should look next. "We have nothing now. At least, no more idea of who West is today than we did yesterday. Unless Basuto can tell us specifically who targeted him."

"We'll figure out who contacted him and dragged him into all this."

She started to move. Ted went with her, but Jess's gait quickly faltered. She stumbled as she headed toward the house. He wanted to support her, only Jess was the kind of woman who tried to do everything on her own. Like facing down his father while also making sure her sister was entirely protected while she took the brunt of a flash-bang impact.

"I can't believe he got away," she muttered as they walked toward the open door and their siblings. "Who brings a flash-bang to the conversation anyway?"

Ted's lips twitched, and he couldn't believe he was amused by that. There was nothing funny about his father. Or the damage that Pierce had done to people that he cared about. That thought served to sober him up.

He looked around to see where the cops and federal agents who had come with them had gone to search for his father. Would they even catch him? It had taken years the first time. They'd wound up amassing evidence against a prominent government figure, the CIA director, and headed into his office with a warrant. It had all been bad enough. Considering what his dad had done to Stuart and Kaylee that was probably an understatement. But the truth was that the feds didn't even know the half of it.

Ellie was the first at the doorway, holding her hands out to grasp her sister's as she entered. "Are you okay?"

The expression on Dean's face was soft as he watched Ellie embrace her sister. Ted hung back, trying to figure all this out in his head.

"I need to get back to the office." If Basuto really was involved with West, then his number would be among the ones Ted had pulled together from the evidence so far. The FBI would need to know so they could ask him more specific questions.

Dean said, "I'll stay with the two of them if you want to head out."

The look he shared with his brother said more than either of the women would know. Dean was about as happy as Ted that their father had been here. That he had confronted the women his sons were in love with.

Because yes, Ted had fallen for Jess. Probably months ago, if he was honest with himself. Since then, he had practically followed her around like a puppy, looking for scraps of attention while she worked the case trying to find West.

When she finally turned her attention to him, he found himself too preoccupied with his father's escape.

The truth was, it was probably all just bad timing. Maybe they were never supposed to have a relationship. This could all just be God proving to them that it would never work anyway. After all, why was it so difficult? Right things should click into place in a way that felt like they had somehow always been like that. Timeless.

Or maybe he'd just watched his brother fall for a woman who was perfect for him, and Ted had finally realized that he wanted that same kind of love for himself—and that it would be just as easy.

He turned away from them and saw Conroy headed toward the house. The chief of police shook his head.

Pierce Cartwright had gotten away. And if he'd wanted to, he could have killed Jess and Ellie here tonight. The way he'd killed Sally Peters in her holding cell.

That realization rolled through him, and he stumbled. Nearly went down.

Conroy said, "Whoa. Easy."

"I'm okay." Ted shook his head. The last thing he wanted was sympathy when the whole reason his father was here was because of him.

"Hold up." Conroy held out a hand, and Ted stayed where he was. The chief answered his phone and had a low conversation. He finally said, "We'll be right there." Then to Ted, he said, "Don't go anywhere. Donaldson just called in a body drop. A woman was tossed out of a car in front of the police station."

The rest of them hurried over. Jess said, "What on earth?"

"We're all headed back to the police station." Conroy indicated Dean and Ellie. "The two of you as well."

After everything that had happened tonight, now there was a murder also?

Before anyone could ask more, Conroy said, "Donaldson says the dead woman has Officer Ridgeman's uniform on." He turned to face Jess. "Her ID says her name is Nicole Collins."

Jess gasped.

25

Jess set her hands on her hips and stared down at the deceased young woman. All the aches and bruises on her body from falling backward and hitting the table before she landed on the floor didn't seem quite so bad considering a life had ended. Her scratched-up arm still hurt though.

Conroy stood beside her. "The medical examiner is on his way here. But I think it's pretty safe to say she was strangled, given the bruises on her neck."

"This is the part where I explain to you who Nicole Collins was. And this woman is not her."

"I read your personnel file from the NYPD. I know you were undercover with vice, working to take down a trafficking ring. I also know that Nicole Collins was your informant from inside, the woman you were trying to save."

"And the strangulation?"

"I know it wasn't your fault," Conroy said. "You couldn't have anticipated the people you were trying to bring down would react like that to finding out the police were closing in."

"So I'm not supposed to feel guilty that they killed her instead of me?"

"Of course you'll feel that way. Because you're a good cop,

one with drive and a heart. That's why I hired you. Not because your grandfather was the previous police chief."

It felt good to hear him say it, even if Jess didn't all the way believe him. She had built a career in New York City on her own merit and abilities as a police officer. However, coming to a department where her grandfather's legacy had proved long and strong was something completely different. Though he was one of the town founders, a group who had proven to be the thorn in the side of the department lately, Alan Ridgeman had been one of the best cops she'd known.

"I'm not going to let this go." She looked at the woman who had been thrown from a moving car—tossed on the ground like a piece of trash. "This was West's doing, and it was because of me. This is yet another warning that I should back off this case. And now that a woman is dead, he has to know there's no way I'll do that."

Conroy twisted to face her. "He's trying to bait you into losing your cool. Yes, a woman is dead, and that's a tragedy. Because she didn't deserve to have her life end like this. But it's not on you. And you can't let this get to you, Jess. Because if you do? It's only going to end with you dead as well."

"I get that you don't want me to die over this. I don't want that to happen either, but West can't be allowed to get away with this."

She spotted the medical examiner's van pulling into the parking lot, driven by a local doctor who had been on call tonight.

Jess turned and headed into the police station. The reception desk, usually with Kaylee seated behind it, was empty. She was safe, and Jess was glad her friend wasn't here right now. Pierce Cartwright had targeted her for his twisted desires, and with the man currently on the loose, it was better for her to be protected.

However, that didn't make the space where Kaylee should have been any less...empty.

Jess let herself in through the door and headed for the break room where she filled a glass with water and chugged it back.

"If I ask you whether you're okay, will you give me a straight answer?"

Jess turned to her sister and could only shrug. She didn't even know what to say, let alone where to start with all this. "Where's Dean?"

"With the lieutenant in Ted's office."

Jess nodded. "Good." She moved to Ellie and squeezed around her sister, kissing her on the cheek as she moved. But Ellie wasn't fooled. Her sister rolled her eyes as Jess headed for the hall where the interrogation rooms were located.

She found the room where two FBI agents were talking with Sergeant Basuto.

Jess pushed the door open. She lifted her phone and showed Basuto the screen. The three men in the room all flinched as though she'd drawn a weapon. "This woman is laying on our doorstep, dead because of West."

The skin around Basuto's eyes flexed.

"We're being targeted. Baited into getting distracted, losing our cool, and putting our focus in the wrong place."

One of the special agents lifted a hand. "Officer, please—"

Jess ignored him, speaking to Basuto. "Are you working for West—or Cartwright—by your own volition, or because they're forcing you to do it?"

"No." Basuto's jaw hardened. "I am not." He looked at the two FBI agents with intent.

"Then we all need your help out there, because things are unraveling fast, and we can't let him tear us apart."

She almost couldn't believe she was defending him without substantial evidence otherwise. But the truth was, Basuto had been a good cop longer than she had. And she had gone off on her own too many times. Right now, what they needed was to band together.

Would she be able to convince Ted of that fact?

Basuto stood. One of the **FBI** agents reached out his hand and said, "Hold up a minute. You want to just tell us you had nothing to do with this, and we're supposed to believe you?"

Before Basuto could retort, Jess turned to them. "You guys are here to find Pierce Cartwright. So why don't you do that, and let us worry about our problems?"

She thought she heard Basuto swallow a choking laugh but didn't turn to find out if she was right. They might not always see eye to eye. Their methods differed considerably sometimes. But at the end of the day, they were both Last Chance cops.

That meant something to her.

Basuto nudged her toward the door. The special agent said, "This isn't done. You aren't out from under suspicion, Sergeant. Not until you've proven that what you say is correct."

Basuto said, "I hear you, Jenkins."

They strode down the hallway. She kind of thought the sergeant would have maybe thanked her, but he said nothing. That was fine with Jess. She had enough thoughts swirling around in her head. She'd partly stormed in there to see if Basuto had something on West she didn't already have. Some kind of intel, or lead, she could use to find him.

After that, hopefully things would go back to normal, and she'd have the time to figure out what her feelings for Ted meant. And why they couldn't seem to get on the same page at the same time about where they were going.

Until then, she had to stick with her priorities and do her job.

Conroy was the first to speak when they made it to the main office. He waved them both over. "In my office. Now."

Basuto nudged her before she could step in. "I'm not working for West."

She stopped and turned to him. "But I'm guessing there's enough evidence in what we have that someone could make a case for it."

His expression darkened. "It's going to be a long road for me to convince everyone I'm not dirty. But if you believe me, then it's a start at least."

She figured she would likely have her doubts at some point. Especially if, between Pierce Cartwright and West, they had planted enough evidence to convince not only cops but officials and the general public as well.

Basuto would have a long road to walk if he wanted to get back in good standing with everyone.

They headed inside Conroy's office, and she found Special Agent Eric Cullings in a chair in front of the desk. He was looking at his phone.

"Are you going to tell me that Pierce Cartwright got away again?" Jess planted a hand on her hip. She knew she was skirting the line of insubordination. Hopefully Conroy would give her some grace, given everything that had happened to her. Not only today but also in the last few days.

Conroy waved her to a chair and Basuto leaned against the wall with his arms folded.

Jess realized just now that she hadn't seen her sister or Dean. "Where's Ellie?"

"She and Dean decided to get some air," Conroy said.

Since her future brother-in-law was a former Navy SEAL and most likely carrying a gun, she figured her sister was in safe hands. "I would dearly like to know how West managed to get into my NYPD personnel file. My captain kept what happened pretty quiet, and I know they never released the woman's name."

Special Agent Cullings looked over. "So you decided to interrupt a questioning and find out the answer for yourself?"

Jess said, "Pierce Cartwright is under West's thumb. Whether you like it or not, figuring out West's identity could get Cartwright right back into custody."

She didn't bother reiterating to him the fact they'd taken so long to capture him in the first place and had now lost him.

More than once West had proven himself one step ahead of them.

"Yeah, we know that," Cullings said. "And not only that, but we've had an undercover trying to identify West for months."

Conroy leaned back in his chair, pressing a hand against the spot where he had been hit by a sniper. The bullet had done a lot of damage, but he seemed to be healing well enough. "I miss the days when criminals made dumb mistakes, and we got them easily. This guy has slipped through our fingers more times than I can count."

Jess was as irritated about that as he looked to be.

Only, was he talking about West or Pierce Cartwright?

"Given the fact this guy is giving you so much attention," Cullings said. "I'd probably have removed you from the case. If you were one of my people, there is no way you'd be working this."

What she wanted to say to him would probably have gotten her suspended, so Jess just kept her mouth shut. Behind her, Basuto made that choking sound again. Conroy shot him a look.

Jess shrugged. "By now, I figure it's personal for all of us."

Though, why West was looking so hard at her, she had no idea. Why would a local crime boss who'd been nothing more than a ghost to them for months now risk revealing his identity by coming after her? Sending men to hurt her and Ted. Using Pierce Cartwright to deliver a message. Killing a woman—and risking physical evidence.

It had to mean that she was close.

On the desk in front of Conroy was a clear plastic evidence bag. Inside she could see the driver's license and cell phone. "That's all that was on her body?"

The chief nodded. "Except for your uniform, which Cartwright must have stolen when he killed Sally Peters. The cell is on, but it needs a passcode we don't have."

That meant Ted was going to have to try and break into it. Or they would get nothing from the device.

"And the driver's license?"

Special Agent Cullings answered, "Very clearly a fake. Probably a rush job that didn't cost very much."

"But he gets the job done, right?" She figured that was true, at least. "It sent the message it needed to send, and we didn't need to believe it was real."

What she needed was a way to flush out West. But all they had was bait to make her jump too fast into something she wasn't prepared for. She would only wind up missing something because she raced in too fast, determined to get this done. West would have a plan set up. She would fall into it.

A trap.

They needed a plan of their own.

Before she could suggest that to her bosses and the FBI agent present, the phone in the evidence bag rang.

They all stared at it.

Conroy opened the bag and pulled it out. He put the call on speaker and held the phone in front of him. "This is Chief Barnes."

"Conroy?"

Jess knew that voice. She jumped out of her seat. "Ellie? What's happening? Why are you—"

"They hurt Dean. It's really ba—"

The line went dead.

26

A notification popped up. Ted blinked at the computer screen, then frowned. He swiped a paper off the printer and grabbed his tablet as he headed out to the bullpen. Conroy was in his office along with Eric Cullings, Basuto, and Jess.

Right now, he didn't have time to be distracted by her, so Ted didn't even look at Jess as he knocked on the Chief's door and entered the office.

He handed over the paper. "This is the list of everyone who could be identified as West, from every piece of evidence we've gathered so far."

"We have a bigger problem than that right now."

Before Ted could ask the Chief what he meant, Jess said, "Or, at least a more immediate one."

He realized then that her face was unusually pale.

"What's going on?"

Conroy stood. "Something happened to Dean and Ellie." He snatched up his phone and made a call.

As he did this, Jess laid her hand on his arm. "We just got a call on the dead girl's phone. It was Ellie, and she sounded upset. She said Dean has been hurt."

"Yes," Conroy spoke into the phone. "You need to find

Dean and Ellie. They went for a walk outside the police station, and we think they might have been hurt. Maybe even taken by someone." He hung up the phone. "Donaldson is on it. Just pray he finds a witness."

Ted glanced between each of the four of them. All cops. They were the kind of people who knew how to get a kidnap victim back. "Are we thinking that West took them? Is that what this is?"

Jess said, "I can't believe someone could have gotten the drop on Dean, but if he was hurt in the process, then that makes sense. Take out the threat first. Then you have open access to get both of them in a vehicle. As much as I love my sister, she is not trained the way the rest of us are."

Ted had thought Ellie was pretty tough. She'd faced down the town's previous doctor who had turned out to be nothing but a selfish criminal who murdered a young man just to keep his dirty secret. Ellie had faced him down long enough for Dean to find her.

But now they were both gone.

He looked down at his tablet. "So that was what the notification was about. An incoming call from one of the numbers on that list—" He pointed at the paper he'd handed to Conroy. "—to a phone at this location, which also happens to be on the list."

Conroy's eyes flashed. "This phone belongs to one of West's people?" He pointed at the cell phone on his desk. "And whoever attacked Dean allowed Ellie to make a call to us? For what, to spin us into chaos?"

Ted said, "I'll have to figure out which one it is, but we know West has a series of burner phones he's handed out to his people. One of them my father used to implicate Basuto. The dead woman might've simply been a method to get this phone into our hands."

Jess looked at the tablet screen in his hands. "Which phone made the call to this one?"

Ted scrolled down with his finger. If they could figure out which number made the call, they might be able to trace it and find out where Ellie and Dean currently were. If West had left that avenue open to them, it would be by mistake. West hadn't made any of those yet.

But it could happen.

And if that didn't work?

Ted didn't want to consider the alternative.

Was West really determined to destroy more lives? He'd been under the radar so long, now it seemed like he was only lashing out at their attempts to bring him in. Focusing on Jess. Using his dad to send messages. Now taking Dean and Ellie.

Conroy's phone rang. He snatched it up, "Chief Barnes." There was a serious frown on his face as he listened to the caller speak. "Thanks." He hung up and looked at them. "Donaldson found Ellie's purse and signs of a struggle. There are tire tracks in the gravel beside where they were walking."

Jess said, "Any witnesses who saw the vehicle speed away with them inside?"

Conroy shook his head.

"So we have nothing. All we know is that they are hurt and missing?" Ted didn't understand why that would be a good thing.

"We'll figure it out." Jess's voice was soft, the expression on her face one he'd never seen before. Usually she was the first to jump in. Especially while someone she cared about was in danger. This time? She was trying to give him hope.

"Will we be able to figure it out in time to get them back?" There had been far too many near misses lately. And he'd argue they were still not much closer to bringing in the man who'd evaded them thus far. After everything that'd happened, they still had little more than nothing.

Ted tapped the screen and sent Conroy the phone number. On the desk, the chief's phone vibrated. "That's the details of whoever made the call to this phone. I'll run the number and see if I can get a location, but if they turned it off, I may not be able to."

Basuto clapped him on the shoulder. "You'll find them."

Ted shot him a look. Were they all counting on him to come up with some kind of technological miracle? Of course they were. "And in the meantime, you guys are just going to stand around here waiting for me to tell you where my brother is?"

"Of course not." Conroy shot him a look that told Ted exactly what the chief thought of that assessment. "We're going to run down every number on this list. Shake some things loose, and see what falls out."

Ted had never heard such a cop-like statement in his life.

Jess grinned. "That sounds like fun. Much better than standing around here." She pinched Ted's ribs under his elbow and then strode out of the room.

Ted shook his head. "And when you guys realize that Basuto is on this list, along with Hollis from the diner *and* several other people you go to church with?"

Eric lifted a paper from the desk. "They're either involved, or they're being implicated like a lot of other people. It may take time, but we will straighten all of this out."

"I hope so." Ted turned to Conroy. "I'm going to go and run these numbers, see whose location services are switched on."

The chief nodded. Ted strode back to his office and set the tablet on the desk.

Were they going to be so cavalier? Sure, the cops had their way of doing things. They were good at their jobs, and they got results. But this was his brother.

Because he had said that he would, Ted entered the phone numbers on his computer and started searching for GPS locations on each of them. If the cops were going to break up the list, assign officers to visit every place, and look for his brother, then he wasn't going to be a hindrance to that. Not if it might mean they found Dean and Ellie.

Ted had alternate resources. Or, more accurately, just one.

He dug the phone out of his bottom desk drawer and powered it up. Thankfully, this phone—one of the burners handed out by West—was not on the list he had given Conroy. Ted hadn't found it necessary to falsify evidence. Just leave out a little bit. So while it put his career in a rocky place, he wasn't exactly in danger of getting fired.

Yet.

He dialed the only number in the contact list on this burner phone. It rang three times, long enough for Ted to get worried his dad might not even pick up.

"You call me now?"

"This isn't about us." Ted fought to keep the frustration from his voice. "Dean and Ellie are hurt. They've been taken by West."

"And you want me to give up all the pull I have with him to get them back?"

"Of course." Ted didn't bother to keep the bite from his tone. "You would only save your son and the woman he loves if it benefited *you*." Ted moved to end the call but heard his dad's voice.

"Hold up."

Ted figured if his dad would do anything, he would make sure it cost Ted more than he wanted to pay. At least, that would be his justification. Instead, what he didn't realize was that Ted was willing to pay anything. Everything.

Ted gripped the phone. "I need your help. Dean has never asked you for anything in his life. But he needs you to help him with this."

How badly was his brother hurt? Dean had always seemed so strong and capable. The man was a former Navy SEAL, which everyone knew meant that he was the toughest of the tough.

And now he had been felled like a giant oak, cut down.

A lump rose in Ted's throat, and he tried to swallow it down. "Please."

"As much as I enjoy listening to you beg, I have things to do. What exactly do you want from me?"

Jess had already asked him for West's identity. Ted didn't figure he was willing to give that up. At least not without a really good reason, which meant he would get something out of it.

"I need you to tell me where my brother is."

"And if I do that?"

"Then you'll be able to die knowing that for once you did the right thing and saved someone's life."

His dad chuckled.

"It was worth a try," Ted said. "But we both know there's not one single noble cell in your body. So here's the deal." He took a deep breath, wondering if he was going to do this. "We both know you are never going to let Dean and I fake your death, but if you want to disappear, I can get you all the resources you need."

"Money? That's what you're offering me? I can get all the money I want, whenever I want. I don't need you for that."

No, Ted figured he didn't need cash. That was something his father had never seemed to have trouble amassing. But right now, there was a lot of heat on him.

"So not only are you going to let West tell you what to do—" Something Ted figured chafed everything his father thought about himself. "—but you're also going to give him carte blanche with your oldest son."

He heard his father grunt.

"You killed for him, and you delivered a message to Jess. Are you really going to let him control your son's life and his future?"

Because when it came down to it, his father was all about control. The more people whose lives he could direct where he wanted, and end when he wanted, and do with what he wanted, the better. That was what his previous operation had been about. Directing the course of the world through clandestine special operations.

As though he thought he was God.

More than once Ted's father had pointed a gun at him and told him that Ted's life was in his hands. The adage he figured every parent thought at least once in their life. *I brought you into this world, and I can take you out of it.* Only with his dad, Ted figured the old man was completely serious.

"I thought you'd gone soft, going to work for the police." His dad's voice was low and mean. "Now I know what I put in you is still there. Forged in the fire. You'll always be who I made you to be."

Ted swallowed down a sick feeling. If it got Dean and Ellie back, then it would be worth it. But right now, he wanted to hang up the phone and hurl in his trash can. Even just the thought of being anything like his father was enough to make him want to quit his whole life and walk away.

Just so no one found out the truth. That deep down inside him, Ted's soul was black.

His dad was right. Nothing was ever going to change that.

"I'll get you what you want," his dad said. "You get me access to my Cayman accounts. The ones the feds don't even know about."

Ted clenched his stomach muscles. "Fine."

27

B asuto led the way through the warehouse, Jess right behind him. Conroy had also assigned Special Agent Jenkins to go with them, but the guy was outside on the phone. The whole police department had been divided up into teams. All of them out searching for the spot where Dean and Ellie were being held.

She and the sergeant had been given the same warehouse Jess had searched only a few nights ago. Had it really not even been a week? The place where the former bank manager had been receiving his "entertainment." Supplied by West.

This was the spot where—as far as they knew—several women had been held and used in a prostitution ring.

Jess's most recent theory was that the dead woman they had discovered earlier, wearing her uniform, would turn out to be one of them.

Whether or not Ted's father had stolen her police uniform from her locker at the same time he had murdered Sally Peters was at the bottom of her list of priorities right now. But she'd like to know how it got out. However it happened, it was a serious invasion of her privacy. But considering her sister was who-knew-where she was trying not to worry about that right now.

"Upstairs first?" Basuto glanced back over his shoulder as he spoke.

Jess shrugged one shoulder. "Sure."

The special agent would probably wonder where they had gone. Considering she and Basuto both had their weapons drawn, she wasn't too worried about needing additional backup. She just hoped he announced himself when he did show back up. To keep from being shot by them when he reappeared.

They headed up the stairs where Kaylee had been held for a while by the bank manager. Just one more piece of the puzzle, considering the fact Pierce Cartwright had intended to marry her in his role as the CIA director. Jess didn't even want to think about the mess it all was. Kaylee was happy now and on an extended vacation with her husband until the threat was back in federal custody. That particular threat, at least.

Considering she'd stared the man down in her kitchen right before he threw a flashbang at her, she could understand why Kaylee wanted to be anywhere but here.

Pierce Cartwright might be Ted's father, and there was some family resemblance, but the man was a sociopath. Only, when she considered the fact that he was currently under West's thumb somehow, didn't that mean the man she was currently chasing was so much worse?

Jess shivered, turning to prayer. God in his sovereignty could make sure that nothing lasting happened to her sister. Ellie had finally found the best kind of relationship. It would destroy all of them if that was taken away.

She and Basuto cleared each room between the stairs and the end of the hall before he turned and said, "There's no one here."

Jess nodded. "It was too obvious, anyway. This location has been burned. We know all about it, and we've been through it with a fine-tooth comb many times over. There's no way West would have risked bringing them here."

Jess figured he hadn't evaded arrest this long without having plenty of places all across town where he could hide people. And himself.

"We'll find them." Despite Basuto's words, his tone indicated he didn't quite believe it.

"We have to."

After all, she didn't even want to consider the alternative. Her sister. Ted's brother. Jess wanted to find them with a desperation that was stronger than any urge to solve the case. Even the determination to take down the person who had murdered Nicole so many years ago.

West had sent Ted's father. Then he dropped a woman's body in front of the police station with the name Nicole. He wanted her to lose it. To be swallowed up by her fear and unable to keep a cool head.

She wasn't going to let him win. They needed to get West *and* Pierce Cartwright. Both of them. In a way that saved Ellie and Dean's lives.

"Sergeant?" The special agent called out down the hall.

"There's nothing here," Basuto told him. Then he turned to her. "Have you heard anything new from Ted?"

She didn't even want to think, or talk, about Ted. Despite everything that connected them, he hadn't even suggested they work together. And then Conroy had sent her out here with Basuto.

She shook her head. "Nothing new. Let's get out of here. This warehouse is a bust."

An understanding look crossed Basuto's face. "One more place we didn't find them is one step closer to finding where they are."

That sounded like something Ted would have said just a few months ago. These days it seemed as though he was nothing like the guy she had been falling for.

Jess was ready to hit the next place on the list now. The quicker they got on with this, the better. "Let's roll out."

Searching for her sister and Dean was a good distraction from thinking about her non-relationship with Ted. Even if redirecting the two men with her made it clear to them that she just wanted to avoid all conversation.

Besides, he was busy anyway. What was the point in bothering him? Ted would call them if he found something in any of the computers or phones they had confiscated so far.

Special Agent Jenkins nodded. "I talked with our undercover here in town. He's with a group of West's men right now. He'll keep eyes and ears open for your sister and her boyfriend."

She nodded.

As they descended the stairs, Basuto said, "What I can't believe is that someone got the drop on Dean." He shook his head, in the lead as he pushed out into the ground floor space. "I kind of figured that guy could do anything."

The special agent said, "He hasn't been a SEAL for a while, right? Plus, he was with his girlfriend. Maybe he was distracted and not paying attention."

Jess shot him a look he should have felt, there was so much fire in it. "Dean isn't losing his skills. He lives and trains with a private security team." Sure, he might be an unofficial EMT and working on his therapy license, but it wasn't like the man didn't keep up with his workouts.

She also knew for a fact that Ted trained with them on occasion. He wasn't muscled like the rest of them, but it was clear he didn't maintain his lean build by sitting behind his desk all day.

And that was the end of that discussion. She ignored the special agent from then on, right up until they stopped at the front doors to see two big trucks pull up outside.

Basuto put out a hand in front of her. "Hold up. We need to find out if these guys are friendly, or if we need to head out the back way."

She was right there with him. Neither wanted to waste time on a confrontation.

Behind them, the special agent snorted. "We're cops. These guys don't have a choice except to let us through."

"Unless they're here to cause trouble, or even take us with them at gunpoint." Jess didn't want to sound pessimistic. Unfortunately, that exact thing had happened several times in the last few days. They'd managed to escape, but now her sister and Dean had not.

Were they West's new target or just more leverage for him to use to get the police department in Last Chance to do whatever he wanted?

"How did they know we were here?" She backed up from the door, thinking through the situation, even while she looked for a way out. They'd have to circle the building to get back to their cars. But she was pretty sure the police forensic scientists who'd been here had shut the back door with a padlock. It hadn't affected her the other day, coming in the side, but it might prevent them from getting out now considering the lock was on the outside.

She turned to Basuto. "Is there another side door?" These guys would see them come out of the entrance she used.

"If there is, we need to find it fast."

They both turned to the special agent. "Are you coming?" she asked Jenkins. "Or do you want to throw your 'cop' weight around and see what happens against a bunch of armed men?"

They were almost at the door now. At least six of them, all carrying heavy weapons.

Jess said, "Either way, we should call for backup."

The special agent snorted again at her assessment of the situation. But what did she care what this guy thought? Cops backed up other cops, and in their department, that counted for everything. Too many times recently had someone been hurt or put in danger. They weren't going to let each other down now.

Basuto got on his radio and confirmed with the on-duty

dispatcher what they needed. It struck a pang in her that it wasn't Bill on the other end, but she couldn't think about that now either.

All Jess could think was one thing.

Between the two men with her, one of them had told West where she was.

Jess turned and headed for the hallway. Basuto jogged right behind her. She said, "The door at the end of this hall, around the corner, is padlocked from the outside. We'll have to find another way out."

"Take a left at the end instead. Go through the offices on the north corner. I think there's another fire exit out there."

She nodded and pushed through the door, glancing back once before stepping into the office. Special Agent Jenkins was coming after them. Not so determined to face all those men by himself.

At the end of the hall, glass shattered. Gunshots sang down the hall. The special agent yelped and ducked his head as he ran toward them.

Jess could hear multiple pairs of boots pounding their way. She turned to the office and raced through, using the flashlight on her gun to light her way. Even so, her hip clipped the corner of the desk, and she nearly went down.

The door swung open and slammed against the wall. Another gunshot rang out. The special agent yelped and went down, sprawling to the floor. He'd been shot.

"Stop!"

Multiple gunmen repeated that word. But Basuto and Jess didn't even slow down. Everything in her wanted to go back and try and help the special agent, even if Jenkins had been irritated with them. That didn't mean he needed to be left behind where he could be shot again and killed. She hadn't seen any blood, but he could be bleeding out.

In the hesitation where she considered turning back, Basuto

slammed into her. They almost went down but both caught themselves on the next desk.

"Go." Her sergeant's order was unnecessary but welcome. He agreed with her assessment of the inherent risk in going back to try to help the special agent.

Another bullet whizzed past them. She dived behind the closest desk, came up, and fired two shots. Both hit a gunman square in the chest.

A bullet slammed into the desk in front of her face. Jess ducked back down and saw Basuto crouched by the desk across from her. "How long until backup?"

"Too long."

She lifted and fired two more shots. Soon enough she would run out of bullets, making her wonder if she had enough to take them all out.

"I'll cover. You get out of here."

She was already shaking her head before Basuto finished talking. "I'm not leaving you."

"That is an order from your sergeant."

Jess gritted her teeth. All she was going to do was go outside, meet their backup at the front door, and bring them back in straight away so they could help Basuto and the special agent. Just that. Out and back in. Still, she didn't like it. It might get the job done, but she would be leaving the sergeant alone.

"Go." Basuto lifted and started firing.

Jess used the cover of gunshots to head for the fire exit at this corner of the building. She reached the doorway and ducked behind cover, turning back to get one last look at her sergeant.

Just as he took a bullet to the chest and flew back onto the ground.

Jess screamed.

28

The spot where his father had told him they would meet was half a mile past the end of a road that dead ended in the foothills. That was Ted's first red flag. But what else was he supposed to do? Stuart was out of town protecting his wife. Dean had been captured with Ellie. The team was off on a mission.

He had no choice except pack the gun Zander had given him for his last birthday and go by himself.

He wasn't going to trust his father. But Ted would do everything he could to get his brother back.

The cops couldn't help him. No one could.

A breeze ruffled the trees, carrying with it the scent of some musty mountain animal. Ted didn't want to think about the kinds of creatures that roamed these mountains. The four-legged as well as the two-legged kind. Threats were everywhere, and he'd never been more aware of that fact as he walked alone up the trail.

To meet his father, a man who had terrorized so many.

Help me be brave.

Ted knew how his brother and Ellie felt about their relationship with God. Maybe he would get there as well, someday. He figured their faith meant even if God wasn't willing to accept everything he'd done, He might help Ted anyway. The kind of God he wanted to believe in helped those who were close to Him. Even vicariously.

He got to the clearing a few minutes later where his dad was already waiting for him. Despite the fact his father was sitting alone on a tree stump, Ted was never going to be fooled that the man wasn't cunning and dangerous.

"Where is he holding Dean and Ellie?"

His dad glanced aside, up at the trees. Sitting like this, he almost seemed like a regular guy, but maybe that was the point. Get people to let their guard down—assume he wasn't as dangerous as he was.

"I don't have time for the runaround right now. This is about saving their lives, not about anything that needs to be said between you and me."

For too long he had allowed his father to dictate his actions and view of himself. Ted wasn't willing to allow that to distract him from his mission here.

His father sighed.

"Am I keeping you from something more important than saving your son's life?"

"You have no clue what's even going on in this town, do you?" His father sounded almost wistful. "Blind. All of you."

Ted didn't care about that, because he thought they *did* have a decent handle on it. He was only here right now for one thing. "Why did you even come back to Last Chance?"

Why ask Ted to meet him if Pierce had no intention of helping get his family back? Unless this was just another game.

Ted pulled his phone out and glanced at the screen. No signal? That was less than helpful. "If you're not planning to help, I'm leaving." He turned away.

His father's clothing rustled. "This is bigger than you. It's always been bigger than you."

"You think I don't know that?" Ted twisted back around.

Given the way his jacket hung, he figured his father had a gun as well. Ted shouldn't have been surprised, but a pang of grief shot through him anyway. Why couldn't they be a normal father and son? All he'd ever wanted was to be raised by a man he could look up to. Not a man he hated. One he would always resent.

It turned out the man he could look up to was Dean.

"Just tell me where West is holding them, and I'll go." Ted lifted his hands, then let them fall back to his sides. "You won't have to see me again." And he would get his brother back.

"You think that's what I want?"

"Why *wouldn't* I think that?" The last thing he wanted right now was to get into a conversation about why his father was the way he was, or why he'd never loved Ted as he should have. Or even if he was capable of that kind of love. The old man should've just handed him over to child services years ago. Instead, he'd packed Ted along with him. Just another tool to be used for his own ends.

Ted studied the old man's face. Despite the lines and shadows, he wasn't going to feel empathy for a man like this. Not ever. "Tell me why you came here. Because I don't buy that you want something from West, or that you're under his thumb."

His dad almost looked proud. "All part of the plan."

The old man only ever had one plan, and he stuck to it religiously.

Ted studied him. "So you keep the cops looking elsewhere. Or, if they get too close, you convince them the threat level is too high. Not worth going after, too risky to try to take you down."

"So you do remember."

"As much as I've tried for years to forget everything about you." Ted couldn't get off track though. "What have you got going on with West?"

Ted figured he was here for the money. A way to run—forever. But that didn't seem like his dad. Nothing about this jived. He should be on a beach somewhere, hiding out in a hut where the authorities would never find him.

Instead, he was here. The FBI was here. And his dad didn't seem too interested in running.

So why stay? To tie up loose ends or pick up what he needed to get going?

Not knowing the answer to that question was enough to drive Ted insane. Perhaps he would plead that way when the cops brought him in for shooting the man in front of him.

He looked at his phone again. Still no signal.

"Technical problems?"

Ted's head snapped up to survey the look on his dad's face. Amusement stared back at him. *A signal jammer.*

He was in over his head, but he couldn't do anything about it. He needed a result. Ted pulled the gun from his waistband and held it on his father, effectively shifting the balance of power in his favor.

Until his dad laughed.

"Tell me where West has them." Ted gritted his teeth. "Or I leave you here to bleed out while I walk away, call the FBI, and tell them exactly where to find you."

Something flashed across his dad's face. Not exactly fear, just a healthy acknowledgment that Ted could do that. *Good.* His dad would be back in federal custody. Not where he wanted to be, but where he belonged.

The old man's face rumpled as he scrunched his nose for a second. "Doesn't matter. I'd escape again."

"Then I'll kill you right here, right now."

"That would accelerate things. Unfortunately, for West." The old man frowned. "And then you'd never find them."

"Tell me where they are, and I'll walk away." He held the gun steady, as though everything in him wasn't shaking at the thought of taking a life. His first kill; his own father.

Then it would be Ted who walked away. Living anonymously, hiding from the authorities. Or they would give him a medal. He wasn't sure how it would play out.

Just so long as it got Dean and Ellie back.

Ted heard an accelerated movement behind him. He let his focus slip to assess who it was. A crackle sounded a split second before the effects of a stun gun rolled through him. One knee hit the ground, but, miraculously, he kept himself from collapsing.

Ted's gun tumbled from his fingers onto the dirt of the trail. His father swiped it up while Ted just tried to breathe through the pain.

Finally, he was able to stand. Behind him, two men dragged a woman toward them. Jess.

A gun pressed against his spine. "You want to know where your brother is? Don't worry. You'll be finding out soon enough."

A myriad of thoughts swept through his mind, most too fast to catch hold of. Except one. "You're handing us over to him?"

Before his father could respond, Jess let out a long moan. The two men dropped her face down on the ground, then turned to him. He braced to fight them off, but the gun dug deeper into his back. "This will be much harder if you're bleeding out."

They taped his hands, stuffed a rag in his mouth, and tied something like a strip of cloth around his head so that it held his mouth open. He couldn't speak, only make muffled sounds that meant nothing.

The gun jabbed at him. "Everything is ready?" That was his father.

"Yes, sir." One of the men nodded, his body taut. He was scared of Pierce Cartwright. Like Keeley was, or even Stuart. Was he one of Ted's father's mercenaries?

You don't have to do what he says. Yet the guy clearly didn't share Ted's thoughts.

What was going on? Ted spun, wishing he could ask all the

questions rolling around in his mind. But he had no power here. Why had he ever thought he did?

Help us. The two men watched Ted's father walk away. Until he disappeared into the trees. Ted wanted to run, but he couldn't leave Jess. He moved to her.

Both men reacted. One shoved him back. Ted fell to the ground. Jess was hoisted up over one guy's shoulder. The other man grabbed his hands, lifted him, and stood back up. He carried Ted much the same way. They bumped and jolted through the trees until they reached a clearing and a couple of ATVs.

Ted flopped onto the ground. His head hit a rock, and he moaned. Never mind the pain in his wrist. He wanted to pass out like Jess. But if he did that, then he would never see where these guys were taking them.

Some kind of final destination. Where the four of them—Ted and Jess, Dean and Ellie—would be killed. West would dispose of them. His dad would walk away clean.

Was that why he'd come home? To bargain with West and walk away to a fresh start; his sons, dead? Nausea twisted in his stomach, and Ted tasted bile in the back of his throat. Just another asset at the end of its usable life. His father had no feelings at all. Let alone any care for his offspring. It was a wonder he'd ever managed to stay with a woman long enough to have made the two of them.

Ted had long ago figured they were step brothers and not full brothers. Maybe his father had killed both women after they birthed him a son, and now he planned to be done with them too.

Using West to achieve that aim.

It was complicated enough that Ted was having a hard time trying to reconcile it all in his head.

The ATV engines roared to life. Ted was loaded on the back of one, and it set off through the foothills. He couldn't tell where they were going. Just that night was ticking on, the temperature falling. His skin chilled, raising those bumps. Sweat gathered at his hairline.

Someone called out. The man driving the vehicle he was in answered, "Just up ahead."

They turned left, the trees parting to a clearing. Ted heard a familiar sound but couldn't place it. Then he smelled algae.

The lake.

The ATV driver slowed them to a stop. Both vehicle engines shut off, leaving the sound of a regular car engine still running. Someone else was here?

Ted was hauled upright and then deposited on the ground. At the edge of the shore, a fishing boat had been dragged onto the sand.

A suited man stood in front of them, the running car behind him.

"We get paid now, right?"

The man sighed. "That was what we agreed. My men will take it from here."

Two guys rounded the car, and the suited man moved closer to Ted. He leaned down so Ted could make out his face. The suit was a white shirt under a jacket, but Ted saw the badges and emblem there. The familiar face frowned. "Not as satisfying as your brother's capture. But still necessary."

Ted stared until his eyes burned.

This was West.

29

The man, obviously West, spoke again, "Now I must leave, and you both are going to die. After all, we can't have any more loose ends."

Jess knew then that the clock had nearly run out. If she didn't move now, she would lose the chance to find out who West actually was. And not only that but take him down in the process.

The only problem was she didn't know if she could move.

Hoping and praying nobody was watching her where they'd tossed her on the ground, Jess rolled to her back slow and quiet.

She narrowly swallowed her gasp as she saw the man who was West.

Steven Hilden, the Last Chance County fire chief. One of the founders of this town, and probably the last person she would've considered to be in the running as West except for that Vietnam photo. Especially given how long he'd been a pillar in this town. Respected. Admired. He was a hero, and yet underneath all that, he had been running a prostitution ring. Among other things.

Anger fueled her muscles. Jess managed to scramble to her

hands and knees, and then she launched herself up into a sprint. She raced between Ted—whose hands were tied much the same as hers—and one of the men who had stormed the warehouse.

Both men jumped back.

As she slammed into Steven Hilden, Jess remembered she'd done this more than once the past few days. And it usually wound up hurting.

She really needed a new fighting move.

When she was in her right mind again, she would figure it out. But right now, that thought was quickly followed by the memory of the special agent's betrayal. How Jenkins had probably called those men in, and Basuto had been shot. If no one knew about that, then her sergeant was probably dead by now.

Hilden fell back and hit the ground. Jess landed with her knees on either side of his ribs. She swung her bound hands from right to left, landing blows across his face. He cried out. "Get her off me!"

Hilden slammed his fists down on her thighs and tried to get a grip on her while she fought him off. Each hit of his closed fists numbed her legs, but she ignored the sensation and lifted her hands to swing at his face again.

"Now!" His gritted teeth flashed in the moonlight. "I said get her off me!"

As she swung her hands, someone behind her said, "That'll cost you extra."

Hilden spat blood, trying to get her in the face with it. "Fine!"

She grasped his neck with both hands, grabbing as good of a grip as she could with them taped together. "Where are the girls?" No, that wasn't the right question. "Where is my sister? Where is Dean?"

Hilden sneered. "The girls? I sold them all *weeks ago*. Back when Silas Nigelson blabbed about everything, and I had to shut down the entire operation." He seemed irritated about that.

Strong hands lifted her off him, and Hilden sat up. "I kept one, though. My favorite."

Given the look in his eyes, Jess could figure out who that was. "Nicole."

That wasn't her name, just the name on the fake ID left with her body. A name designed to affect her so much that it threw her off her game.

He laughed as he stood up. The hands that had lifted her off him still gripped her, entirely too tightly, around her ribs. She tried to wiggle out, but the man shifted his hold. His arms banded around her waist, cutting off her air supply as he restricted movement of her diaphragm.

She gasped. "You didn't need to kill her."

Hilden laughed. "She had her uses, and then she was useful because she was dead."

Jess screamed in his face. The guy holding her chuckled.

Ted shifted closer to her shoulder. "Jess, calm down."

The guy holding her said, "Feisty thing, isn't she?"

Hilden shook his head. "You can't have her."

The guy grunted. His arm around her rib cage didn't loosen.

She figured that meant they were going to die. "Did you already kill my sister?" She didn't want to think that life might not be worth living if Ellie wasn't around anymore. It felt as though it would be that bad. But it would also mean that he'd won, which was the last thing she wanted to happen.

When he said nothing, she began to struggle once more against her captor.

Ted glanced between her and Hilden. "You don't have to do this. Whether or not you're West doesn't matter. There's no evidence yet, just our word against yours. Tell us where they are, and then walk away. Because when the feds bring down Pierce Cartwright, you aren't going to want to be anywhere near him —or whatever he has to say about you."

Hilden wiped the corner of his mouth with the back of his hand. Jess saw blood reflected in the moonlight. Why were they here? She didn't want to consider the fact Dean and Ellie might be already dead—drowned at the bottom of the lake—or the fact she and Ted might be next.

"Shame." The guy with his arm banded around her lifted her off her feet.

She kicked at his shins and tried to pry his fingers from her. Ted stepped closer toward her. Probably intending to intervene, but he was intercepted by the other man who brought the butt of his gun down on Ted's temple.

Ted, the man and friend she had so much feeling for, crumpled to the ground. Jess gasped, renewing her fight to get away from these men.

The man who had knocked out Ted turned to her. "Is that how it's going to be with you, too?"

Jess deflated, her legs dangling down. But she didn't stop trying to push the man's arm away from her waist. She was never giving up that struggle so long as there was even a slim possibility Dean and Ellie were still alive.

"Where are they?"

Hilden shook his head and looked at the men. "Take them away."

She had never heard him speak that way. As though he was Lord of the Manor, not a local hero who had saved so many when their property caught on fire. This man was someone she had never met before. A total stranger who used others, who made arrangements with Pierce Cartwright, and tossed precious life away as though it was garbage.

The man holding her adjusted his grip. One arm migrated up and his fingers clasped her neck, his other arm still holding her waist. The second man looked on, as did Steven Hilden. Black spots picked at the edges of her vision as she began to pass out.

After a minute or so, darkness swallowed her. The last thing she recalled was the feeling of being lowered to the ground.

Sometime later, Jess blinked. A moan escaped her lips. Her throat felt like the worst strep infection she'd ever experienced. She tried to swallow, but her neck was so swollen it was hard to make her throat move.

Finally, the room came into view as did her realization of why pain sliced through her head. On the ceiling, a bright-white bulb illuminated what appeared to be a small room, probably no bigger than a prison cell.

She managed to push herself to a seated position and realized she was all wet. Around her was a puddle…of lake water. Why was she wet?

Ted lay on the other side of the room, facing away from her with his face to the wall.

"Ted." Not much noise emerged from her mouth, but she managed to croak out his name again.

He didn't move or even stir.

Across the other side of the room, the door was closed. The top half had a window with clear glass, and the door handle seemed simple enough. Jess just had to get up off the floor.

She didn't think too much about the bruises in various places as she crossed the bare floor, one hand braced against the wall as she clambered over Ted's foot. Her injured arm had blood soaking through the bandage, and she didn't even want to think about the staple that had been put in her head.

None of that mattered now.

Wherever they were, this was where West had intended for them to be. The place they would die. Or was some other horrible thing going to happen to them, as Pierce had intended for Kaylee only a few weeks ago before he was arrested?

Things were such a mess.

She was supposed to have brought Pierce in, or at least told the FBI where to find him. She was supposed to have given her intel on West's identity to Conroy. Instead, she'd only managed to identify West after coming face to face with him on that shore. Not because of great police work.

The lake. Was that where they were now? She couldn't think of any buildings close by that were set up like this. Kind of like a school. That was what the finish reminded her of. Stark and barren like a place of learning, supposedly designed to inspire creativity in young minds.

Jess halted her progress and took a breath. She was officially losing her mind. Why else would she be having crazy thoughts about schools right now?

Finally, at the door, she shoved down the handle. Part of her expected it to be locked. That there would be no way to get out of this tiny room. Sure enough, the handle didn't go all the way down, and the door didn't open. But she was still dressed for work, even if she was all wet, so Jess lifted her foot and kicked beside the door handle. The flimsy lock broke, and the door swung out with a new dent where the sole of her boot had hit the wood.

If they planned for her and Ted to be stuck in this room, then it was a bad plan.

She glanced out into the hallway and didn't see anyone. The long corridor was a lot like the room they were in, with bare bulbs hanging down every few feet. Now it reminded her of an underground room or basement. Maybe even at the local high school. Could that be where West had taken Dean and Ellie?

She turned back to Ted and wandered to him, crouching to gently shake his shoulder. "Wakey wakey, sleepyhead. Time to get out of here."

She tugged on his arm, halfway pulling him to a seated position, as he blinked and came awake.

"Whoa." He glanced around, his body jerking away from hers as he pulled his arm from her grasp. "Where are we?"

"I have no idea." She straightened out of her crouch, which was preferable to falling over, and leaned against the wall. "Are you okay?"

"No."

She wasn't either.

Ted stood.

"Need help?" She waved a hand at the door and started to explain what she'd done, but instead realized something. "They cut me loose." Her hands were no longer bound together.

"Me too."

"Why would they do that?" She shook her head, her brain not able to compute any of this. It barely made sense. "We were by the lake. Where are we now?"

Ted frowned. He reached up with his good hand and swiped the hair back from his forehead. "We should look around."

She nodded. "See if Dean and Ellie are here."

He returned her nod but didn't look at her. Ted went first toward the door even though she was the cop. She considered again how different he seemed now. Still aloof, though. He had plenty of secrets. Things he held close to his chest. And maybe that would be true of him always. She didn't know.

Jess followed him into the hall. "Which way?"

At one end was a closed door, a dark LED display above it. The kind found on the subway in New York that told you what the next stop was. The other end was a similar door, but with no sign. Down the hall were several doors like the one they'd escaped.

Jess looked in each window, separating from Ted so they could check each one quickly. Just in case.

"Over here."

She raced to him, stumbling as she nearly tripped over her feet. Ted caught her. A second later, he stepped away, letting go of her arms as though she'd burned him.

Jess tried to brush off the hurt. "What is it?"

"In there."

She peered in the window, the room much like where she'd regained consciousness. "Dean." She touched the glass. "Ellie!"

Jess slammed her palm on the window, over and over. Neither looked up.

Dean had blood on his forehead. Ellie lay collapsed over him.

"Wake up, Ellie!" She turned to Ted, her eyes filling with tears. "What is this place?"

A frown crinkled his brow. "I think I know."

30

Jess didn't respond. She slammed her hand against the glass, over and over, while Ted's thoughts spun on this whole thing.

His part in it.

His father.

The founders.

Ted couldn't believe he'd been so stupid, when he and everyone else considered him so smart. The truth was far from that.

Ted turned to survey the hallway around him. Renovations had been done at some point in this structure's history, but the whole thing—the underlying construction—was from several decades ago.

Given the problem they'd been having with the founders the past few months, it jived. There had been a dead man not much younger than he was, discovered by Ellie and buried in a cave in the mountains. Now this? Some kind of holding facility. A place the founders had constructed. Or placed here. Could be a shipping container—or several, welded together.

His brain spun, working out the problem like trying to unravel a tangled wire.

"Did you find anything?"

He turned to find the desperation in Jess's tone matched on her face. "Like what?"

"A way to get them out of there." She motioned to the door.

"Can't you kick it open?" He figured there wasn't much point finding a way out if there was no way to get in the room to Dean and Ellie in the first place.

"I did the last door. You do this one."

"Why are we arguing about this? You're the one who wants to get in there." He could feel the anger burn in his stomach. Or maybe it was fear. He couldn't tell.

"Because you don't?"

Ted started to speak, then stopped himself. He turned away to walk down the hall. Even though the act of moving farther from his brother felt like his heart was being torn from his chest.

Her footsteps padded on the floor as she scurried after him. She grabbed his arm and spun him back around to her. "What is your problem?"

"Right now, you are."

"We have to get in there."

He shook his head. "We need a way out."

"Well, yeah," she said. "But we also need to see if they're even okay. For all we know…"

He finished for her. "They could be dead."

She sucked in a breath.

"You think I don't know that? They might not be passed out. They could already be dead. The fact we can't see any blood means nothing. We have *no idea* what was done to them, or why we're here."

"Ted—"

"Don't." He shook his head, not interested in the softening of her features or the fear still in her eyes. "Find a way in there. I'll find a way out. If we split up the tasks, we'll be able to do both, rather than making all this take longer."

Between the two of them, they would be able to do this,

right? To divide and conquer made so much more sense than Ted going in there to face his brother's lifeless body. He'd rather work to find a way out before someone came to stop them.

"Why are you convinced he's dead?"

Ted wasn't going to touch that one.

"I'm not giving up hope. I'm sorry you have." She turned away.

Now that he didn't have to maintain his composure because she wasn't looking at him anymore, he let the façade fall. Tears filled his eyes, blurring the image in front of him. Jess trying the handle. Her backing up, a limp obvious in her stride.

She lifted her foot and kicked the door beside the handle. It didn't open. She sucked in a breath and let out some frustration in a groan.

Ted turned away and went to look in some of the other rooms. They were decorated as sparsely as the one he had woken up in. No phone. Or a computer or even a keypad. Not even some kind of control panel.

He needed a network closet. But he still wouldn't have access to it if he didn't have a device to hook in with. He would have no access to the computer system that worked this place—if that was even how it had been set up.

Though, he figured he knew how it worked. Of all people, *he* knew.

Still, how was he supposed to figure out where this facility was located—and how to get them out—if he couldn't hook into the control system? The whole place might look like a seventies throwback bunker, but there had been some upgrades to security and the HVAC system. At least as far as he could tell from a quick survey.

Jess grunted loudly. At the same time, he heard wood splinter. Ted spun around just as she headed into the room.

A second later, Jess called out, "They're alive, just unconscious."

Ted sagged against the wall, and a wave of relief rolled over him. His brother wasn't dead. As he gasped through that realization, he gave himself a minute before moving into the room after her.

Jess lifted Ellie from his brother and laid her back on the floor. Ted knelt by Dean's elbow and felt for the pulse himself. A faint but steady beat thrummed under his fingertips. Ted closed his eyes and took a minute to just feel the sensation.

"They look beat up, but okay." Jess was breathy with relief. "Maybe it's better if they don't wake up right now. I hurt enough, and I didn't go through half of what it looks like they did."

He opened his eyes and saw she was right. Dean's face was far more injured than her sister's, but both had been punched and hit repeatedly. "Is this what it took to bring them down?"

Jess huffed. "You'd rather they just gave up?"

Now there was a loaded question. But seriously, when had he and Jess ever seen eye to eye? They could barely agree on the best way to make a pot of coffee, let alone what their relationship would be. Now that both of their siblings were injured and unconscious, they were going to have to figure a way out of here.

At least he didn't need her for that. Though, he wasn't going to discount an extra set of hands. He couldn't carry both of them.

"What now?"

"There's a door at the end of the hall." Ted swallowed the lump in his throat. If his emotions hadn't gotten the best of him so far, he didn't think they would overwhelm him now.

He stood. "I'm going to go and see if I can get it open."

He turned away to the door and was almost to the hallway before she said, "What aren't you telling me?"

Ted glanced over his shoulder. "We don't have enough time for that right now."

"Okay, then I have another question for you. What is it

about our immediate situation that means we need to be in a hurry to do something about it?"

Ted gritted his teeth together. "I'm going to find a way out."

"Good. But I want to know what will happen if you don't do that fast enough."

When he said nothing, she simply stared at him. His brother and her sister laying on the floor on either side of her. "How about...Dean and Ellie could be in an emergency medical situation?"

She studied him. "You know what this place is, don't you?" Jess got up and moved to him, closing the gap between them. "Where are we?"

"I can't be completely sure."

"But you have an idea. Right?" She shrugged. "What is this, some kind of facility? A prison? We can't be in Last Chance anymore. There's nothing like this in town. So where are we?"

"We haven't left town. And this facility is my father's doing."

"And you know that because?"

"I designed it."

Ted turned and walked out of the room, not wanting to see the look on her face when she realized what he meant. Yes, his father had been involved in some terrible things that involved manipulating and hurting other people. Even back here in Last Chance County. Pierce Cartwright had done whatever he wanted to secure his own end—even going so far as to change the course of covert operations across the world. Simply so his financial backers made even more money, and his father could get promoted to the job of CIA director.

Her footsteps scurried across the floor behind him. "Ted, please tell me you haven't been working for your father this whole time."

He shook his head but didn't stop looking for a way out of this place. "Not for a long time, but so much of it is still in play." He waved around them. "Like this place."

She looked like she might be sick. Ted figured he would just get it over with and tell her everything right now.

"He had me puzzle out a whole lot of things, researching security systems. Penal facilities. Even advanced psychology. There was barely a single part of military or covert operations that I didn't study extensively. So if you ever want to do some enhanced interrogation, I can tell you some really sketchy but extremely effective methods. Too bad for me that's what Dean is trying to fix in the people he helps. People like me are the reason his work exists."

"As soon as we get out of here," she said. "You and I are going to have a conversation about how you still seem to think the bad things your father did reflect in any way on you."

"What happened is what happened. I'm not going to be a victim. But I'm also not going to pretend I'm a good person who's done good things."

"Is any of us a good person? Sure, we're capable of great love and kindness. Even self-sacrifice. But there's a reason why those things are fruits of the Holy Spirit."

"So you're going to be all spiritual now?" They hadn't talked about any of that stuff, but they probably should have. "This is the time for that?"

Ted wanted to talk it over with her. Who else would he do that with? She was the only one who understood. The only one —or so he'd thought—who was in the same spot he was. Questioning. Searching. Had she decided to accept all those things the pastor talked about on Sunday mornings? The stuff about every day, not just salvation.

"What's the rush?" She shook her head. "There has to be a phone around here somewhere. We can call for help."

"You won't find any communication with the outside world. This facility is completely self-contained, designed to keep everyone here isolated."

"So it's a prison?"

"You remember what they said about the place where

Kaylee was held?" She had to remember, considering they'd heard all about it from Dean and the rest of the guys who'd gone to rescue her with Stuart. "This is a lot like that. Somewhere my father—or in this case, more likely the fire chief—can keep anyone he wants to be contained while he convinces them around to his way of thinking."

"Well, isn't that a horrifying thought."

"To us, yes. To him, it's just a game."

"The fact you just said that means you're nothing like him or your father." Before he could respond to that comment, she spoke again. "And I don't think you know how much you mean to me. So don't shut me out."

He wanted to say there was no time for more. Instead, Ted pulled her to him and hugged her, planting a kiss on the top of her hair. "I have to find a way out of here."

"But it's designed to keep people in, right?"

"We can't call for help, and no one knows where we are. That means it's up to us to get out."

"Do you know where we are? Or why we're all wet like we were thrown in the lake or something?"

Ted had been thinking the same thing, asking himself the same questions. Trying to figure it out from the moment he regained consciousness.

He was about to answer when an alarm beeped in the hallway. Through a speaker high on the wall, an electronic voice made an announcement while the display at the end of the hall scrolled the same words in glaring red letters.

"Airlock containment breach. Five minutes to airlock containment breach." The alarm beeped again, and the message repeated itself

"Uh…Ted." Her voice contained a wealth of worry.

"We're under the lake."

31

J ess gaped at him as she realized the implications of what he'd said. "We're going to drown down here?"

She couldn't wrap her brain around believing him that they were at the bottom of the lake. But since she couldn't prove he was wrong, there wasn't much point in arguing. And it seemed as though there wasn't enough time for that, either.

Five minutes.

He looked about as happy over this entire situation as she was as he shook his head. "I, for one, don't plan on still being down here when the whole place fills up with water."

"I can't believe we're at the bottom of the lake." How was it even possible that there was a facility submerged at the bottom? "Surely someone would have found this place by now."

He opened his mouth to reply but was cut off from speaking when the alarm sounded again.

Jess winced as the noise sliced through her temple, making her headache worse.

"You think I'm lying?"

She shook her head as he'd done. Unfortunately, that didn't help her head feel better either. "Of course not."

She didn't say anything else. Not when she could see the fear in his eyes and knew he was purposely pushing her away, because he thought he was responsible somehow. Ted wanted nothing more than to never have to confront his fear. And yet, here it was, staring him in the face.

"Hello?"

Jess spun to the open door. "That was Ellie." She wasn't above being the police officer who took control of the situation, so she said, "Find us a way out."

She heard him mutter as she raced back into the room, but ignored it. Whatever had happened between the two of them, they could wait to figure it out when they got out of here. When Ted didn't have such visceral dread rolling through his whole body the way she did. The only difference between them was that she pushed away the feeling for later. When they knew they were safe, it would hit her, and she could fall apart in a place where it was okay to do so.

Until then, she was going to work the problem while she pretended fear didn't have a hold over her.

"Ellie." She knelt beside her sister and saw her eyes flutter. Jess laid a hand on her sister's shoulder. "Ellie, are you awake?"

Her sister moaned and opened her eyes. "I heard someone in the hall. I guess it was you. Where are we?" She looked around.

Jess only had the time to say, "A place we need to get out of. Quickly. Do you think you can walk?"

Her sister nodded. "If I have to." She sat up abruptly, breathing a sigh of relief when she spotted Dean beside her. "But we have to wake up Dean because there is no way I can carry him."

Jess figured that given the man was heavier than either of them and all muscle, that was probably true. Maybe Ted would be able to help the two of them, and they could get Dean to whatever exit doorway he managed to find.

She told her sister, "Ted is looking for a way out right now. As soon as he finds one, we need to be ready to move."

Her sister pushed up to a seated position. "Okay."

On Ellie's face, bruises and abrasions had swollen the skin around her eyes and mouth. Despite that, she turned to the man now beginning to stir. Jess had never been more proud of her sister's strength.

Dean's fingers flexed by his sides, and he shifted. His lips parted, and a moan escaped as his eyes began to flutter.

Jess turned to her sister. "Stay here with him. I'm going to go check on Ted's progress."

Her sister nodded, all her focus on Dean.

Jess winced, just thinking how much worse Dean had been injured than her sister. That was a good thing. She and Dean would agree on that much, while Ellie might argue against it. But whichever way they viewed it, this was bad. She wondered if her future brother-in-law was going to come out of this with a concussion.

Or something much worse.

She found Ted down the hall, around the corner. A place she hadn't explored yet. As she approached him, that alarm sounded again. Along with the electronic voice alerting them of the containment problem.

"Is it just me," she asked him. "Or are those announcements getting closer together?"

She didn't want to correlate it with contractions. This was nothing like having a baby, and she didn't know anything about that anyway. But still, there was a sense of impending inevitability.

Ted shot her a look.

"Any luck with this?"

"If we get out of here," he said. "Then it won't have anything to do with luck."

Did that mean he was willing to concede the fact God was the one in ultimate control? Her sister had been talking to her about spiritual things and that had started bleeding into her conversation with Ted earlier. She was still reasoning it all out but didn't figure trusting Him to help them out of this would necessarily be a bad thing.

"Okay. So is it possible?"

She didn't exactly want to die down here. There were a lot of ways Jess had imagined the end of her life. Especially as a cop. She hadn't exactly thought that drowning in an underwater facility at the bottom of the Last Chance Lake was anywhere on the list.

"I'm working on it," he said. "I need a couple more minutes. What about Dean and Ellie?"

"They're coming awake. I told her they need to be ready to go." She didn't want to ask but figured she had to. "How long do we have?"

"Given how far apart those announcements are, if they continue to decrease at the same rate, then we have less than three minutes until this place starts to fill with water."

"Unless the leak has already happened, then three minutes is the time we'll all be submerged."

He shook his head. "I don't think so. That would be a full breach, not just the opening of the airlock. But either way, I'd rather not be around to find out. So in three minutes, let's plan on being at the surface."

"That sounds good to me."

She moved back towards the room her sister and Dean were still recovering in, racing down the hall as fast as she could despite the chafing of her wet clothes. She'd never been as uncomfortable in her life as she was right now. And yet, had never been able to brush it off as easily as this either.

She reached the room. "How are you guys doing?" She crouched, just as Ellie pulled Dean to a seated position. "Ted is about ready for us to get out of here."

She didn't bother asking Dean if he could walk. Not when the alternative meant he would still be here when it was flooded with water. Not only were none of them prepared to leave him, but they would also do whatever it took to get him out if he couldn't manage that on his own. All of them. Together.

After all, that was what Dean would do for any of them.

Her sister's gaze met hers, and she knew that Ellie understood exactly what she was thinking. It didn't happen often, but when it did, it certainly counted.

They helped Dean to his feet while he gritted his teeth and tried not to let out the moan she knew was there. He was trying to remain stoic for their sakes. He probably figured Ellie could deal, and for once she didn't mind so much. As long as they all kept moving. Working the problem, figuring a way out of here.

"Let's go." She ducked under Dean's arm and steadied some of his weight as they moved.

Her sister did the same thing on the other side, proving that part of Ellie's assessment of her future brother-in-law had been incorrect. He was willing to accept their help. Not so macho that he'd try and do everything by himself when he had the worst injuries of all of them.

She said, "End of the hall, and then we're going right."

"Copy that." His voice was gruff, and she could hear the discomfort and pain he was in. What else had Hilden's men done to him?

"Just a little swim, and we can get you to a hospital."

Air escaped Dean's lips.

"Oh, you think I'm being funny." They ambled around the corner. "It turns out I'm not. I'm telling you, if I'd made a list this morning of everything that might happen today, this probably wouldn't have been on it."

He grunted. "You can tell me everything later."

Jess was the one who said, "Copy that." And nodded to her sister, whose worried face was on the other side of Dean's chest. Jess stopped, her arm still supporting Dean. "Ted?"

"Of course." He frowned in her direction, surveying his brother's physical state for a split second before going back to his bundle of wires. "I have a miracle all ready to go. Let me just put the finishing touches on, and we'll be all good."

Dean shifted and leaned against the wall. Ellie stood close to him while Jess moved to what was an exterior wall. She gaped at the tiny circle window. "We really are underwater, aren't we?"

The alarm sounded again.

"We have less than two minutes before the flood gates open."

Ellie gasped. "We're…*what?*"

Dean said to his brother, "Later on, you're going to explain all this to me."

Jess figured she could cut down on some of the time that would take. "Stephen Hilden is West. His guys dumped us down here, and he's trying to kill all of us because there's no way an 'airlock containment breach' is just a coincidence."

Ted spoke without taking his attention from the panel of wires in front of him. "He probably plans to destroy this facility with us inside it."

"That won't go unnoticed." At least, she figured that was true. Surely there would be some kind of disturbance on the surface of the lake.

This time of night, would anybody even see it?

"So what's the plan?"

Ted glanced over as he answered his brother's question. "I'm trying to override the airlock mechanism. With the containment breach, the safety measures have kicked in."

Dean's said, "But you're trying to turn off the safety and open the door."

Ellie gasped.

"At least it will be a quick death."

All of them turned to stare at Jess. She shrugged.

Ted said, "One more second," and went back to his wires. A few seconds later, there was a spark, and she heard a metal clang inside the wall. Shortly after that began the slow roll of a mechanism turning, like a great wheel beginning to rotate inside the wall.

"Is that a good thing?" She glanced between the three of them. Her sister and the two men here were all smarter than her. They all probably understood what was happening, at least better than she did.

Not for the first time in the last few days, she felt at a distinct disadvantage. But West hadn't killed her yet. Jess was still a police officer, and she was as determined to take him down as she'd been before. Whether or not she gained any recognition from doing that.

The truth was, Basuto could be dead. And the FBI might sweep the entire operation into their jurisdiction. The Last Chance Police Department could wind up with nothing left to show for months of investigation.

Ted waved for them to follow him, moving down the hallway to a big door at the end. The one with the light display above it. He glanced around, as though looking for something.

Ellie said, "We can all swim, right?"

After they all murmured responses, Ted slowed. "Grab on to something. The door is about to open. After that, water from the lake will come rushing in and fill this whole place."

Jess gaped. "I thought the idea was to not drown!"

He shot her a look. "Like Ellie said, we're going to swim."

Her sister and Dean didn't look super surprised by this. But Jess couldn't believe it. They were just going to stand here while water rushed in?

That didn't sound like a good idea at all.

32

Ted looked over at his brother. He was about to say something when another alarm sounded. This one was different from those that had gone before. It was a continuous beep. The kind you resented at six in the morning on a Monday after a busy weekend.

Dean gave him a long look and then nodded. Ted was glad his brother was on the same page. He was counting on his older sibling's trained skills to get them out of this.

Through the airlock door, Ted heard a thunderous clang as metal hit metal. Heavy and at high speed.

Everyone braced. Ted said, "Put your back to the wall and grab something to hold onto."

Jess hugged the wall beside him. She grasped a pipe with both hands. "For the benefit of the whole class, maybe you could explain to us what's going to happen in this demonstration."

Ted figured she was scared enough to want to know what they were about to face. He just hoped there was time enough to explain the whole thing.

"The exterior door just blew open. Whether it was sabotage, or for some other reason, I won't know until we get out there. So right now, beyond that door, there is nothing but lake water. And probably some fish."

The metal door groaned as water pressure built up on the other side. The airlock's interior door wasn't built to withstand the weight of the lake pushing against it. This far under the surface, it could probably hold for a minute or two, and then it would buckle.

He continued, "In a minute, the contents of the lake will come rushing through that door."

"And that's our only way out?" Ellie asked.

"Yes."

Jess said, "You'd think they would build a back door in a place like this. Enclosed underwater."

"We have to assume that anyone watching has their eyes on the back door." Though he figured they would have their eyes on both, he also figured they wouldn't expect the four of them to emerge from the front. "If they are even watching. Which they might not be. They could be convinced that we're trapped and will drown, so maybe they've left already."

"If they did, they're probably right." Jess rolled her eyes. She was about to say something else when the bulkhead door began to groan. "What kind of a place is this, anyway? Underwater facility. Holding cells. Probably some kind of reconditioning thing, like they were going to do with Kaylee."

She was scared and using humor to combat it.

"And just like her," Ted said to her. "We're going to get out of here."

"She was rescued." Apparently, Jess was still mad that she hadn't been included in the operation. But she'd been on shift in Last Chance that night. "We have to get ourselves out."

He nodded. "We will."

Ted had one eye on the bulkhead as he continued, "In a minute, that will crash open, and a wall of water will come rushing in."

"You said that already."

He pinned Jess with a stare. "As soon as this place fills up, we're going to have to swim out of here and up to the surface of the lake. Are you ready for that?"

She opened her mouth to respond when, at that moment, the hallway exploded.

The rush of cold water hit Ted like a brick wall. He gasped for breath, unable to suck in air as the water shoved them all sideways. He managed to hang onto his pipe. Until the force pushed his feet out from under him.

He was swept to the side on the surface and heard one of the women yelp. He didn't know which one. As the water battered him, and he tried to hold on, Ted tracked the level as it rose up the wall.

Past halfway up, just above the light switch, all the electronics flickered and went dark.

He yelled, "Everybody holding on?"

"We're good," Dean said.

"I'm okay." Jess's voice was full of all that fear he'd seen on her face—more than he had ever heard from her before. She was holding on, but from the sounds of it, it was getting difficult to maintain her composure.

He prayed then. It was the only way to say he'd done everything he could to get them the best outcome. Not that it was a checklist, but more that he didn't want to leave one single inch that could lead to failure. He wanted to know he'd covered all his bases.

And that included asking God to help them.

Ted gritted his teeth against the freezing temperature of the water. He took a couple of big breaths and shouted, "Time to swim."

He didn't waste even a second, just took another breath the way Dean had taught him the SEALs did to hold their breath longer underwater. And then he went under.

The current was intense, but it got easier the more he swam. His eyes struggled to adjust to the darkness. He could barely see more than a foot or so in front of him. Mostly he only got his bearings when something swirled at him, and he had to bat it away. Debris and other objects. Things that had been laying around. Even a fish.

Someone's body collided with his, and he realized Dean and Ellie were passing him. Powered by his brother's strong legs.

Ted looked around for Jess but didn't see her in the murky water. *God, please help us all get out.*

He swept his arms through the icy liquid and kicked his legs. He glided forward from the force until his whole body jerked, stopped from going any further. His foot had snagged on something.

Air bubbles escaped from his nose in a rush.

He looked down at his foot, but couldn't make out what he was tangled in. It was way too dark down here. Maybe in the daytime he would have been able to see. But right now, all the light was from the moon and stars that shone overhead.

Down at the bottom of the lake, there was barely any light.

Ted curled up his body and reached down to his foot. It felt like twine. Maybe wire or some kind of net. He wasn't sure if that was better than having been caught by a bad guy. Either way, if he waited too long before he managed to get out, he would meet the same end.

More bubbles escaped his nose.

His lungs screamed in his chest, and his head swam as his oxygen levels depleted. Ted understood the mechanics of what was happening to him. But even as his mind tried to logically explain the science behind spending too long underwater with no air, part of him screamed and raged against it. As though determined to believe that the impossible could be true.

Forget about having a growth mindset. If he was about to die, what good was thinking positively? Especially when he wasn't going to make it to the surface.

Ted kicked and thrashed in the water. His actions stirred up silt from the bottom so that his vision grew even more clouded.

He grasped at the netting, or whatever it was holding him fast. But try as he might, he just could not wiggle his foot free. He was completely tangled up and stuck.

His strength floated away. His arms and legs grew heavy, and he could no longer move them as he'd been able to. A numbness descended over him. The last few bubbles of air left in his lungs released from his mouth.

Ted floated, overcome with cold and a sense of nothingness. Not peace, more like an absence of anything. Just a single, quiet flicker inside him. Not quite a flame; it held no heat.

Help me.

Dean barreled into him, grasping Ted with his arms. His brother felt down Ted's legs. A second later, he was free. But Ted had no strength left to swim.

Dean hauled his limp body up toward the surface. Instead of making it out of the water on his own, he had to rely on the strength of his brother and his brother's love for him. The fact his brother would never allow him to drown on his own, alone in the dark and cold.

They broke the surface, and Dean tugged Ted toward him, one arm around Ted's back and the other one lifting his head. "You need to breathe. Because I don't want to give you mouth-to-mouth. You're not nearly as cute as Ellie."

Ted wanted to laugh, but he didn't have the strength.

He managed to suck in some air and then coughed out water, hacking and gagging on it as his body continued to expel the lake water and take in precious air.

"There you are." Dean patted his cheek, as though that would get Ted to breathe more.

"Stop hitting me."

His brother chuckled. Ted could only groan since he didn't have the strength to speak.

Dean hauled him like a lifeguard toward the shore, while all Ted could do was blink up at the stars and try to make some sense out of what had just happened. His brain could hardly keep track. But eventually he managed to piece together Stephen Hilden and the facility. The one Ted had designed for isolation and underwater reeducation.

If it was blown up so no one could ever go in there again, that would be fine by Ted.

Give or take several arrests and probably a lengthy hospital stay for several of them. His wrist that had been injured a day or so ago had no feeling left in it. Dangling in the water, pretty much useless.

"Ellie." Dean's breath left his mouth in a rush.

Ted managed to twist his torso, but trying to look at what his brother was seeing didn't net him any results.

Seconds later, he could finally feel the ground underneath his feet. Ted tried to stand, but his legs didn't want to hold his weight.

Dean dragged him to the shore and set him down with his feet still in the water and upper body on the sand. All Ted could do was lay there.

Two men ran past his vision, up on the grass. Or the path. He couldn't really tell. Ted tried to warn his brother, but all that emerged from his mouth was a breathy moan.

"Hey!" His brother's yell rang out across the expanse of the lake.

Ted realized that Dean needed help. He managed to get his hands, or at least one of them, to shift underneath his shoulder. With his forehead braced on the sand, he lifted up enough to raise his head off the ground and see what was in front of him.

One man held Ellie, his arms around her, lifting her so that her feet were off the ground.

As Ted watched, Dean punched the guy in the head. A gun went off. These were the men who had brought them to West. The ones who had given them over to be put in that underwater facility. Or maybe they'd even been the ones who swam them down there and shut them inside.

From this distance, he couldn't tell if their clothes were wet.

And given Dean had just tackled a man holding Ellie to the ground, this probably wasn't the right time to figure that out.

A woman screamed. "Ellie, run!"

Jess.

Ted found her at the tree line, being dragged away by another man.

Ellie started to run while Dean fought the man on the ground. Ted could do nothing but lay there completely helpless. Unable to even summon the strength to get his legs under him.

The man holding Jess hit her over the head.

She slumped in his arms, and he dragged her away.

33

T here was nothing else Jess could do but go limp. After all, he had hit her over the head. What would come next, except her being knocked out? Too bad for her she was still fully conscious. And now with an even more massive headache that made her feel as if her skull had split open.

At least she didn't have to expend extra energy on walking. Her clothes dripped, heavy from the water that soaked through to her skin. An extra ten pounds of weight, even after she'd kicked off her shoes before she broke the surface of the lake.

Jess had been concentrating on making sure Ellie got to the shore as well, after Dean went back for Ted. She hadn't even noticed the two men approach. The same guys that turned them over to Stephen Hilden, and who probably were responsible for putting them down in that facility.

Jess could hardly believe it had been under the water. Now it was destroyed and completely waterlogged—both terrifying and actually kind of cool if she could admit that to her terrorized self. More denial to keep from thinking about the awful situation she was in yet again.

Again.

Again.

Was this never going to end? *Lord, I need Your peace. Please.*

The man hauled her away. Once he had put some distance in, Jess would've had enough time to figure out what she would do about it. Before he killed her. Or put her in a car. Whatever his plan was.

But instead, she'd yelled for her sister to run. It was all she could do. Plead for her to get away. It wasn't the only thing that mattered, but Ellie's survival was seriously more important to her than her own.

Now she had to focus on saving herself.

When the man shifted her weight in his arms, Jess let out a low moan. She wasn't sure if it sounded real or not. Who could tell? At least the man didn't seem to be worried she might be faking her current physical state.

She blinked and focused on the ground. It was difficult, given how hard she'd been hit over the head. Plus, the swim. And the tension, and the staple. She probably should've tried to pass out. That would likely feel better than this. But it wouldn't fix her problem of yet more gunmen running loose around Last Chance.

Nor would it help her get Hilden in cuffs.

She moaned again, tracking their progress along the ground. They were headed down a path by the lake. To the parking lot? Where he would do...what, exactly?

Jess wasn't sure she wanted to know. Their plan to murder the four of them in that facility had failed. Why not just kill them the moment they surfaced, instead of now abducting her —and trying to abduct Ellie—for some other inexplicable reason? She had to figure out what he was doing so she could stop it.

Just as soon as she figured out how.

All the while...wondering if Ted was even still alive.

Had Dean saved him? She didn't even know why he hadn't surfaced with the rest of them. The swim had been tough, and she'd realized they were at the far end of the lake where the water was deepest. Maybe it wasn't so strange that no one had ever discovered the facility. It wasn't like people went diving over here, what with nothing there to search for. No one swam at this end.

How wrong everyone had been.

Not just about the lake, but also about the fire chief.

Frustration gave her a surge of energy. She tensed her muscles a split second before planting her feet and elbowing the guy behind her. He grunted and let go, enough she could reach down and grasp a branch on the ground beside the path.

She spun, swinging the branch as she rotated her body toward the man. She used every bit of strength she had to slam the branch into the man's head.

Except that she misjudged his height and ended up hitting his shoulder. The branch splintered under the force of the blow, shattering. With the last pieces, she managed to clip the side of his head at least.

Her head thundered, and she gagged back bile.

He roared at her attack, and Jess scrambled to figure out what she was going to do next. Then he reached for his gun. She settled on simply tackling him the way she had done many times during the Thanksgiving pickup football games with the other cops. Never mind that she had sprained her wrist once. They had still won, hadn't they?

Besides, it was pretty much her signature move at this point.

The man's back struck the ground, and she managed to get her weight on his to pin him down. She slammed the hand holding the gun down on the gravel path, trying to get him to let go of it. The familiar movements helped her to focus despite the pain…everywhere. Not just her head.

His grip was iron tight, and she wasn't going to be able to keep this up much longer. One of them was soaking wet, injured and exhausted, and the other one was a gunman.

Finally, he managed to let go. She reached for the gun, but he used the momentary distraction to flip her onto her back.

Jess grunted as her head bounced off the gravel. But she didn't lose her grip on the gun. The man punched her in the side of the head. Jess barely managed to absorb the blow, wrenching her neck in the process. She gritted her teeth and swung as hard as she could with the gun.

She couldn't knock him off of her.

The man started to reach for her neck. Jess pressed the gun into his ribs, her finger on the trigger. "Back off. Down on the ground, hands behind your head."

He chuckled as he continued reaching for her neck. The second he began to squeeze down, his intent very clear, Jess pulled the trigger.

The blast muffled against his clothing and flesh. But she knew what'd happened when his whole body jerked, and he slumped down on top of her.

Before his weight fully settled on top of her, Jess shoved him to the side, breathing hard. Just trying to process the fact she had taken this man's life. As long as she had been a cop carrying a gun, Jess had never killed anyone. She had only pulled her weapon a few times, never actually using it on another person.

She stared up at the night sky and took a few gulping breaths before she flung herself over to search the man's body. If she couldn't get a phone, there wasn't much else she could do without getting into a car and driving away from the lake.

They had to get help. And if they were going to leave, the four of them needed to do it together.

She sat up. The man's phone was in the front hip pocket of his pants. She couldn't see the lake now. They'd walked too far away from it and around the corner. Once she got the phone out, Jess would be able to find the others and figure out a plan to get them away from here.

The phone used facial recognition, so she held it to the bad guy's face to access it. Then she changed the security settings, so it wouldn't require his image again. She also deleted the passcode.

Then she made a phone call as she stood up to walk back toward the lake. *Ugh.* Walking hurt a lot.

She held the phone to her ear and listened to it ring, wincing as even the tone hurt her ears. Her legs each felt like one-hundred-pound weights. The fact she was completely soaked didn't exactly help either. She was freezing, her teeth chattering so much that when Conroy picked up the phone, she had to fight to get the words out.

"It's…Jess."

"I'll trace the call, find your location, and send someone to you."

"The lake. West side, right in the corner."

"I'm putting the call out now. Hang on."

She was grateful for his quick thinking and explained to him what had happened. When she explained about the fire chief, she heard him bite back a word he wanted badly to say but knew he shouldn't.

"Just as long as you're all okay." Then he muttered. Finally, he said, "This is going to take a long time to unravel. An underwater facility?"

"Given Pierce Cartwright and his crazy ideas about keeping people in captivity, it doesn't seem quite so bizarre." She had to suck in a few breaths after the exertion of getting all those words out.

"I still don't like it," Conroy said.

She figured it didn't matter whether he liked it or not, the truth was just the truth. Though, everyone in town would have to deal with that since Steven Hilden was a local hero. No one would easily accept the fact he was the one who had been West all along.

She turned the corner and the lake came into view. Dean was kneeling over a man on the ground, punching him over and over again while Ellie sat a few feet away, her eyes wide as she watched.

"Dean!" Jess yelled his name so that he could hear. So he'd

be distracted and realize he'd probably punched this man more than enough times. When he looked at her, she said, "Conroy is on his way."

She wanted to ask them all where Ted was, but Dean had his full attention on the man who had tried to abduct Ellie.

Dean called out over his shoulder. "Where's the other guy?"

"I killed him."

Her future brother-in-law looked like he wanted to do the same with the man he had. But didn't.

On the phone, Conroy said, "Everyone available is on their way."

"Thanks, Chief." Jess turned, looking all around to find Ted. Where was he? Dean wouldn't have left him to drown for the sake of saving Ellie, right? Then again, she had no idea.

"Jess."

She realized Conroy had been talking to her. "What?"

"Are you guys all okay?"

"I can't find Ted. I don't know where he —"

Stephen Hilden stepped into view.

Jess nearly dropped the phone, but managed to tell Conroy, "Hilden is here." And speaking of, the man had a gun pointed at Ellie. She blinked, and he shifted it between the three of them. Equal opportunity with his aim.

Conroy said, "Two minutes."

"Hang up the phone." The man who was West, who hurt and sold people for financial gain, pointed the gun at her.

She heard Conroy say, "Don't —"

Jess didn't end the call. She tossed the phone to the ground. They could continue to track her location here. All she had to do was keep him from shooting anyone for the next two minutes.

And Hilden looked like he thought he had all the time in the world.

Ellie whimpered. Dean stood, moving his weight off the unconscious man on the ground. Did he have a gun? She prayed Dean had grabbed one from the man's body. She'd left the other one with the man she'd killed, not wanting to touch his weapon after she had already used hers to shoot him.

She hadn't thought she would have to try and kill someone else tonight.

Of course, that meant, once again, she was a complete and total failure at keeping people from being killed. If Hilden decided to shoot, she would have no way to stop him from taking a life.

Jess lifted both hands, palms out. "Don't shoot." She wanted to ask him what he wanted, but the words just wouldn't come out. She was more likely to sag onto the ground right now, into a heap, unable to move.

Hilden pointed the gun at Dean. "You, back up. Ms. Ellie comes with me."

He reacted at the same time Jess did. She said, "No way. I'll go with you, but you aren't touching Ellie."

She knew Dean felt the same way as her. *Help us find a way to take him down. To not let him hurt anyone.*

Ellie backed away from Hilden, toward where Jess stood.

"I will shoot both of them if you don't walk toward me."

Ellie shook her head. Jess grasped her sister's hand and, in one fell swoop, swung her around behind her while she stepped in front.

Just as the gun went off.

The explosion erupted into her chest, and everything went black.

34

———

Ted flinched as the sound of a gunshot echoed across the shoreline. He heard a woman scream, then a serious commotion.

"Keep going."

Ted lifted his hands an inch higher. Whatever it took for his father to think he was cooperating. Dear old dad had found him on the shore and dragged him to his feet. Ted should have played dead, since he was pretty sure now that if his father had been forced to carry him, Pierce Cartwright would have just left him there.

Though, he would likely have killed Ted right then and there since he couldn't take him with.

Like he was trying to do now.

"As if I'm going to let Steven Hilden kill my sons," the old man muttered behind him.

"He was going to drown us in that facility."

Pierce huffed. "But you *escaped*."

"You gave him the plans, right? That's how he got this whole place built down there."

"Plans? It's *my* facility, you should know since you've seen it for yourself. It was my pride and joy, back in the day. Some of my first operations happened in that place. In some ways, it's going to be my crowning achievement forever, regardless of what else I manage to achieve."

Multiple gunshots echoed to him. A woman screamed, "Jess!"

Ted's footsteps faltered.

"Move it." Pierce shoved him in the back with the barrel of his gun.

Ted glanced over his shoulder at his father.

"You think I'm going to let an asset like you slip through my fingers?"

Ted swallowed. "Someone will be looking for me. Kind of like how the FBI is looking for you."

Pierce chuckled.

Evidently he didn't consider the feds he'd escaped from to be much of a threat.

"They'll think you drowned in the lake."

Ted pressed his lips into a thin line. It was that or rage at his dad. Actually, maybe he should do that. Making a lot of noise might help now. He'd tried it before when he first saw his father standing over him. Didn't work then, but this could be different. It might.

Please.

Pierce stabbed his back with the gun, and Ted took another few steps. "They'll spend days dredging the bottom of the lake for your body, trying to figure out what happened."

Ted's body shuddered. *Dean.* His brother would believe he'd died.

A tear rolled down his face. By the time they realized he wasn't in the water still, he would be long gone. Captive to Pierce Cartwright—again. "I don't want to go with you. I never wanted to stay with you, and I won't do anything for you."

Pierce chuckled. "Did you practice that?"

Ted spun around. "*I hate you!*"

His father's expression darkened, and he swung the gun at

Ted's head. He lifted his arm to counteract the blow, but it was with his wrapped wrist—the sprained one.

Pain shot up his arm. Ted fell to his knees and threw up—mostly lake water. He gulped a few heaving breaths until his father kicked him in the ribs.

"Get up. It's time to *go*."

"Sorry." Ted looked up at him, not sorry at all. "Didn't realize we were on a timetable."

"You've gotten mouthy since I saw you last."

Ted said nothing, bile in his mouth and tears still drying on his face. He sat back, holding his injured arm to his front.

Jess had been bleeding. Her arm. She had a staple in her head. *And now she's been shot.* He hardly wanted to even think about seeing her fall. She was dead. That was all there was to it. Nothing to be done, no way to get her back.

Dead in her uniform, killed in the line of duty while bringing down the town's worst enemy.

She'd have liked that.

Ted wanted to have that kind of parting satisfaction. "Just kill me." Someone would hear the shot. They would come running, right? The FBI would get Pierce back, and he'd die knowing he had a hand in bringing his father down.

A man whose stain infected those around him. But no more, Ted didn't want anything to do with Pierce this time around. He hadn't exactly been a willing participant before, but he had no intention of being a witness to his destruction. His dad wasn't going to take him anywhere.

Ted wanted the chance to choose his future. Whether that was five minutes or fifty years, it would be up to him.

And no one else.

He was done being controlled.

"Get up." Pierce waved the gun at him.

"No. I won't go with you." Ted lifted his chin. "Last Chance is my home."

"You're gonna stay here? This place is a joke. Why do you think I left the first moment I could?"

"On to bigger and better things?" Ted planned to drag the conversation out long enough for someone to find him.

"Well, *yeah*. The founders do whatever they want. The cops think they're making a difference, but they're not. Small time, every bit of it."

"And you've made a name for yourself in much bigger things."

"There could be more for you if you get on board again."

Ted shook his head. "I was never on board. You have to know that."

"A moral failing on your part," Pierce said. "Now's the time to change your mind. Or I can put you through a program. That'll change it for you."

Ted's body stiffened.

"They're very good at what they do. But you'll probably not enjoy the experience, so it's best to just comply." His dad looked like he might feel bad about making Ted go through something like that. Despite all he'd done, and the countless people he'd hurt, it seemed Pierce Cartwright had some feeling for his youngest son.

"You've done enough to hurt me, don't you think?"

Pierce huffed.

"Just leave me alone now." Ted looked at the trees beside the hiking trail. "I'm tired of you, and all the pain you cause." Let his dad think he'd hurt Ted more thoroughly than he'd imagined.

He would either walk away, or he would suddenly decide he didn't care after all.

Ted wasn't sure which way it would go. "I'm not leaving with you. You're nothing but a sociopath. I won't be a part of any of it."

"Well, I need your expertise, so I guess you have no choice." Pierce shifted, a rustle of clothing. He was growing impatient.

"You think they'll take you in after they find out what you've done?"

"I think they'll be hurt," Ted said. "But they'll forgive me. That's what family does. Something you know nothing about."

Pierce huffed. It sounded vaguely like a chuckle.

"Just go now. Because I'll never go with you. It was a waste of time, you coming back here." All his father had done was ruin Ted's life further.

"That's a shame." Pierce shook his head. "I would've given you the world."

One that was truly demented. A world where his father had planned to terrorize Kaylee into being his wife, all because Pierce had some sick obsession with her mother back in the day. "I don't want anything to do with your world."

"I guess I'll have to make things a bit clearer to you then."

Ted stilled.

"You don't have a choice. So let's go."

35

"**H**elp me."

Conroy huffed but did as Jess asked. He held her upright while she stumbled to Steven Hilden. Pain sliced through her chest with every gasp.

She grumbled. "Why does no one say getting shot in the vest hurts so much? Gah. It feels like I broke my sternum."

"That's why EMTs are here to help you."

"I just want to talk to him." She stumbled to the grass beside the fire chief and knelt. "Hilden."

He gasped. Blood covered his chest from where they'd taken him down after he first shot Jess. *Thank You, God.* She'd been wearing her vest.

The last thing she'd done before being captured and put in that underwater facility was put on a vest and walk through that building with Basuto.

She whirled around to Conroy, pain slicing through her. Jess gasped. "Basuto."

"Hit in the vest. He's here, somewhere."

There was another thing, a thought that began to stir in her head. But when she opened her mouth to speak, the thought evaporated. She closed it again and shook her head…whatever she had thought was so important, it was gone now. Chased away by more pain. Her grandpa always told her that if it was important enough, the thought would resurface. She let that settle her for the time being.

"You're a mess." Conroy shook his head. "Whatever you've got on your to-do list, it happens in the next thirty seconds, and then you're going to the hospital." Before she could ask, he added, "We'll find Ted. They're already looking for him."

Jess nodded. That was good, she was glad they were looking for Ted. Trying to figure how he got lost in all the confusion.

She turned to Hilden.

Conroy cut into her thoughts. "What are you doing?"

She didn't look at Conroy but answered his question. "I want to talk to him." Jess put her hand on Hilden's arm, ignoring the sharp pain in her shredded forearm. She seriously needed a new bandage. Dry clothes. Medicine. And then about six months of vacation time. "Hilden."

He gasped. The man didn't have much time left, considering all the damage from those gunshots. Blood bubbled on his lips.

She glanced at the closest EMT. He shook his head. She turned back to Steven Hilden and saw his gaze had snagged on her. Face pale. Seconds left to live. "I want to hear you say it."

Behind her, a man sighed. "Why can't someone just put him out of his misery?"

Jess leaned down to the fire chief. "Are you West?" She wanted to hear him say it. "It's all over for you, but you can do this one last thing right. Tell me. Are you West?"

She wanted to tell him to just admit it already. But he might fess up just to get her to stop asking. Even if he did confess, this wouldn't exactly be a lawful confession. Still, she wanted to hear it from his lips.

Hilden's lips spread into a bloody smile. "West." His chest shook, as though that was funny. "She..."

He coughed. His whole body jerked, and he gasped. This one more desperate than the last.

A second later, the life bled from his eyes the way it seeped from his wounds.

Conroy laid his hand on her shoulder. "He's dead." The chief didn't allow her to do anything else, he simply hauled her up in his arms. As though she couldn't walk herself. Which was probably true, if she was being honest.

Jess allowed her whole body to sag in his arms, her forehead resting against his neck. "Where's Ted?"

"I know," he crooned as he walked toward the ambulance. "Don't worry about Ted."

"You know Basuto isn't a traitor, right?" Was that it? The thought she'd had was about Basuto, the memory of concern for her sergeant. Or someone related… Someone who had also been shot.

"Yes, I do."

There was something else he wasn't saying, but she couldn't put her finger on it. At least he knew. Meanwhile, Jess couldn't get her mind to process the thought fully enough to say it aloud. Something wasn't adding up in her brain.

She spotted some FBI agents and tried to shift out of Conroy's arms, not fully realizing what she was doing. "They need to find Pierce. He has to have Ted."

Where else would he be right now?

"I'll tell them." He sounded like he was simply trying to placate her. "You need to be in the hospital, Jess. It's time to lay down the fight and let us take over."

He was mad. She knew he was.

Because she hadn't told them all her concerns? Because she hadn't brought them in to help when things got hot. He had to know she wasn't wired that way. This was a fight that belonged to her and Ted.

Jess lifted both hands. She realized then that she was barely walking on her own. Her feet were only slightly touching the ground he was holding her so tightly upright. Shoving away all other thoughts except what needed her attention, she clutched

Conroy's cheeks. "Find Pierce." No, that wasn't it. "Get Ted back."

"You get in that ambulance. Don't worry about Ted, we'll get him back for you. Okay?" He still sounded like he thought she was simply overly distraught and should only be told what was absolutely necessary right now. That she wasn't capable of handling any kind of truth.

"Find. Him." He had to understand, and saying that was the only way she was willing to get in the ambulance and concede the fact she couldn't go after Ted herself. *Where are you?* She knew something was wrong. She could feel it.

"I know you're worried about him. But don't be."

Strong arms assisted her into the ambulance, and a man said, "I'll get her statement. You find your guy, but keep me posted on the hunt for Pierce Cartwright."

Jess frowned. The EMT had her lay back. She stared up at his face, her attention snagging on his shirt collar. Why would…

Her head swam. He patted her shoulder. "Just rest. We'll have you taken care of in no time."

Jess briefly wondered where her sister was, too. She opened her eyes and lifted her head off the bed. She saw Ellie standing beside Mia just for a fleeting second before the chief closed the doors. The FBI agent settled across from her.

She sighed. What was Jenkins doing here? He'd been shot. He had to know there was no strength left in her to give a statement right now. And the last thing she wanted to do was go over everything. Ted was still out there. Until she knew he was all right, she hardly wanted to think about anything different. Or do much else besides praying for him and the cops and agents trying to find him.

That he would be safe.

His dad in cuffs, or dead like Hilden.

Jess was exhausted. She kind of hoped the EMT would just stick her with a needle—hopefully with something that would make her fall asleep. That would show the agent what was what.

That he'd wasted his time here when he should be out there doing his job.

She heard someone shift, and she opened her eyes. Her body swayed on the bed, as the ambulance set off to the hospital. Jenkins grunted. He was closer to her now. And there was the needle that would take her to the sweet oblivion that could only come with sleep…wait, why was the agent holding the needle? Where was the EMT?

"What…" She couldn't form the rest of the words.

"Don't worry." Jenkins held it to her arm. "This will all be over soon."

"Hey." She tried to think of a whole sentence. "No. Hey!" She needed help. He was trying to…

He jabbed the needle into her arm.

An elbow swung out and cuffed the special agent in the head. He fell to the side, let go of the needle, and slumped away from her. Jess stared at the thing poking out of her arm.

She pulled it out, wanting to throw it away from her. Instead, she held onto it. She might need a weapon.

The EMT jumped, clearing the space between them. "You're done. Traitor." He punched the special agent and then hit him again three more times. Jess frowned. A red knot erupted on the agent's forehead. One more and Jess heard his nose crunch. "How much pain have you caused, turning people over to Pierce Cartwright? You'd better *pray* they find him."

The ambulance was still moving, causing Jess's body to sway as she pushed up into a sitting position.

Special Agent Traitor pulled his gun. The EMT swiped it away so that it flung across the ambulance and hit the back wall. Then he hauled Jenkins up by the collar of his shirt and got in his face. "Now, you're going to call Pierce."

Jess heard a muffled, "What on earth?" from the front of the ambulance as they started to slow.

The special agent grinned. "Too late. He's already here."

Jess gasped.

The EMT dumped Jenkins on the floor, kicking him in the ribs for good measure, and moved to the front where she could no longer see him.

The ambulance came to a complete stop, and the special agent scrambled to his feet and grabbed up his gun. Jenkins closed in, pointing it at her, a menacing grin on his face. When he was close enough, Jess jabbed out with the needle and shoved it into his side.

He grunted. And then chuckled, brushing it away. It clattered to the floor. "Nice try."

Jenkins moved away then and shoved open the back doors of the ambulance. Where did her EMT hero go? She'd never seen him before. Or, at least, she didn't think she had.

A shadow filled the back of the ambulance. She lifted her head, shielding her eyes with her hand. Not the EMT hero.

"Ted?"

He stood in the open doors, a look on his face she'd never seen before.

"What's wrong?"

His throat worked as he swallowed. Pierce Cartwright stepped into view beside him.

The Special Agent stepped out right then. "The other guy already hit me plenty, but you should still knock me out. Make it look good."

Pierce lifted his gun and shot the agent clean in the forehead.

Not indispensable after all.

Jess whimpered as he fell out of sight onto the ground.

Ted didn't even flinch.

Pierce shoved him forward. "First you kill her, and I'll take care of Dean. Then we're done with Last Chance. Forever."

36

"I would rather die." Ted tried to turn around and face his father.

Pierce shoved him to the edge of the ambulance. He fell onto the floor, half in and half out. *What am I supposed to do?* He had nothing to fight his father with, but he wasn't going to allow Jess to be killed. "You aren't going to hurt her, and neither am I."

Jess *and* Dean. No way. That just wasn't going to happen. Not if he had anything to say about it.

Ted had to figure out how to finish this. Jess looked ready to pass out, sitting up in the ambulance bed. She shouldn't have to help. Even if he needed it *and* she was in any condition to help, Ted planned to do this himself. It was time for him to finish this once and for all.

If he could.

Help me.

He hoisted himself to a standing position and glared at Pierce. His father. Except that he didn't deserve the title. It didn't matter who he was anymore. Ted had to end his father's destruction and the dominance he held over his life.

A swift movement caught his attention, over in corner of his vision. A uniformed EMT rounded the back door, gun first. Before Ted could even react to his appearance, the man lifted a gun and shot Pierce Cartwright in the head.

Then he turned to Ted. "Bro, you good?"

Ted just blinked at the guy. "Hammer."

"Yep. You're good." He pulled out a phone, shifting, and Ted couldn't help but notice the spider tattoo on his neck. Into the phone, he said, "Clean up on aisle four."

"Ted?"

He turned to Jess at the sound of her voice, stepping over his father's dead body, wincing at the quietness and pain in her voice. He clambered up to her, sat on the bed, and pulled her into his arms.

"I thought you were dead."

Ted smiled against her dark hair. He liked it better blond but would take Jess any way she came. "I thought *you* were dead." To his consternation, more tears ran down his face. How many times had he cried recently?

He was too wrung out himself to figure out the answer to that question.

"Dude."

He tensed at the voice, glancing at the open doors. Dean stood there. Ted said, "Hey."

"You good?" His brother lifted his chin.

Ted nodded.

Dean said, "Jess?"

She lifted her head from Ted's shoulder. "Can I go to the hospital now?"

Ted smiled. "I love you."

She shifted further, so she could look in his eyes. "That's good." She smiled. "Because I figure that might be the only thing we have in common."

"You love you, too?"

Dean snorted. "You guys suck at this."

Jess frowned at his brother, then said to Ted, "No, dork. I love *you*."

"You've both lost your minds." The tattooed EMT, Hammer, folded his arms.

"I think we've gained some sanity now." Ted shrugged one shoulder. "But the hospital sounds good." He glanced at Dean. "Ellie okay?"

Dean nodded. "She's worried about the two of you. I'm going to call Mia and give them an update so she can tell her." He frowned at the EMT.

"That's Hammer," Ted said. "He's undercover FBI."

"Taking down traitors. Generally kicking some butt." Hammer made a brushing motion over each shoulder.

Dean looked impressed. "So your work here is done now, right?"

Ted figured that was true. They'd taken down West, and Pierce Cartwright was dead. He tried to feel sad about that. The emotion didn't come. Maybe later it would, but he would deal with it when that happened.

If it did, or not, he figured his family would be around him when it happened. Dean and Ellie. The Last Chance Police Department.

Jess.

He held her close to him while Hammer turned to Dean, one eyebrow raised. "Done?" Hammer shook his head. "Not even close."

EPILOGUE

One week later

Ted stood at the open car door when the orderly pushed Jess out of the hospital entrance in a wheelchair. "Ready?"

She frowned at the guy behind her. "Ready to walk on my own two feet."

Ted moved to her. The orderly put the brake down on the wheelchair. Ted lifted Jess to her feet, his arms supporting her.

"Conroy told me he doesn't want to see me in uniform for another two weeks."

"Yeah?" Ted felt his eyebrows rise.

"So kiss me, and let's get this party started."

Ted laughed.

I HOPE you enjoyed *Expired Game*, please consider leaving a review, it really helps others find their next read!

Turn the page for the first 2 chapters of the 6th story in the Last Chance County series: *Expired Plot*

U.S.A. TODAY BESTSELLING AUTHOR
LISA PHILLIPS PRESENTS
EXPIRED
PLOT
LAST CHANCE COUNTY BOOK SIX

1

———

There wasn't much to pack for her interview, and she refused to contemplate the fact her entire life amounted to not even enough to fill one suitcase. If she got this job, Hollis wasn't coming back to Last Chance.

Not ever.

She looked around the quiet of her apartment to make sure she hadn't forgotten anything. She had the rest of her clothes, not counting the black pant suit and white shirt she was wearing, and she'd safely stashed the emergency wad of cash she'd been amassing the past few months. A few toiletries. Enough to get her started somewhere else.

The closet. Hollis pulled her leather jacket from the hall closet and stowed the final item in the suitcase. That brown leather jacket was the only thing she'd ever splurged on in her life. It had been on sale at two hundred fifty dollars. It would really be quite fitting if she wore it while leaving the only town she'd ever lived in. The place she'd spent every day of her life.

No. It didn't matter what she wore. It only mattered that she was finally free of it all. No more trying to do the right thing. No more trying to get everyone to see what was right in front of their faces. She was done. Her life was going to be lived on her own terms from now on.

Hollis grabbed the letter she'd written to the man who owned the lease on the diner she'd run ever since her stepfather, Frankie, had been in an accident. She would leave the letter in the office after she said her final goodbyes to the place she'd spent nearly half her life and the only job she'd ever had.

A lump rose in her throat.

"No." Her voice sounded thick, but still hollow. She wasn't going to cry.

She pulled out her phone and sent a text to the guy she'd been seeing for the past couple of weeks now.

I WON'T BE ABLE TO MAKE DINNER TOMORROW. SORRY.

They were supposed to have been going to some concert for date number six. She didn't feel super bad about leaving him— or so she was trying to convince herself. After all, she was pretty sure there was something he was keeping from her. It was mildly irritating that she would never find out what it was. But not irritating enough to stop her from doing what she had to do.

She breathed a big sigh of relief. She was finally leaving Last Chance, going somewhere none of them would ever be able to find her. Where the past wasn't going to hold her back, or hold her down.

"No more."

It was like an addiction. She had to cut them all off cold turkey, or she'd never get free of it. She would never find something genuine that was just hers. People with no ulterior motives. Hollis was going to get a fresh start where no one knew her.

Her phone buzzed. The repeated buzzing told her it wasn't a text. She turned it to look at the screen and saw *Dad* illuminated. He was actually her stepfather, but given how flaky her mother was, it wasn't a surprise that Hollis had gravitated to the only supportive parent she'd ever had. Frankie's first love would always be the diner, which was why Hollis had worked there since the day she turned fourteen. All she'd wanted was to be absorbed into his world.

She swiped to answer. "I've been trying to reach you all day. Where are you?"

"Holl—" His voice cracked.

"Frankie?" She'd never actually called him dad. Not after the first time, and the way her mother had laughed at her for twenty minutes. "What's wrong?"

There was a shuffle on the other end of the line. After that, a voice came on. "We have your father." It sounded like a recording, like in one of those kidnapper movies.

The voice sent a shudder through her, and she swallowed. "What?"

"I won't repeat myself."

Only this wasn't a movie.

"Who are you?" She'd stood up to plenty of bullies in her life. She straightened her shoulders and didn't betray one ounce of fear in her tone. "What do you want?"

The voice let out a low chuckle, detached and emotionless. "They told me you could be cold. Now I believe them. We have your father."

"Where is he? Don't hurt him." She gasped out a breath. "What have you done with him?"

"Enough questions." The voice said, "He stays with us, and we'll send instructions. If you don't do as we ask, he dies. If you involve the police, he dies. If you fail to respond…" The voice didn't finish.

"I get it." Hollis squeezed the phone so hard her hand started to cramp. "I need to speak to—"

"Don't waste my time."

"No—"

The line went dead.

"Frankie!"

Hollis lowered the phone and stared at the screen.

Kidnapped. This was insane. What was she supposed to do,

sit around and wait for instructions? She was supposed to be at an interview! And yet, suddenly, the interview and her plan to leave seemed so pointless.

Trying to leave town.

Starting a new life.

He dies.

Her hand shook, and she had to fight for a steady breath. *We have your father.* He'd been kidnapped. *Father.* That was the word he'd used. Interesting, considering it said he only knew what he'd been told about Hollis. This wasn't someone she considered a friend—who'd know Frankie was no relation of hers.

She looked at the packed suitcase and her purse. She'd been about to walk out the door, leave town, and never come back. Now she was going to have to do…what?

Hollis glanced around her apartment. What could these people even want? And worse, what would they ask her to do to get him back? She didn't even want to imagine. It had to be serious, otherwise why go to the trouble of kidnapping a man and holding him hostage?

She shifted her phone in her grasp and tried to steady the shake in her hands.

She could call the police. Conroy, the Last Chance police chief, was a long-time acquaintance. His fiancé was always nice when she came into the diner to order their lunch. The police detective, Savannah Wilcox, was someone Hollis liked. She could probably consider them all friends. But Hollis didn't have friends. It was just easier that way.

Less of a chance her mother could make a mess of everything, the way she'd been doing for Hollis's entire life.

She winced. Her mother.

Hollis slipped her cell phone into her purse, grabbed her suitcase, and locked her apartment. She slipped the door key into an envelope and put it in her purse so she could mail it after she accepted the new job. The suitcase went into the trunk of her little compact SUV, the car Frankie had handed down to her for a year of low payments when he'd upgraded his own ride.

She drove over to her mother's townhome where Sharleen lived in by herself—that is, when she chose to be alone. The other times, when she didn't want to be by herself, she invited over whoever she wanted. But not Hollis. Sharleen had kicked Hollis out the day she'd turned eighteen, walking away from the lease on their tiny rental house to buy a classy townhome.

Hollis had slept in the diner on the cramped office couch for a month until she found a place of her own.

Before she walked up to the front door, Hollis switched out the suit jacket for her leather one. The brown jacket would hopefully distract her mom from making any sort of conclusion that Hollis had been headed to an interview—or maybe a funeral. Her mom likely wouldn't care either way, but Hollis didn't want to field any questions right now.

And it was none of Sharleen's business.

Her mom answered the door. She took one look at Hollis's jacket. Jealousy flashed in her eyes, but she didn't comment. Then she flipped her hair back and said, "What?" while bracelets slid down her slender, bare forearm.

Hollis lifted her chin. "I need to talk to you."

Sharleen said nothing, even though she had to know something was wrong. She also didn't move. Just stood there in a blouse that probably cost more than what Hollis made in two days, and a pair of jeans Hollis wouldn't be able to fit into even if she went on a starvation diet for two years. Which she knew all too well about—because her mom had actually put her on one. That is, until Hollis had figured out that fast food places had dollar menus. From then on, she'd supplemented her food intake with money she found on the sidewalk on her way to school.

"I need to come in."

Her mom opened the door, but only wide enough for her to

get her own body through. Hollis had to turn sideways. Her mom still didn't budge, so Hollis had to squeeze her way in.

This was a mistake.

Hollis walked all the way to the open living and kitchen area. Then she turned around.

"Frankie's been kidnapped." She took a breath and tried to figure out how to continue. "I'm not supposed to involve the police, but I need help. Why would someone kidnap him?"

"How should I know?" Her mother strode to pour herself a drink at the breakfast bar and slung it back in one gulp. "Why should I care?"

"Maybe you didn't hear me, but he was *kidnapped*. I have to do whatever they want, or they'll kill him."

"Like I said. I'm supposed to care?"

Hollis wanted to scream at her. "There's no one else I can go to. Surely you know…someone who might know who took him. Or why. Or maybe they know who did. You have contacts in town, right?"

Her mom was the only person in Last Chance who might be able to help her and not put Frankie in danger.

Sharleen only chuckled. "I am connected. Maybe I can make some calls."

"I would appreciate it." Hollis gritted her teeth.

"You can do whatever with the information."

"Thank you."

"Don't thank me yet." Her mom slung back another drink. "I haven't done anything."

Hollis stood between the leather couch and the entryway table and waited.

Her mom just stared at her. "What?"

"You're going to make some calls."

"With you here?" She tipped her head back and laughed.

Hollis strode around the breakfast bar and got in her mom's face. This was exactly why she had to leave.

"I know Frankie isn't your favorite person. You both have

your own things going on." It had been years since they were together. "But you must still feel *some* kind of affection for him. Or are you as cold and heartless as you tell everyone I am?"

"Of course, I think fondly of the good times," her mom said. "We aren't all like you."

Hollis didn't have time to even touch that. "So, make your calls, because I'm getting him back."

"You?"

"At least one of us cares."

"Because you've gotten all emotional, suddenly that means you care?" Sharleen poured another glass. "It just means you can't handle yourself."

She lifted the glass to her lips.

Something snapped within Hollis, and she swung out with her arm and hit the glass out of her mom's hand. It hit the sink across the kitchen and shattered into tiny, glinting pieces.

Her mom actually flinched.

Hollis said, "As soon as I get him back, I'm leaving town."

"I know, dear." There was no affection in the word, though it was technically an endearment. Sharleen was the sun, orbited by every planet in the solar system. Shining its light. Shame this sun had no warmth to it whatsoever.

Hollis didn't need to get on a tangent about how her mom could've possibly known that. "Find out who has Frankie."

Hollis had no idea who was holding Frankie, or what they wanted. Maybe her mom could help, or maybe she'd make everything so much worse that Hollis would regret involving her. The way she always regretted involving her mother in anything…for as long as she could remember.

Frankie was the closest thing she had to family. It wasn't like she would leave without getting him back. She'd never be able to live with herself.

Didn't matter that her family was fractured. If you could even call it a family. Her stepdad cared about the diner. Everything—and every*one*—else was a distant second. She'd planned to tell him goodbye, but doubted he'd have stopped her from going to her interview. Or that he'd have done or said more than give her a hug and wish her well.

"Why do you even care, if you're leaving anyway?"

She turned back and saw something in her mom's expression that she couldn't decipher. Not surprising. Sharleen gave nothing away. But that only made Hollis all the more curious. "Because it's Frankie."

Her mom shrugged like she was confused.

"He can hire another general manager." She shrugged. "But he needs to know why I'm not showing up for work on Monday."

She didn't want to leave him in the lurch. And on the off-chance he'd be worried, or even compelled to file a missing person's report, she'd rather have communicated clearly to him.

Not that she expected anyone to come looking for her.

But then, that was the whole idea.

She said, "Just tell me if you come up with something. Because he can't help himself at all right now. He's been *kidnapped*, Sharleen."

Her mom rolled her eyes. "Yeah, I *know*. I said I would make calls, and I will."

Hollis closed the front door behind her. She strode to her car, looking at her mom's street. It was the other end of town from where she lived. Between the two houses were her stomping grounds—all the places she'd walked her whole life. History.

Don't get nostalgic.

The grass wasn't greener anywhere else, but that wasn't what she wanted, anyway. She was only looking for different grass where no one knew her. A place she could make a fresh start with genuine relationships.

Her phone buzzed. She climbed into the front seat of her car and pulled out her phone. An image sent by text. A private number.

Frankie had been roughed up. His hair was matted down on one side, and he had a swollen black eye. He'd been gagged by a roll of cloth.

A whimper escaped her lips. She sent a reply text.

Don't hurt him.

She could imagine the voice on the other end of the phone laughing. Could remember the amusement in his tone. A tear rolled down her cheek. Why take Frankie? What could they possibly want and why hurt him? She could only assume they needed her to do something.

It had to be bad if they thought they needed that much leverage. And it had to be something *she* could do—an asset, or a scapegoat.

Hollis swiped away the tear, and then sent another message.

Just tell me what you want me to do.

2

———

Will shut the door to the interview room in the Last Chance Police Department and tossed the file on the table. "I'm FBI Special Agent Will Briar."

The man across the table lifted his brows. "Yeah, I remember you." Stuart Leland had lived in Last Chance for a few months. This was a good guy. A solid guy who was now married to the police department receptionist, Kaylee.

"Yeah?"

"We were in Utah, when Kaylee was kidnapped." Stuart studied him. "Tate said he was bringing the FBI."

"Ah." Yeah, he'd been in on that operation. Taking down a facility owned and operated in secret by a man who talked his way up to the CIA Director job. The FBI had arrested him, lost him and then Last Chance cops had helped them get him back in custody. Will had a hand in that, but it was mostly their doing bringing down Pierce Cartwright.

"Thanks for your help, by the way."

Will nodded. Kaylee had been the focus of Pierce Cartwright's attention, but she was safe now.

And despite Jess Ridgeman and Ted Cartwright's recent

attempts to bring in the local bad guy "West," he wasn't so sure they'd actually accomplished it.

"And this is about…"

Will pulled out the chair and sat. "This isn't a formal conversation, and you're not in trouble."

"But you are fishing for information." Stuart's eyes narrowed. "About what?"

Will saw movement out the door, in the hallway. Conroy—the police chief—stood there, watching. Beside him was Kaylee, this man's wife and the receptionist. She might be happy, married to Stuart, but she wasn't happy right now.

He was out of options. Will had been living in Last Chance for nearly a year now, using the persona of a biker and going by the name "Hammer." A guy who had a spider web tattoo on the side of his neck.

"You work at Hollis's diner, correct?"

Stuart shrugged. "Everyone knows I cook there."

Will could've opened the file, but he knew what was in there. He'd written it. "A week ago on Tuesday, Hollis left the diner around four pm."

"I doubt it," Stuart said. "Considering she never leaves before six."

"And that specific day?"

"Can't say I remember specifics on a random Tuesday."

"Only last week. So, try." Will had a lot riding on this. He needed Stuart to give him something he could go on, because they'd all been trying to bring down West for months. Had they cut off the head of the snake? Will didn't think so.

He'd even tried getting close to Hollis to see if she would let him into her life. All the way in. Because too many things had pointed in her direction.

She hadn't opened up, though.

"Tuesday was the day a couple of kids spilled soda in their macaroni," Stuart said. "I remember because I ran out, so I told them they'd have to wait while I remade it. The mom didn't want to. She got mad. I talked to her, but Hollis wound up giving them something else for no charge. The lady still stomped out."

Will nodded. He'd seen Hollis handle irate customers before and respected the way she was with people. She gave modestly. Neither was she a pushover. Some people would simply never be satisfied.

Will said, "What time did she leave that day?"

"After she closed out the cash register and doled out the tips it was after five."

That was the same time Will had in his notes from the surveillance he'd been doing. "She's the one who handles all the money?"

Stuart nodded. "Though, if I asked, she would let me look at the books. She said that to me the day she hired me. Straight up, if I wanted to make sure I was being paid fairly, I could just ask."

"And she logs all the tips?"

"Notes it all down. Her records are meticulous." Stuart frowned.

Will wasn't going to explain why he was asking about Hollis and the diner money. Her being meticulous could be both a good and bad thing as far as Will was concerned. Either she insisted on everything being above board, or she was particular because she was hiding something and needed to make sure the deception was all straight. So, which was it?

"That's what you want?" Stuart leaned back in the chair. "Information on whether Hollis is dirty, like she's hiding something from everyone? The FBI has better things to do than investigate a waitress in Last Chance. Surely." He shot Will a look.

One he had little trouble deciphering.

Stuart thought Will was an agent no one cared enough about to give significant assignments to, and so he'd been relegated to this.

It was on the tip of Will's tongue to tell this Last Chance resident his current theory about West's real identity. Considering he had no evidence it would only sound outlandish. What he needed was to get the FBI colleague who operated as his handler—FBI Special Agent Eric Cullings, a guy with plenty of local contacts—to send him the tax records for Hollis's diner. Then he might have more than a theory.

He might know for sure who "West" was. The criminal behind every bad guy activity in Last Chance was a person who remained elusive the past few months while Will had investigated drug smuggling. Then the founders emerged, and the cops had been taking them down, one by one. Going up the ladder while the police searched for West as well. A series of cases had led them through the founders of Last Chance—all the way to the boss. The head of the snake had been outed as the fire chief, responsible for most of the crime in town.

Only problem was, the cops were convinced he was "West."

Will was not.

Someone else pulled the strings, and the fire chief was simply the last in a line of scapegoats.

Hollis was a business owner. The diner had been in her family for years, right? He had reason to believe she was "West." Alternatively, if she wasn't, and he was wrong, then Will was almost positive she knew who West really was.

At one point, he'd believed "West" to be a group of people even. Now there was an unpopular theory. But it had weight nonetheless. West, a collective persona. He had that possibility on the back burner, and he would continue to until he figured out exactly what Hollis was hiding.

Will had an idea. "You said she would show you the books if you asked. How about you make me a copy."

Stuart snorted. "Wow."

"Something funny?" If he could get the financial records, then maybe he could prove she was receiving money she should never have access to. Washing it for the criminals in town so they could have it back as legit bills.

"You want me to copy it all to a flash drive while she's not looking?"

"I'm sure you can find the motivation to cooperate."

"All her records are on paper." Stuart shook his head and got up. He strode to the door. "Good luck with your fishing expedition. Though, I'm not thinking your odds are great for catching anything."

He left Will alone in the interview room until Conroy walked in. "You wanna tell me what that was?"

Will glanced over at the police chief. Conroy had worn suits every day as the department's lieutenant. Will would bet he probably wore a suit on the weekend nowadays, too. Now his fiancé held that rank, and he'd been promoted to chief. No one knew when the two would be married. So far in town Tate and Savannah had eloped, and Stuart and Kaylee had been married in a tiny ceremony a few weeks ago. Dean and Ellie were seriously dating, and his brother was seeing her sister.

As far as Will could tell, they were all good cops. Effective and upright. There hadn't been any red flags. Not that he'd seen so far, at least. For a police department anywhere, that was basically unheard of. Which meant, either they hid their wrongdoing well, or they were the most moral bunch of cops he'd ever met in his life.

Will swiped the file off the table as he stood. "Just a couple of questions. Getting a feel for the situation over at the diner."

"Because you think Hollis is West."

It wasn't a question, so Will didn't take it as one. "That's part of an ongoing investigation."

"What Ted and Jess heard was…" Conroy shook his head. "It had to have been a red herring. There's no way Hollis is involved."

"Until you can prove that," Will said, "I have to continue as though it's at least a possibility."

Conroy worked his mouth side to side. No way to argue with that. "Just…tread lightly with her."

"You want me to go easy when she could be West?" Would this be evidence that Conroy wasn't as upright as he'd always thought?

"Of course not." Conroy said, "It's just….you don't know her."

"And you do?"

"I know enough, so I'm telling you this." Conroy folded his arms. "You'd better be sure. Because if you're not and you move on it anyway, I don't want you back in my town. Ever."

"Fine." Will headed for the door while Conroy muttered behind him.

"I know you're trying to date her, too. As Phil Tilley."

Will turned. "So?" He'd made several plays. Hung a few lines out there, both as his undercover biker persona and as the buttoned-up, straight-laced guy Phil. Either the biker discovered evidence his way, or Hollis would give something up. The two personas moved in such differing circles, it wasn't hard to keep someone from recognizing him. So far, at least.

Too many people knew who he really was. Sooner or later he would be outed.

"I get that you wanna finish this undercover assignment. To know you got the guy at the top," Conroy said. "I just don't like how you're going about it."

Didn't matter. Will was going to do this, and how the locals felt about him wasn't his problem. He was beyond tired and wanted to finish it. The need to close the case and walk away was a desperation that wouldn't let him get a full night of sleep. He'd never left anything unfinished.

And this wasn't done.

If he felt any peace at all these days, it was when he saw Hollis's name light up on his phone screen. Whatever that was even about.

Of course, it was Phil Tilley she was calling. Not him. Will had no reason to reciprocate her phone calls at this point. Not when she didn't even know who he really was. Once she found out, he could kiss all their rapport goodbye.

She would know exactly how much he'd been stringing her along this whole time.

That was why he had to push aside his feelings and get this case closed. Get the evidence he needed, and contact his handler for an arrest warrant. Eric would take care of all the paperwork. All Will had to do was make sure there would be no doubt as to the identity of this "West" person they'd been chasing for months.

After that, he could walk away clean.

Done.

Will's phone rang as he walked out. He expected it to be Hollis, following up with her text—as if she'd know he had just been thinking about her—but it was Eric. He sent his FBI agent handler to voicemail and slid the phone into his cup holder before driving to the diner.

From across the street, he watched the front windows.

Hollis opened seven days a week for breakfast and lunch. He knew she ran the place essentially singlehandedly since her father's accident. He'd broken both his legs, which put him in a wheelchair, or occasionally on crutches, depending on how his day was going, but no one knew how it had happened.

Will also knew West was a woman, with a witness description that matched Hollis, and intel that suggested she used her diner to launder money. He was going to prove she'd been behind everything sinister going on in Last Chance this whole time.

The fact he was attracted to her was simply further proof of how convincing she was. Manipulating everyone, all the time. Whenever she wasn't alone, the woman was spinning a line. Creating a story that had the town convinced of how nice she was.

Not him.

He'd seen through her, as much as he'd rather believe it wasn't true. As though she were some kind of innocent bystander caught in the middle.

He didn't believe in that. No one was innocent. Will was even beginning to wonder if the police department here wasn't covering up for her. Perhaps she'd paid them off. Given how Conroy talked about Hollis, it could be that he benefited from some kind of arrangement between the two of them.

That made enough sense that Will decided he'd have to include this new theory in an email to Eric tonight.

Will got out of his car and took a walk around the building, just in case something was happening.

He wandered nonchalantly until he saw the back door was ajar, then pulled his gun and headed inside, still dressed as Will. Jeans, boots, and a dark green Henley. Hard to explain the style change to someone who only knew straight-laced Phil, but he would if he had to. At least he wouldn't have to explain why the biker known as Hammer had no tattoo right now. Will had covered it with makeup, but hadn't bothered to wipe it off when he changed clothes.

By the time it did fade, he planned to have this case all wrapped up. He'd be far from Last Chance and the people here who knew him only as a biker.

Will crept down the dark hall. A light was on in the office, and he could hear someone rooting around in there.

Two steps toward the door, he heard a shuffle. The blow came out of nowhere.

Pain reverberated through Will's skull.

His body slammed onto the floor and everything went black.

Continue reading *Expired Plot* now - Find out where at
LastChanceCounty.com

OTHER BOOKS IN THE LAST CHANCE COUNTY SERIES

Find ALL of the books at:

LastChanceCounty.com

In this Series:

Book 1: Expired Refuge

Book 2: Expired Secrets

Book 3: Expired Cache

Book 4: Expired Hero

Book 5: Expired Game

Book 6: Expired Plot

Book 7: Expired Getaway

Book 8: Expired Betrayal

Book 9: Expired Flight

Book 10: Expired End

Also available in 2 collections!

Books 1-5

Books 6-10

ABOUT THE AUTHOR

Follow Lisa on social media to find out about new releases and other exciting events!

Visit Lisa's Website to sign up for her mailing list to get FREE books and be the first to learn about new releases and other exciting updates!

https://www.authorlisaphillips.com